"What was that all about, Donner? Don't do that again."

"I think you meant to call me *Oliver*," Isaac corrected her. "And I'm not only going to do it again, you are too, *Cassandra*. This is what we both signed up for."

"I didn't sign up for that kind of kiss," Rory said, her lips still tingling. "Married people's kisses last for like a half a second. That was the kiss of people having a forbidden affair."

"I thought it was a pretty good kiss too. Exactly the sort that will convince Washer we're legit. As soon as he sees one."

Back to business. She'd been seared from the inside out and all he could talk about was the job.

As he should. She should be thinking about the job too. That's all this was. Her partner was a great actor, one who could obviously fake a lot more than his name on paperwork. She could take a lesson.

"Point taken," she told him briskly. "Public kisses only though. From now on. I mean it."

He grinned. "Wanna bet?"

Dear Reader,

I'm so happy you picked up this book! When I found out I would be writing the twelfth story in The Coltons of New York series, I got really excited because (a) Coltons! and (b) I can include characters from all of the preceding books. Then to top it all off, it's a Christmas book. And a fake-marriage story. All of my favorite things wrapped up in one edge-of-your-seat ride.

Rory Colton spilled out onto the page, a no-nonsense detective who wants to see the most notorious serial killer behind bars... Only she gets stuck with the arrogant, annoying new guy on the force, Isaac Donner, who turns out to be her ideal partner in so many more ways than she'd have ever guessed. He's even a pretty good husband. Too bad it's all fake. Or is it?

I adore heroes like Isaac, who surprise the heroine, surprise readers and maybe even themselves in the course of falling in love (while catching bad guys on the side!). I hope you like him too.

I'm new to writing Harlequin Romantic Suspense novels, but from the first page I fell in love with this book and with the whole line. I hope to bring you many more new adventures between the pages.

PS: I love to connect with readers. Find me at kacycross.com.

Kacy

COLTON'S YULETIDE MANHUNT

Kacy Cross

HARLEQUIN
ROMANTIC
SUSPENSE

Special thanks and acknowledgment are given to Kacy Cross
for her contribution to The Coltons of New York miniseries.

Recycling programs
for this product may
not exist in your area.

ISBN-13: 978-1-335-59386-3

Colton's Yuletide Manhunt

Copyright © 2023 by Harlequin Enterprises ULC

For questions and comments about the quality of this book,
please contact us at CustomerService@Harlequin.com.

Harlequin Enterprises ULC
22 Adelaide St. West, 41st Floor
Toronto, Ontario M5H 4E3, Canada
www.Harlequin.com

Printed in U.S.A.

Kacy Cross writes romance novels starring swoon-worthy heroes and smart heroines. She lives in Texas, where she's seen bobcats and beavers near her house but sadly not one cowboy. She's raising two mini-ninjas alongside the love of her life, who cooks while she writes, which is her definition of a true hero. Come for the romance, stay for the happily-ever-after. She promises her books "will make you laugh, cry and swoon—cross my heart."

Books by Kacy Cross

Harlequin Romantic Suspense

The Coltons of New York

Colton's Yuletide Manhunt

Writing as Kat Cantrell

Harlequin Desire

Marriage with Benefits
The Things She Says
The Baby Deal

In Name Only

Best Friend Bride
One Night Stand Bride
Contract Bride

Switching Places

Wrong Brother, Right Man
Playing Mr. Right

Visit the Author Profile page at Harlequin.com for more titles.

To Jessica Alvarez, who introduced me
to the idea of writing for
Harlequin Romantic Suspense—thank you!

Chapter 1

Detective Rory Colton had dedicated her life to putting criminals behind bars, but despite interacting with the dregs of society, she generally believed people deserved a fair trial. Hopefully that same sentiment would apply to her when she strangled her new partner.

Surely a jury of her peers would nod appreciatively and vote to acquit when she testified how Isaac Donner tormented her constantly just by existing.

"Doughnuts, Detective?" he drawled as she bustled past his desk, which happened to be next to hers because for some unknown reason, the universe hated her. "That's so cliché. You couldn't have stopped at that bakery on the corner? The one with the kolaches. I love those."

Rory shifted the box of doughnuts in her hand away from Donner, suddenly self-conscious at the pastry selection visible under the cellophane window. "Then buy your own. These are for people who appreciate thoughtful gestures."

"I appreciate you, Detective," he said with that gleam in his eye that she'd call flirting on anyone else, but she hadn't figured him out yet, so she mostly ignored him.

When she could. Which wasn't often because…partners. "I wish I could say the same."

"Aw, and here I thought I was growing on you." He laughed like her grumpiness didn't bother him, and probably it didn't. Not much seemed to. "When you're done playing doughnut delivery girl, meet me in the conference room. I want to go over the case again."

Rory stifled a groan. He always wanted to go over the case again—no need to mention which one. The Landmark Killer. Until she brought the perp to justice, there was no other case. That was the one thing she and Isaac Donner had in common—they both wanted Xander Washer in handcuffs, and while Donner might've been the bane of her existence, the fact that they knew the identity of the killer and still hadn't caught him ranked as worse.

So she'd grit her teeth—again—and go back to work because that was what she did.

She handed off the box of doughnuts to one of the beat cops who made the streets of New York safer but never got enough recognition. Then she jerked her head at Sergeant Wells Blackthorn, the lead detective on the case, indicating the conference room where they'd posted a giant board with a spiderweb of details and clues, all threads leading back to the suspect in the center.

Blackthorn followed her through the door, Cash and Brennan right behind him, and Rory took comfort in the fact that while her new partner lived to irritate her, the rest of the team was solid. Both Cash and Brennan shared her last name—cousins, officially—but they were sharp FBI specialists with skills she appreciated. The fact that they were family came second.

Technically Blackthorn counted as family too, since he'd married Sinead, Rory's sister. Half-sister. The specifics shouldn't matter, but they did. Maybe one day she'd be able to think about Sinead without the qualification, but they'd never been close. They'd barely spoken until they'd landed this case, honestly, and then Sinead had up and fallen in love with Rory's boss. Madness.

Mixing business with pleasure sounded like a recipe for disaster in Rory's mind, though she wouldn't argue if someone wanted to point out that work was her *only* pleasure. Relationships weren't her cup of tea.

Predictably, Donner had taken the seat at the head of the table, the one normally reserved for Blackthorn as the lead detective. It was a formality, not a hard rule, but still. The guy was such a *jerk*. She and Blackthorn glanced at each other, but he'd obviously elected not to say anything to the new guy.

She had no such reluctance. "That's Sergeant Blackthorn's seat."

"Then he should have gotten here first," Donner said with another of his trademark grins that lots of women probably found perfectly charming.

Rory was not lots of women. "This is not a competition. There's no prize for the first person to the conference room."

"Everything is a competition," Donner corrected her as Blackthorn made a noise in his throat that even her partner couldn't ignore.

Mercifully, he shut up, letting her regain her legendary control.

Of all people—why did *this* one get under her skin so easily?

Her face a mask that told everyone in the room she meant business, Rory waited as Blackthorn slid into a seat next to Cash. Then she pointed at the board, where she'd personally placed a picture of the iconic Rockefeller Center ice-skating rink, complete with the famous Christmas tree ablaze with colored lights. "We know Washer is going to hit Rockefeller Center next. The FBI team put the text we all received through several tracer programs, and while we didn't get any hits on his location, the landmark profile fits."

Off to sharpen my skates.

All of Washer's other murders had taken place at notable landmarks, so it didn't feel like a stretch to interpret the message literally. Brazenly announcing your next target certainly wasn't the standard way most criminals went about doing things. The killer was taunting them, and he'd gotten bolder the longer this case had dragged on.

Rory burned to take Washer down.

Donner rolled his hand obnoxiously. "Yeah, yeah, we already know all of this. What I want to know is when I can get cleared to execute the undercover operation."

Wells shrugged as all eyes shifted in his direction. "Not my call. It's the captain's. Last I heard, she's thinking about it."

"What is there to think about?" Donner interjected

with a scowl, scrubbing a hand through his short silver hair that contradicted his age. "It's the perfect plan."

"No," Rory cut in, matching his scowl. "The perfect plan is the one we already have in place. We have half the force taking shifts at the rink, as well as others like Madison Square Gardens, just in case the read on his target is wrong. There are more eyes on ice in this city than during Game Seven of the Stanley Cup Finals."

"You like hockey?" Donner's eyebrows scrunched together as if this might be the most unbelievable thing he'd ever heard in his life.

"I'm allowed to like hockey. It's not a crime." Shifting her focus back to the board, she started to recite the remaining known facts about this case, the same as she did every morning.

It was tradition, and the routine of police work soothed her.

"We should catch a game together sometime," Donner interrupted smoothly. "Use it as bonding time."

That was not where she'd expected him to go with his hockey segue, and it flustered her for a moment. "I'm not going on a date with you."

Donner shuddered. "Not as a *date*, Detective. Please. I have a feeling not many men escape a date with you with all their original parts still intact—especially those below the belt. I value all the stuff down there."

"You are definitely in the category of men who need to lose some stuff," she agreed cheerfully to cover the slight sting over his implied insult.

She wasn't that emasculating. Was she?

It didn't matter. She didn't date for reasons that had nothing to do with whether Donner had anything worthwhile below *or* above the belt. And she wasn't in the habit of explaining her personal life in front of her team, even though they were family. Especially because they were family.

"All right, children," Blackthorn said as he raised his hands to settle the squabble once and for all. "Take this outside. *Later*. The Landmark Killer doesn't care whether either of you like hockey or need to be taken down a peg or two."

Rory tried—and failed—to hide the smile that climbed on her face at her sergeant's choice of wording. Obviously he didn't like Donner much either, and the fact that he'd opted to get in a dig while shutting down the exchange pleased her to no end. If she could have anyone's approval in this room, she'd pick her boss over everyone else combined.

"Exactly," she said, and shot Donner a look. "So our current plan to keep eyes on the rink—"

"Is useless," Donner broke in to finish for her, even though that had *not* been what she intended to say. "Since you told all the blond-haired blue-eyed men to stay home. Who is Washer going to come after? At best, he'll find another landmark target, one we *don't* know about. This is our chance to capitalize on the perfect scenario that you've already set up. I go undercover, voilà. We have a target who is not a civilian and is new to the investigation. Washer doesn't know me. With the surveillance we already have in place, it should be a piece of cake to draw him out."

"That's not going to work," she argued. "We've had a police presence at other landmarks, and he still manages to get his victim anyway. Which would be you, by the way. You'd be the dead one."

And she'd lose another partner in less than six months.

The never-quite-healed ache flared up again, and she snuffed it, like she always did when the subject of Zach Holleran came up.

The big difference between losing Holleran and the idea of losing her new partner was that she'd learned the hard way to stop caring. Caring about people only brought pain, so why bother?

Brennan cleared his throat. "Detective Donner does have a point."

Cash nodded in support of his brother's assessment. "He's right. We had to warn the employees. The last thing we want is civilians caught in the crossfire. But if you drain the field of targets, you change the equation. We don't know what Washer might do if he realizes his preselected landmark won't work for his next step."

Just as she opened her mouth to contradict her cousins—because, of course, they had to be wrong—she forced herself to take a breath before she jumped all over not one but two special agents on loan from the FBI.

They were here because this killer was different. She knew that. Donner was the changed equation here. He was deliberately baiting her, needling her, doing whatever he could to stick his obnoxious personality straight into her craw. Distracting her. Causing her to lose focus.

But that didn't erase the man's reputation. When Captain Reeves had first brought up the idea of a new partner and dropped Donner's credentials into her lap, Rory had breathed a sigh of relief. Detective Isaac Donner had a stellar record. He excelled at working harder than anyone else, to hear his former captain tell it. No one in his old precinct had as many closed cases as Donner.

On paper, she'd landed the perfect partner.

In reality, they couldn't stand each other. Or at least that was the reason she'd sold herself on why she sometimes looked up from her desk to find him quietly studying her as if he couldn't quite get his head wrapped around her.

She had news for him. That went both ways.

Sure, he was easy on the eyes, if you liked super masculine types with the kind of body that didn't lend itself to partaking in community doughnut offerings. Which might've been part of the reason she'd made it a point to bring some in this morning—he was too perfect. He could use some fat on that frame to tone down his look, which was made even more striking by his silvering hair. He didn't even bother to use that color-wash shampoo she'd seen in commercials. No, he just owned his prematuring gray as if it was the hottest style around.

Normally she appreciated confident guys. The other three at the table exuded self-assurance, and she'd never felt particularly threatened by any of *them*.

Which meant Donner was the problem. And that was not okay.

"We don't know what Washer will do," she agreed as she gave up the ghost on walking through the remaining intersections on her spiderweb board. "But I can't imagine he'll pick another target. That's not his MO."

"But he's been quiet for a week or so," Brennan pointed out unnecessarily because Rory had been living and breathing that reality. "The only thing we do know is that he won't hesitate to strike once he decides to. He might very well pick a different victim profile, just to be sure he keeps us occupied. We can't have that on our shoulders."

"He won't pick a different victim," Blackthorn interjected firmly. "That's not his MO either, and it's clear he's acting out both his admiration for the Black Widow Killer and his grievances against a blond, blue-eyed father figure. He's going to hit a male in his thirties whose name starts with *O*. Period. The FBI profiler on this case is top notch, and I'm not just saying that because she's my wife."

The last victim had been a male in his thirties with blue eyes and blond hair, like the others. He'd been found with a note in his pocket: *Until the brilliant and beautiful Maeve O'Leary is freed, I will kill in her honor and name. MAEVE down. O up.*

Blackthorn was right. Washer would go after someone with an *O* name. They had all the pieces here in front of them. Except the Landmark Killer's location.

"Sure, we get it," Cash said with a short laugh. "No one is disparaging Sinead's work on this case. We're all just edgy."

Donner drew Rory's gaze as if he'd become magnetic. She couldn't look away. He fit the profile, if he dyed his hair blond. The undercover idea wasn't completely off base, and she wasn't daft enough to keep arguing the point—she just hated the idea of his being the one to take down Xander Washer. This was supposed to be her moment to shine, to show everyone that she was fine after losing Holleran. Zach. Her partner.

How had it been six months already?

They'd had a mutual respect for each other. Holleran got her. He'd been married to his job too—the best combination for a law enforcement team she could think of. He never left early to go home, and he never had to worry whether she'd be equally focused.

And then he'd made one small mistake. A bad read on a suspect. A gun in the perp's pocket that Holleran hadn't detected.

Rory would never forgive herself for not being there, for having crept around the other side of the building despite the fact that they'd agreed he'd go left, she'd go right. Luck of the draw.

Except she knew it hadn't been luck but fate—as in hers, to never have a true connection with anyone, only pain. Even her own father had tainted their relationship by leaving Sinead's mother to marry Rory's mother. How fair was that to any of the people involved? He'd torn apart two people's lives due to his own selfishness. She could barely stand to be in the same room with him, let alone trust him not to do the same thing to her and her own mother.

Donner wasn't her father. Or even Holleran. She knew that—except Holleran hadn't volunteered to set himself up as bait to entice a deranged serial killer out into the open.

Numb all at once, she let the others talk over her as she wallowed in a moment of remorse that she'd even jokingly thought she might strangle Donner. She shouldn't care what happened to him. But she couldn't go through losing another partner. She didn't even *want* a partner. It was too hard.

The four men at the table hashed out some of the clues—again—without getting any further than they had the day before, mercifully not seeming to notice that Rory had stopped participating. Well, most of them didn't notice.

Donner did. Of course. The man had some kind of extra sense that told him exactly when to shift his focus to her, and when he did, his gaze caught on hers, holding, probing, assessing. And finding her wanting, surely. Because that was what he did—make her feel inadequate and unprofessional.

They split for lunch, and she took a moment to collect herself in the restroom. She couldn't do this anymore. That much was clear.

Resolute in her course of action, she strode to Captain Reeves's office before she could change her mind, before she could stop herself from changing the status quo. Two firm knocks and then she opened the door, determined not to be put off her path. Poking her head in, she nodded at Captain Reeves, who stood behind her desk.

"Sorry to barge in," Rory said, banking on the fact that her years of good service and the captain's general high opinion of her would make the action forgivable. "But I need to speak with you about removing Isaac Donner as my permanent partner. It's not going to work out long term."

Captain Reeves crossed her arms, an oddly amused look stealing over her features. "I'm afraid he beat you to the punch in that regard."

"Detective." Donner's voice slapped her from inside the captain's office, and her gaze landed on him a beat too late. He was already inside, standing off to the side with that expression on his face that brought her up short every time. "Looks like great minds think alike."

Chapter 2

If you had asked Isaac Donner his number one turn-on in a woman, he'd have said stilettos. A woman in a sky-high pair of slinky, strappy ice-pick heels? Yes, please.

New York was full of them. Even in winter. No matter how many blocks a woman had to walk, the streets teemed with legs strapped into architecturally impossible shoes that never failed to make his mouth water.

Rory Colton never wore heels. Or anything that could be remotely called feminine. She didn't have a sweep of long, luxurious curls or a deft hand with a mascara wand. Nor did she seem to have any interest in showcasing a blessed thing under her serviceable long sleeve shirt and black pants that blended her into the background. A great asset for a plain-clothes detective, and she wore it so well that none of the other cops in Isaac's new precinct ever looked at her.

He wouldn't have given her a passing glance on the

street either. So he got it. What he didn't get was why he caught himself seeking her out across a room, just to see what she was doing. To see if he could catch her watching him. Sometimes he did.

Those were the most interesting times, because she never looked away. She owned the fact that she'd been checking him out, that slight sneer in place as if she'd found him wanting.

It fascinated him.

Far more than if she'd stepped into a pair of stilettos. In fact, he'd started to think he found her intriguing because she was so far off center from his normal type. Those women were a dime a dozen, but he'd never met anyone as focused on the job as Rory Colton. He couldn't stop thinking about her.

That made her a problem. One he needed to solve immediately.

Never had he expected that his trip to Captain Reeves's office would result in his new partner upping the stakes so dramatically as to interrupt his own plea to be let out of this arrangement early.

Detective Colton had proven herself to be his biggest competition once again. And that was not going to work.

The detective stormed right into the captain's office, uninvited, to confront him, her short dark hair framing her face, which had the strangest effect of softening her features.

He couldn't stop himself from staring at her. "You want out of this marriage too?"

"What?" she snapped. "We're not married. This is a partnership, one that has already outlived its usefulness. I work better alone."

"Funny, the Landmark Killer is still at large. If you

worked better alone, you'd think that wouldn't be the case, now, would it?"

Her gaze glittered with challenge as she raked him from top to bottom with her full attention, and dang if he didn't like that. She had so much focus that she fairly vibrated with it, enlivening her, and he liked that too, much more than he should've.

But she'd been so different a week ago, the first time he'd met her. A shell.

He couldn't quite pinpoint how he'd arrived at that conclusion, but Detective Colton had seemed off. Quiet. Too much so. He'd made it his mission to spark something inside her, and boy, had he, creating a green-eyed vixen who lived to vex him.

And all the credit for that went to Isaac. Not that he thought he'd get a thank-you or anything.

"I can't work with you distracting me all the time," she countered with a hint of primness that told him he'd gotten to her on a much deeper level than he might have supposed. "That's the problem here, which is what we need to focus on. You. Causing problems. You need to go back to where you came from."

Hands shoved into his pockets, he bit back a grin. "And leave you here to have all the fun? No, thank you."

"Why are you even here?" she asked, eyeing him suspiciously. "No detective with your reputation just ups and leaves his current beat to come hang out in another territory without an agenda. It's far past time to clue us all in on that. Let's have it." The detective spread her hands to encompass Captain Reeves as well as herself.

The captain shrugged, her smile still a bit more amused than the situation warranted. "Don't drag me into this. You two need to work this out yourselves, which is what I was going to suggest to Detective Donner before you joined us."

That got his attention in a hurry. "It's a no? You're not going to consider my request to work this undercover operation?"

The captain raised her eyebrows. "Did I say that? I'm still thinking about it. There are ramifications beyond your ambition, Detective Donner."

"Yes, ma'am." He knew when he'd been dismissed, but this seemed to be a day for not knowing when to cut his losses. "Forgive me for beating a dead horse, Captain. If Detective Colton is still my partner, how is that going to work for the undercover operation? We can't be seen together. It only makes sense that we sever ties immediately and let her work with the existing team to lift rocks."

"What's that supposed to mean?" The detective jumped back into the fray, hands on hips as she faced him down. "You want us to let you charge into Rockefeller Center by yourself? You really are going to end up in the morgue before this is done."

Or…he'd end up solving this case, putting away a serial killer before he destroyed more innocent lives, before he took up more headspace in the minds of New York's finest. Before he got away with it.

If not, that would be the ultimate failure. One Isaac could not live with. No one had caught Allison's killer, and each time he closed another case, he marched closer to avenging her. The Landmark Killer would be the final step. He could feel it.

"I'll be fine, Detective," he commented mildly. "I'm a big boy, and I've gone undercover before. This is the only way to handle the situation. Trust me, I've thought it through more than once."

"You're not the only brain involved here, Donner. We have some of the finest law enforcement personnel in the country on loan to this department, specifically to stop Xander Washer before he kills again. You can't waltz in here and act like you're in charge—"

"Okay, that's enough." Captain Reeves held up her hands, her amused smile vanishing. "You two are something else. You need to figure out a way to work together, or I'll do it for you."

Detective Colton's eyebrows came together, but she seemed to be absorbing the captain's warning. "So you're officially rejecting my request to dissolve this partnership?"

"Officially official," the captain said in a no-nonsense voice that Isaac recognized despite not having worked under the woman that long. "Washer is dangerous. So is the rest of New York. Two cops is always better than one, and you're good together, even if you can't see it yet. Spend some time actually collaborating on something, and show me I'm wrong if you think I am. I'll wait."

That sounded like a challenge Isaac could get behind. "I do like showing other people they're wrong."

Detective Colton rolled her eyes. "You would. Why is everything a contest with you?"

"Because winning beats losing every time?" he said with a laugh because come on—no one liked to lose.

"Or because you have something to prove?" she countered, the glint in her gaze far more knowing than he was comfortable with.

"Doesn't everyone have something to prove?" They stared at each other for an eternity. "Besides, you don't think we'll work well together either or you wouldn't be in here. If you're not showing the captain she's wrong, you're verifying she's right. Can't have it both ways, Detective."

Her internal struggle played out across her expressive face. That was another thing about the detective. You never had to guess where you stood.

If he somehow lost his mind and asked her out to dinner, he would never wonder what she thought of him, the venue, his choice of attire, the waitstaff efficiency, the temperature of the food... How great was that? The women of New York he spent time with drove him batty with their indecision, their constant need to pretend they weren't hungry and pick at their food. The detective ate sandwiches at her desk like no one was watching or cared.

Or maybe *she* didn't care. Either way, everything about her screamed authenticity, and he lacked that in his life. Who knew? Not him.

"Why do you want out of the partnership?" the detective asked him point-blank. "And it isn't just so you can go undercover, which is a dumb plan in the first place."

"It's not dumb, it's brilliant," he said as adrenaline pulsed through his body. Man, this woman challenged him at every turn. It was invigorating. "After you and your crack team of the country's finest warned off all the employees, there's no other choice. Washer is bound to be frustrated and will move on to another landmark or worse. We have to move fast. We've been over this."

No choice, and no other way to prove to his father that Isaac had made a good career choice. This case had national attention. The cop who caught Xander Washer would be a hero. Finally, Isaac could point to an accomplishment and say, *Look, Dad. I'm good at what I do even if I'm not the chief detective like you are.*

That was why everything was a contest. He was competing against himself, as a version that wasn't quite good enough for Francis Donner but could be. And he planned to win.

"Fine," the detective said with a decisive nod. "I withdraw my objection to the plan. Going undercover at the ice-skating rink is the only option."

Isaac shook his head as if she'd clocked him, and honestly, he almost felt like she had. "I'm sorry, what? Did you just admit that I'm right and you're wrong? Is that what I'm hearing?"

"Don't be obnoxious, Donner, or I'll change my mind," she sneered.

"Too late—you can't take it back. Just out of curiosity, and I can't believe I'm poking this bear, but what spun the dial in my favor? Surely it's not because you suddenly had a change of heart and realized I'm quite good at what I do."

He crossed his arms to wait for her return volley and realized he hadn't had this much fun with a woman in... well, he couldn't quite remember the last time he'd had *fun.* He'd *enjoyed* the company of women, sure, but that wasn't the same thing.

"Not even close," she chirped cheerfully, and that was when his palms started to sweat.

Detective Colton in a good mood about an idea she'd been super clear she hated did not bode well.

Not one to draw things out, he curled his fingers in a *gimme* motion. "Then lay it on me."

"Simple. Washer needs a target, you're willing to volunteer, and the captain is insisting we work together.

The answer obviously is that we have to go undercover as a couple."

"As a *what*?" His voice rose an octave as he blinked at the detective. "You're not horning in on my operation."

"That's a good plan," the captain interjected thoughtfully. "I approve."

Just like that. Dazed, Isaac slumped down in one of the chairs ringing the captain's desk. This was *not* what he had in mind. At all. Sharing credit for the collar was only the first of many objections, and the long list grew by the second.

"A couple," he repeated, thoroughly unable to wrap his brain around the concept. "What, like, we're dating, and you come to work with me one day? I don't get it."

"Married," the detective clarified, and she didn't even choke on it the way he would have. "And we work at the rink together. That's how we watch each other's backs. It's the only way we can do as the captain asks."

Detective Colton glanced at Captain Reeves, her eyebrows raised as if to question whether she'd gotten the sentiment right. The captain nodded, beaming as if the detective was her star student.

"I like this plan," the captain reiterated. "It's perfect."

"Wait, wait, wait." He threw up a hand as if that alone could ward off the sheer insanity of the words coming out of the mouths of both females in the room. "You want me and Detective Colton to pretend to be married. Like legit, with PDA and living together and the whole nine yards?"

"Exactly," the captain said.

"What, are you worried you can't pull it off?" the detective threw in as if he hadn't been having a conversation with the captain. "I'm shocked that you don't think you can do it."

"I can do anything I put my mind to," he snapped. "Maybe you're the one we should be worried about. You know this means you have to kiss me in public, right?"

Oh, dang. That was something he hadn't quite thought through either. The cool look she shot him belied none of her thoughts, which made it seem an awful lot like it didn't bother her. Maybe because she had no issue with keeping it professional where he was concerned.

He shouldn't have had an issue either. But suddenly, this whole plan felt precarious and difficult for a number of reasons he didn't like, the number one being that he couldn't stop thinking about kissing that smug smile right off her face.

His unholy fascination with her was about to be indulged in a very big way. Not only would he be allowed to kiss her, it was a *requirement*. They'd go on dates. Live together. Take showers in close proximity.

"I'm good," she said. "Are you?"

"Yeah," he growled because what was he supposed to do, argue that going undercover as a couple wouldn't work?

He had no leg to stand on. The solo plan was only better inside his own head—plus the captain hadn't gone for it. The couple plan she loved, which was the only opinion that mattered.

"You don't seem all that thrilled with this idea," the detective noted, one finger to her mouth as if perplexed. "Are you sure you're not going to undermine the operation because this wasn't your idea? After all, you came into this office to request that our partnership be terminated, and instead you got the partnership of the century out of the deal. How do I know you're not going to try to figure out a way to ditch me after all?"

Oh, that was *so* not the problem any longer.

Before he could spit out a defense, the captain's gaze swiveled in his direction as she contemplated him, clearly weighing out Detective Colton's point. "That's not going to be an issue, is it, Detective?"

"She came here for the same reason," he protested hotly, aware that his rising temper wouldn't help plead his case, but wholly unable to get control of himself or the situation, which never ended well. "If you should be concerned about anyone, it's Detective Colton. Have you even done any undercover work?"

"Some," she said breezily. "I'm counting on my enthusiasm for catching the Landmark Killer to make up for any holes in my résumé."

Which meant no experience. She'd come up with this whole plan to needle him, that much was clear. Putting Washer away was the bonus in this situation, as long as she made Isaac's life difficult while doing it.

"Be that as it may," the captain said, her gaze wagging back and forth between the two of them, her expression hard and unyielding. "Even with a lot of previous undercover experience, you've never done it like this and not with each other. You're going to have to learn to work together while faking a marriage and do your jobs at the same time. That's a tall order. You should practice before you hit Rockefeller Center, otherwise you're going to wind up losing Washer because you're bickering over who gets to hold the gun."

Practice. Being married. Baffled at the turn of events, Isaac scrubbed a hand over his jaw. "I'm assuming you have marching orders."

The captain nodded. "The precinct is involved in a local school outreach program in the neighborhood, to hand out donated school supplies to the kids. It's a tradition every Christmas for a few officers to volunteer. You two get to be the tributes this year."

That wiped the smile right off the detective's face. "You can't be serious."

"Problem, Detective?" he asked sweetly, glad to finally be back on the offensive for once. "It sounds like a good cause. I'm looking forward to it. Great idea, Captain."

"I think so too," Reeves said with thinly veiled sarcasm. "Except it's not an idea, it's an order. Figure out how to do that without killing each other, and you'll be in good shape for the undercover job."

"Wonderful," he said enthusiastically. "Can't wait to start. Let's head over as soon as possible."

"Oh, we'll be making another stop first. At a costume store," the detective told him, arms crossed over her chest as she watched him absorb that. "We have to hand out the school supplies while dressed as elves."

Chapter 3

Married. To Detective Isaac Donner. The refrain set itself up in Rory's head on repeat, and she couldn't make it stop. Or the point he'd planted in her head—on purpose—about having to kiss him.

They hitched a ride with one of the beat cops to the costume store the precinct worked with in the Theater District. The place was on 45th, but construction forced them to take 47th, which was a mess most days anyway, with all the foot traffic and clueless tourists who thought nothing of stepping into the street so they could take a selfie with the iconic signs in Times Square. Add in construction detours and the street became a parking lot.

Which meant more time trapped in a small vehicle with the man about to become her fake husband.

Fortunately, he seemed similarly shell-shocked over

the events of the day and stared morosely out the window of the squad car.

Fine by her. It gave her more time to look out her own window.

Rory loved the bustle of New York, the lights, the energy. At Christmastime, the city became even more magical. The buildings sported holiday cheer, decorated trees popping up all over the place, ornaments dripping, red ribbons and bows overflowing. The weather had been perfect thus far, crisp and clean, the stiff breeze sweeping the streets free of its normal debris.

Somehow they made it all the way to the costume store without speaking a word to each other. As they both jumped out of the squad car, Donner even went so far as to veer out of her way so they didn't accidentally touch when they stepped up on the curb.

"I didn't expect you to take the captain's suggestion to practice so literally," she commented, sarcasm creeping into her tone because she was just that done with his childishness. "Except I think we're supposed to be a newly married couple, not one who is already at that 'can't stand each other' stage."

"Is that what you think I'm doing?" Donner's voice, on the other hand, sounded faintly amused. "Practicing being married to a woman I can't tolerate?"

"Isn't it?" she shot back cheerily. Two could play that game.

Though what game they were playing, she hadn't quite worked out yet. She'd messed up his undercover plans, sure. But he hadn't seriously thought she'd allow him to barge ahead with that alone, had he? This was her job, one she'd worked hard to excel at, and he wasn't waltzing in here and taking away a case on which she'd already logged a zillion man-hours.

"Maybe I'm channeling my inner elf in anticipation of what's to come," he countered wryly, and the look on his face almost made her laugh.

But she stopped herself in time. This wasn't supposed to be fun. It was a *test*.

Oh, she'd heard the captain. *Practice being married.* Except that wasn't what this was. No married couples dressed up like elves together. They'd been plunged into this hell so that the captain could get a sense ahead of time whether this undercover plot would be successful or a disaster. Before she inadvertently put her cops into the line of fire.

Washer was smart—too smart, and he'd worked for the FBI for long enough to have amassed a network of contacts as well as the opportunity to stockpile tools the team couldn't begin to unravel. That made him far more dangerous than other criminals.

Rory got it. It was a cautionary measure. But she intended to pass the test. There was no other option— because if she didn't, she might get taken off this case anyway. Not happening.

"If you are channeling your inner elf, you might want to reevaluate," she said with a pointed look. "Elves are jolly and do not walk around looking like they've just swallowed a lemon."

"Then you should look in a mirror," he suggested with a chin jerk at her own demeanor.

"I'm jolly." But she had a feeling she might not have told her face. "Being an elf is fabulous. Pretending to be married is fabulous. Can't wait."

As she took a step toward the costume shop, Donner

slid his hand into hers, nesting their fingers together, bringing her up short. Too shocked at the zing of contact to move, she stared up at him.

He was too close. Why was he standing so close to her? The citrusy scent of something masculine wafted from beneath his overcoat, and it smelled so good that it made her a little dizzy.

"Detective," he murmured as the people traffic around them dissolved, "this was your idea. Own it."

Good night, had his eyes always been that shade of blue? The clear azure pools sucked her in, mesmerizing her to the point where she couldn't quite tell which way was up. "What was my idea?"

"Being married." His voice had gone a touch husky, as if he might be equally affected by her. "If it bothers you to pretend to such a degree, why did you suggest it?"

"I'm not bothered," she said, and it came out far too breathlessly to be believed.

Which he did not miss. A slow smile spread across his face, one that she didn't know what to do with. "You're a terrible liar. We have a lot of work to do if we're going to pull this off."

With that, he released her, and the strange bands around her lungs finally eased off. Dragging air into her body for what seemed like the first time in a year, she let the oxygen influx clear her head.

"What was that all about?" she called as he strode toward the door of the costume shop, leaving her standing on the street as people eddied around her.

"Practice," he said shortly and held the door open for her as if gallantry might be part of the test. "And we need a lot of it. We should go to dinner tonight."

She blinked. "Dinner? What, like a date?"

"Yes, Detective, exactly like a date," he said with a laugh. "Though I appreciate the stunned expression on your face. It warms my heart to see how ecstatic you are about spending time with me."

"I'm not going on a date with you," she snapped.

He just shook his head. "You're something else. I've got news for you. Married people eat dinner together. Plus they do a lot of other things together. And they enjoy it."

The fact that he was right—about everything—rankled. How was she supposed to act like she was in love with Detective Donner when she couldn't even pretend to like him enough to have dinner together?

She was already failing the test.

Steeling her spine, she sailed through the door of the costume shop, determined to flip the script before she lost her career over this madness. Because it *had* been her idea. She just hadn't thought it through very carefully, a fact she suspected he knew and meant to wield as a blunt instrument designed to torture her.

"We need two elf costumes," she told the guy behind the counter and handed over her department-issued credit card to pay for the expense. "One male and one female. Adult size."

The guy nodded and disappeared into the back, returning a moment later with two hangers full of red-and-green felt, then handed one to each of them.

"That is a lot of stripes," Donner muttered, holding his hanger out at arm's length as if afraid the explosion of Christmas colors would leak onto him somehow.

"I've got news for you," she mimicked him. "You have to wear that. So go put it on, and let's get this over with."

"You want me to wear this in the car?"

"You can't change at the school," she said, biting back a grin at the horrified look on his face. "Trust me, this is the easiest way."

In a shocking turn of events, instead of arguing with her, he trudged off toward the dressing room, leaving her with her own costume to deal with, which did indeed have an alarming plethora of stripes.

The costume fit perfectly, which didn't feel like a plus in her book. Surveying herself in the full-length mirror that the costume store had installed in the dressing room to torment customers, she thanked her lucky stars for the first time ever that she wasn't taller or the skirt would be too short. The fur-trimmed edge hit her just above the knee as it was, but no one would be looking at her skirt given the red-and-white-striped leggings beneath it. A hat and shoes with matching curly ends tipped in bells completed the outfit.

"I look like a Christmas tree ornament," she muttered and forced herself to leave the dressing room before she forgot that she'd wanted to be a cop since first grade, when she'd first realized what her teacher had meant by choosing a "profession."

Since then, she'd developed a higher-than-average need for justice, largely motivated by her uncle Mike's murder. He'd been a cop too, a great one, his tenure and his life cut short by a serial killer. She wasn't the only one who carried that weight—all four of her cousins had dedicated their lives to putting criminals behind bars after losing their father, and they'd come together to form a great team. They should've been celebrating having stopped Xander Washer by now. How many others would find themselves mourning the loss of someone important to them because they hadn't caught the Landmark Killer yet?

Donner waited for her in the main area of the store, arms crossed over his green coat, which emphasized the unfortunately large square buckle over his midsection.

"This outfit is ridiculous," he said by way of greeting.

"The kids will love it," she assured him, more amused than she probably had a right to be given that she looked equally ridiculous, but Donner seemed so genuinely put out by the whole thing that it cheered her right up.

He eyed her suspiciously. "So you've done this before?"

"A few times. Usually we make the rookies do it, but obviously this year, we drew the short straw." She shrugged. "It's for a good cause though. So try to keep that in mind as your annoyance level with the bells grows."

Groaning, he followed her out of the shop, his street clothes folded into a bag dangling from his wrist. "I was serious about dinner tonight. Don't think I didn't notice you brushed it off."

Yeah, she hadn't dared hope the subject had been dropped, but she'd at least like to get through one fiasco at a time. "Here's a deal for you—don't make me hate life for the next two hours as we do this elf thing together, and I'll consider it."

Donner's eyebrows flew up as they climbed into the squad car. "Consider it? Like I'm a frustrated Romeo dying for some encouragement from the lovely Juliet, whom I can only admire from afar until you deign to acknowledge my presence? I don't think so. Counteroffer— if *you* don't make *me* hate life, I'll pay."

She'd stuck out her hand to shake his before thinking better of it, and then it was too late. His fingers closed around hers, capturing her hand thoroughly and holding it way too long to simply seal their agreement. Their gazes locked, and this became a contest too—who could stand the electricity arcing between them the longest.

She blinked first. Dang it, he was good.

"We have a deal, then," he murmured, his voice silkier than it should be.

The beat cop in the driver's seat tapped on the wire mesh between them, a smirk splitting his face wide. "Nice outfit, Romeo. You going to PS 212?"

"Yeah," Rory called. "48th Street entrance. Thanks."

"The pleasure is all mine," the cop said with a toothy smile. "Price of admission is a picture of the two of you that I will be printing out and hanging up in the break room at the precinct."

Of course he would. She sighed. This was her punishment for nixing Donner's solo undercover operation. "Do your worst."

They arrived at the school far too soon, especially given that the car ride had felt like an eternity as Rory had pretended Donner's striped thigh hadn't been a mere six inches away from hers. The captain's assistant had arranged for the donations to be boxed and shipped to the school ahead of time, so all Rory and Donner had to do was set up the North Pole decorations provided by the school in the small classroom the principal directed them to.

Then it was go time.

The kids started pouring through the doors, lining up with excited chatter. Their little faces reflected a sense of wonder and awe as they took in the fake snow drifts and miniature trimmed trees volunteers had strewn around the table where they'd also stacked preassembled packages full of Christmas-themed pencils, rulers, notebooks and stickers. Some enterprising volunteer had wrapped each one in paper stamped with snowflakes.

Time passed in a rush as Rory handed each kid their package, watching with a smile as they ripped the wrapping paper off to exclaim with glee that they'd gotten the pencils featuring Rudolph the Red-Nosed Reindeer or the Frosty the Snowman stickers.

One of the little boys, who couldn't have been more than six or seven, stared at Donner with unabashed curiosity, clutching the package he'd just been handed as if it might escape if he didn't hold on to it tightly.

"Are you a real elf?" he asked in perfect seriousness.

"You bet, buddy," Donner said without missing a beat, his voice so mellow that Rory scarcely recognized it. "Straight from Santa's workshop."

"Do you have to go right back to work after this?"

Obviously the little boy was trying to reason out something in his head. Rory handed a package to the next girl in line, her attention half on her job and half on Donner because this opportunity to observe him when he wasn't directly interacting with her was too priceless to miss.

"I do," Donner told him solemnly. "I have the most important job in the world, so I don't want to miss much more of it. But I'm glad I got a chance to take some time off to visit you."

Rory had a feeling he'd spoken from the heart, answering the boy about his job as a detective and not as an elf.

"Me too. This is the only Christmas present I'm going

to get this year. I can't wait to open it." But he didn't. He clutched the package to his chest as if savoring it, then did the most unexpected thing. Instead of racing back out the door like all the other kids, he rounded the table and gave Donner a one-armed hug. "Thank you, Santa's Helper."

Donner's mouth trembled, but he flattened his lips and bent down to give the boy a proper hug. "You're welcome."

Rory's heart rolled and never quite settled back into its original place. It sat there beating, spreading heat and light through her body. Ignoring the stupid stuff going on inside her rib cage, she focused on her own line and stopped watching Donner. Obviously this elf costume had granted her with the gift of amnesia if she'd forgotten for even a second that he was the scourge of her existence.

After the last kid left, they began cleaning up in tacit agreement on who would handle which piece, despite never having done anything even remotely of this nature before. It was a clear sign that they did indeed work well together, and it tugged at Rory in uncomfortable places.

She didn't want to work well with Detective Donner. She wanted him to be a screwup and get fired so she never had to deal with him making her heart squish ever again.

Except that *had* happened, and now she had to pretend this experience hadn't humanized her partner. Which sucked. She had to get back to that place where she thought of him as an obstacle, a jerk, expendable. Because she could not lose another partner she cared about. So that was that.

She brushed off her hands, expertly pushing everything back into the black box where all her longing for connection and meaning lived. That was how she avoided pain, by not setting herself up for it in the first place.

"You know what this means, right?" Donner said with a sidelong glance at her.

What? Her squishy heart didn't mean anything. Her pulse scattering, she busied herself with boxing up the last miniature Christmas tree, refusing to look at him. "You're going to have to fill me in."

"You held up your end of the bargain. I held up mine."

Oh. He was talking about dinner. Somehow she had managed to forget about their deal. "I don't know, Donner. Can you honestly say you don't hate life at the moment?"

She made the mistake of glancing over at him. His face softened so quickly that she wasn't prepared, and now it was too late. This man's face without its normal snarky edge nearly took her breath away.

"I hate life for some of these kids, yeah," he said softly. "It's rough hearing that this might be the only present they get—a crappy set of pencils and notepaper."

"That kid liked you," she admitted, not at all happy that the concept of his being likable had just presented itself to her. "Otherwise he never would have said that to you."

"He thought I was a real elf," he said with a tiny, dazed smile that pinged around inside of her, looking for a place to land. "It was something else."

Oh, dang it, no. She didn't want to start liking him too. Isaac Donner was evil. Or something. He made her life miserable.

Okay, to be fair, she gave as good as she got, but only because she had to hold her own with him. The man would railroad her, stomping her flat if she let him. Just look at how he'd handled this whole case, going to the captain behind her back and trying to get his undercover scheme approved. Thank goodness she'd thrown out her own plan that guaranteed she'd be in on the action. Which he'd graciously accepted, even going as far as trying to come up with some ways for them to practice outside of department-mandated elf duty.

Ugh, this was the part where she had to admit that she might be part of the problem. A tiny, insignificant part. But maybe enough that she could take a step back and give Isaac a fair shot at this fake-marriage-slash-partnership. There was a distinct possibility the experience wouldn't be all horrible, and if they pulled off the ruse, it meant drawing Washer out of hiding, which would be worth a lot.

That meant she had to go to dinner with him *and* she had to let him pay.

Chapter 4

So far today, Isaac had gained a fake wife, transformed himself into an elf and convinced Detective Colton to let him buy her dinner. That should have been enough, and surely anyone would agree he'd earned some downtime. He'd like to spend an hour or two going over Washer's profile, just to see if he'd missed anything the first 547 times.

But no. As soon as he and the detective left the school and returned the costumes, she flashed him a text message on her phone. "The captain called in a favor with her contacts at the FBI and got Ashlynn assigned to help create our fake backgrounds. That's a huge win."

"Ashlynn?" he repeated, feeling as if the name should mean something to him.

"Colton," she said with a smirk. "My cousin. She's a tech expert, with a wide variety of skills that we desperately need."

He'd definitely missed a few cues while he'd been busy playing Santa's Helper. And it kind of irked him that the detective had been conversing with Captain Reeves about the case they were supposed to be working on together.

"Is there anyone in the whole of New York City who is not related to you?" he muttered. "Why do we need anyone's skills again?"

The look she shot him had so many layers he could have peeled it like an onion. "I thought you were the one with all the undercover experience, Donner. She's going to work out our fake backgrounds. Washer is FBI. He might not have ever been an agent, but he knows the system, has contacts and tools. He's also smart. We need an expert in laying out our digital tracks, so to speak. We have a virtual appointment with her as soon as we get back to the precinct."

Yeah, he had undercover experience, but not anything like this. He felt like he'd been plunked down in the middle of an RPG without benefit of the fun part. "So she's going to be like our dungeon master."

"I don't even want to know what that means," she shot back, her nose wrinkled. "You can keep your own kinky stuff to yourself."

That made him laugh, even as he wondered why her mind had jumped straight to that explanation. "You never played Dungeons and Dragons, I take it. It's a role-playing game. The dungeon master works with all the character backgrounds and guides the players through the story he makes up."

The detective shook her head. "Ha, no. I would not let Ashlynn touch one single element of my fake background. That's why we're meeting with her. So we can go over the details, then she'll run down her process to plant the fake data. I mean, we have to have fake driver's licenses and everything, right?"

Well, honestly, he hadn't gotten that far. This whole scheme had become twenty times more elaborate than he could have ever dreamed. "I kind of thought I'd show up at the skating rink and tell everyone I was the new guy with an *O* name."

"Sure," she said with a withering scowl. "That won't be suspicious at all. Washer won't think twice about the place having been cleared out of employees fitting his MO, and then, oh, look! One magically shows up. Don't pay any attention to that man behind this curtain over here, Landmark Killer. Come out, come out, wherever you are."

"Yeah, yeah," he mumbled. "I get it. We need to be more strategic."

Maybe he should be thanking his lucky stars that the detective had horned in on his undercover scheme. She'd already brought more to the table than he'd expected.

He followed the detective to the nearest crosswalk and zipped his lips while they passed through the crush of people on the street. He'd learned the hard way that someone was always listening in a city like New York, despite the feeling of anonymity the sheer number of people created. Mostly he considered himself a better cop for his mistakes, but he sincerely hoped that agreeing to this fake relationship with Detective Colton wasn't going to be one of them.

How was he supposed to manage all of this when he couldn't seem to focus on anything else but her face? She never rested, even on the subway. Her gaze scanned every person in their car, evaluating, considering. He'd bet she could recount exactly what they were all wearing, their heights, weights, if they carried a purse or a messenger bag, etcetera.

It was fascinating, sure. He'd already accepted the fact that she intrigued him. But after all the elf business, there was this additional layer that he couldn't quite sort, namely because he'd never done anything like that before and it had humbled him. She'd been right there with him, inexorably entwined in his soul with the realization that he'd given those kids something positive in a harsh world. They had done that together.

Which had been the point. But somehow he didn't think the captain had intended for it to be quite *that* kind of bonding experience.

When they got back to the precinct, he had the distinct impression everyone had been waiting for them to make an appearance. As soon as they walked in, all the cops started clapping and hooting, the entire room's attention on the two of them. That was when he noticed the beat cop who had given them a ride had indeed taken the picture of Isaac and Detective Colton dressed as elves and printed it. A lot.

There were hundreds of copies taped up everywhere—two on the coffee maker, three on the door to the captain's office, one on each cop's desk. In almost all of them, someone had drawn a fake mustache on them both.

"Very funny, guys," the detective called out with one of her trademark scowls. "I'm sure the criminals of New York appreciate the head start you're giving them by hanging around here waiting to give us grief."

"We're just disappointed you're not still wearing the costumes," Agent Brennan Colton called from his temporary desk while he worked out of the 130th office.

This was one of those times when Isaac wished the FBI would go back to their own office and leave him in peace, a sentiment he'd bet the detective shared, judging by the look she shot her cousin.

"Where's Blitzen, Detective?" one of the beat cops called, and everyone laughed.

"Har, har. Yeah, I've never heard that one before," Isaac called back, opting not to resort to one of his stinging comebacks when someone made a joke about his reindeer name. Or asked where the rest of the Donner party was.

He'd been a cop long enough to know that this was how they relieved tension, not to mention the requisite new-guy hazing, so he let them have their fun and their catcalls, then hustled the detective to one of the private conference rooms so they could get on with their dungeon-master appointment.

"Tell me again why we're doing this virtually?" he murmured as she booted up the laptop she'd snagged from her desk and positioned it on the table in front of them so they would both be in the camera's range.

"Ashlynn is—was—friends with Washer. They worked together at the same FBI office. There was some concern that he might come after her, so she's lying low."

Apparently Isaac wasn't in the circle of people she trusted to know her cousin's location. Noted. And it wasn't relevant for him to know either. But it did sit funny that the detective had intel, no matter how minuscule, that she hadn't shared.

What else had she kept close to the vest?

A woman in her late twenties or early thirties materialized on the screen when the call connected. She and Detective Colton had the same cheekbones and the same shade of dark brown hair, but the similarities ended there. Agent Colton could be described as classically pretty with a nice face, but it wasn't very interesting to him. He'd skip right over her if he scanned a crowd she happened to be standing in.

The detective, not so much. She had this energy that played out across her features, snagging his attention thoroughly. Against his will sometimes. He'd never call her classic anything, let alone pretty, but *stunning* fit.

And that marked the first time in history he'd acknowledged a preference. Normally his criteria lay in whether he'd grown tired of a woman yet.

"Hey, Rory," Ashlynn chirped when the audio connected. She glanced at Isaac. "You must be the new guy."

"Agent Colton," he said with a chin tip. "Donner's the name. For the next few minutes, I guess. I'm told you're the wizard who will be magicking up new identities for us."

"Yup." Agent Colton typed for a few seconds and glanced up. "So we're going with Orlando Walken and—"

"Orlando?" he broke in. Obviously the hazing extended much further than the microcosm of the precinct. "Surely you're joking."

Agent Colton squinted at Isaac. "What's wrong with Orlando? Rory said we needed an *O* name. That's an *O* name."

"It's the name of a city, for crying out loud." And the actor who had played an elf…oh. Now he got the joke. Obviously one of the wise guys at the precinct had spread the tale of his afternoon's activities. "I'm not giving myself the same name as Legolas. Get over it."

The agent and detective glanced at each other, and the woman on the laptop screen shrugged. "Fine. Oliver, then. Or do you have objections to that too?"

"Oliver is fine," he growled. Oliver Walken. It would take some getting used to.

"Rory, you'll be Cassandra Walken," Agent Colton said briskly, only to throw up her hands when the detective shook her head. "What now?"

"I'm keeping my maiden name," the detective told her. "Let's pick something easy to remember like... Smith."

"Okay, done."

Isaac threw up his own hands. "Hold on a minute. You give me grief because I don't want to be named after Orlando Bloom, but it's fine for her to want to have a different last name than me? That's not going to work."

The detective stared at him. "Do you have a problem with women who want to keep their maiden names?"

"I have a problem with the fact that this is fake!" he burst out. "And yes, I realize that my first name is fake too, but I have to answer to it. If you have a different last name, it might cause Washer to dive deeper into our backgrounds. It's a red flag that may cause extra scrutiny that we don't need."

"Lots of women keep their maiden names," Agent Colton said with a sniff. "It's not unusual."

They'd ganged up on him. Of course they had; the women were related.

"Fine, keep your maiden name," he said wearily, but the detective shook her head.

"You might be right, as much as I hate to admit it. Washer may have unconscious bias that a different last name could trip. It's more important to have bulletproof backgrounds than for me to get my way."

Would wonders never cease? Isaac crossed his arms and settled back in his chair, wishing he felt more like he'd won. This was the first time he'd ever thought about whether he'd care if a woman took his name when they got married. Because he'd never thought about getting married before. He'd just kind of assumed whoever this mythical woman was would want to share his name since they would be sharing everything else.

But maybe marriage didn't work like that. What else had he missed?

He didn't like missing things, and it seemed like a day for it.

What was he doing agreeing to do this thing that he had no experience with? It had seemed like it would be simple—lots of people did married things every day without breaking a sweat. Shouldn't it come naturally?

Agent Colton went through a few more items including their new hair colors, which she'd digitally alter on the photos she'd taken. Then she announced that she'd cross-referenced everything with their new address, a small condo owned by the US Marshals Service but that the agency had buried their connection to. And like that, he and Detective Colton were officially a couple, with a marriage certificate on file with the city clerk.

"I'm working on the hard copies of everything," Agent Colton said by way of wrap-up. "My guy will overnight your driver's licenses, Social Security cards and passports, but fair warning, they'll come from a legit delivery service so that it's not suspicious that you immediately have weird activity at your new lodging."

New lodging. He'd have to move some of his personal stuff to this condo near Rockefeller Center and try not to think about how completely upended his life was about to become.

"Good luck," Agent Colton said with no small amount of sympathy, as if she truly got the need for the sentiment.

The detective clicked out of the virtual meeting, shut the laptop and shoved it under her arm, her gaze on everything except him.

"Problem, Detective?" What was wrong with him that he enjoyed poking at her so much?

Her gaze finally rose to meet his. Oh, yeah, that was why.

So many things snapped through her expression that he couldn't keep up with all of it. He could spend a lifetime learning to interpret her. And it would probably take that long, especially when she did stuff like letting her lips turn up in an enigmatic smile that hit him in places inside that he wouldn't have said a woman could touch.

"For one thing, you should start calling me Cassandra," she noted.

Yeah, he definitely should not. "Oliver isn't the kind of guy who would whole-name his wife. You'll be Cassy to me."

She bristled visibly, which brought a smile to his own lips. "Not if you expect me to answer, I won't be. In fact, I might insist you call me Cassandra Walken every time you address me, just as a reminder."

"That we're married and you belong to me?" he asked, in genuine shock that she'd go there.

"Don't be ridiculous. That this is all fake," she shot back. "We're not really married."

"I'm aware. But we have to act like we are, and this constant one-upping me isn't going to help. Come on."

He jerked his head toward the door. "Let's go to dinner and get started."

She sailed through the door ahead of him without comment, then plunked down her laptop on the desk next to his and snagged a tiny handbag that looked as if it couldn't hold more than a wallet and some lip gloss.

Not that he'd ever seen her wear anything of the sort. She had natural beauty that would not be improved by slathering cosmetics all over her face, so he appreciated that she didn't.

She said goodbye to several of the beat cops by name while he stood near the door cooling his heels. A few of them laughed as if she'd told them a joke, and that was when he realized what he'd thought of as her prickly personality applied only to him.

Detective Colton wasn't like that with everyone. She'd been sweet as sugar to her cousin, so he hadn't noticed it right away. And Blackthorn she treated with respect, but the sergeant had recently married her sister, so he'd again chalked it up to personal history. Maybe not so much, then.

Rubbing the back of his neck, he had a come-to-Jesus with himself about it.

Had he brought this on himself somehow? Or was there something deeper going on that he'd missed?

He was starting to get the impression that he'd missed a lot where Detective Colton was concerned. And that it was far past time to start paying attention.

Maybe if he got it right, she'd be the asset he'd already started to see she could be. They'd take down Washer together, and then he could finally put the ghost of Allison to rest.

Chapter 5

Rory had a bit of experience with the concept of dating—at least that was what she would have called it prior to tonight. But the way Isaac Donner did it wasn't even in the same ballpark.

He did not "buy a woman dinner," not in the traditional sense. No, that would be too easy.

Instead, he'd turned it into a whole thing. A *date* in capital letters, complete with picking her up at her walk-up and producing a bouquet of flowers from behind his back.

"For you," he murmured and handed her the riot of blooms in every color.

Mystified and not a little moved by the gesture, she inhaled the heady perfume of fresh flowers. No one had ever given her flowers before. For any reason. The fact that he'd thought of it, coupled with the strange fluttery sensation in her belly, made her instantly suspicious.

"What's this all about?" she demanded.

"They're flowers, Detective, not an envelope full of anthrax," he responded mildly. "You say *Thank you, Isaac*, and you put them in water so we can make our reservations."

Reservations. Had anyone ever made *reservations* for her before either?

She murmured her thanks, refusing to tack *Isaac* on the end because it felt too intimate all at once, and ended up sticking the flowers in an iced-tea pitcher since vases weren't a thing in her world.

Donner had managed to find a restaurant near Chelsea that she'd never heard of, tucked away on one of the lesser-traversed side streets. The owners had taken over an entire brownstone before it could be split into multiple apartments, or else they'd done extensive renovations to make the upper floors accessible. The place had an old-world feel with heavy wooden accents and a switchback staircase leading to the second floor.

"This is exquisite," Rory murmured to Donner, a bit intimidated by the grandeur of the house turned restaurant, the likes of which she didn't often come in contact with. "When you said you'd pay, I envisioned standing in line at a fast-food place."

Which meant she might be severely underdressed in a serviceable pair of black pants and button-down shirt. It was hard to tell. The tables all seemed to be secluded behind screens or in alcoves, so she couldn't get a good look at any of the patrons. Though she suspected that was the point.

"Nothing but the best for my wife," Donner said, a thread of silk in his tone that she didn't recognize. Or like particularly.

Okay, a small part of her liked it fine. There was something about being called "wife" that wrapped around her, warming her like a cup of hot coffee on a frosty holiday morning while the city still slept.

That warm bit inside was the part she needed to find and squish.

This was not a date. Just because it felt like one—the best one she'd ever been on—didn't matter. Donner was not an interesting man she liked and hoped might become more. That was the qualifier here. One she needed to remember.

The hostess threaded through a warren of rooms and passageways, leading them to a small room with a bay window and a fireplace. And only one table. Theirs. Donner had sprung for an exclusive room, and she couldn't imagine what it had set him back. Nor could she ask without coming across as crass.

He held out a chair, waiting for her to sit, which she finally did after a brief internal war.

"You don't have to act like this when no one is even watching us," she mumbled.

"I'm watching us," he said, his expression thrown into shadow as he sat in his own chair with his back to the fireplace. "And I wanted to treat you like I would if we were really married. It's easier to get into the habit if you do it twenty-four seven instead of only when necessary. That's how you slip."

This was what would be in store for Mrs. Isaac Donner? "You're a cop. I'm pretty sure I have a handle on your salary, and it doesn't include seventy-five-dollar bouquets and a restaurant that requires bribes to get reservations last minute."

Apparently crassness wasn't something she could suppress all that well.

"I'm flattered that you're concerned about my portfolio, Detective, but don't worry about me or my finances. You're worth it."

Unsettled to the point of speechlessness, she focused on her menu, only to find that this was a fondue restaurant. "I, um…have no idea what to order."

Donner smiled and did the strangest thing—reaching out to catch her fingers in his, threading them together until they were nested like braided hair. "Don't worry. I'll take care of you."

Jeez. "You're a much better actor than I would have ever thought."

She was really going to have to up her game.

"Maybe this isn't an act."

What rabbit hole had she fallen into? She stared at him as he sipped his water, his gaze never leaving hers either. "Donner, we hate each other."

"Do we?"

He let it sit there in the space between them, not taking it back, not elaborating, forcing her to think about it. The back of her neck heated as she scrambled to figure out how to fill the silence. "You must be aces at getting a perp to crack if this is how you interrogate a suspect."

"I am good at my job, Detective," he murmured, his thumb wandering over her knuckles, almost absently, as if they sat this way on a frequent basis and she should be totally comfortable with his casual affection. "That's why we're a brilliant match."

"You think I'm good at my job?" she repeated, cursing the slight lilt of hope. Why would she care if he thought she was a great cop or should be fired immediately?

"I think you're passionate and dedicated—two things in short supply in any profession, let alone ours."

Which wasn't the same thing as saying she could run circles around all the other law enforcement professionals in the city. But the admiration reflected in his gaze... That warmed her from the inside out. It was clear that he'd meant it as the highest compliment and she should take it as such.

"Maybe I don't hate you as much as I did this morning," she allowed, and his face split open in a grin that did a lot more fluttery things to her stomach.

"Progress. And for the record, I never hated you."

Agape, she blinked, but his expression didn't change. "You're always on my case, giving me grief and generally making my life miserable. How else should I interpret that but you expressing your extreme dislike for me being your new partner?"

He shrugged, sobering. "No one would have been a good partner for me. I'm always going to want to fly solo. But that's my issue, not yours."

The oddest feeling of camaraderie stole over her, as if she and Donner might have more in common than she'd have guessed. "I get that. I'm still not fully ready to commit to a partner either."

"It's tough to lose one," he allowed gently. "I'm trying to remember what you've been through, but sometimes I forget. It's fine if you remind me occasionally. Sometimes I require a swift boot to the backside to get it."

Had she mentioned to him that she'd lost Holleran? Or had someone at the precinct warned him ahead of time? Either way, she'd never have expected him to be so sympathetic about it. "I appreciate that. A lot of other cops would have told me to get over it and move on."

"I'm not a lot of other cops."

No—no, he was not. But maybe that wasn't quite the negative she'd assumed it was. The fire crackled merrily at Donner's back, and the atmosphere in the private room wasn't quite as stifling as she'd been telling herself. Rory actually relaxed, surprised at how easy it was given the company.

Actually, he'd been instrumental in facilitating it. She should give him a break, especially since it seemed that he'd likewise decided to do the same for her.

Donner ordered for them both and then showed her how to use the long metal forks to dip her bread into the cheese sauce, then repeat with the meat and vegetables into a separate pot. For the finale, the waiter brought a pot of chocolate with an assortment of marshmallows and fruit. The chocolate was so dark and so divine that it was a waste to dip fruit into it—she'd rather drink it straight and told Donner so.

He grinned. "I take it you are a fondue convert, then?"

"This is the best restaurant I've ever been to in my life," she gushed, completely aware that he'd be forever tied to it in her memory. But was that so bad?

Her phone buzzed with a text message, and she glanced at it. All of the lovely, fluttery things inside her vanished in a heartbeat. "Ashlynn just had the keys to our new condo couriered over to the precinct."

Our condo. This thing had just gotten real.

"That was fast," Donner commented mildly. "Good timing. Let's take a few to go back to our places to get the stuff we'll need for the next week or so, and I'll meet you at the precinct to get the keys."

"Hold on a minute," she squawked, her throat closing in all at once. "We're moving in *tonight*?"

She had a sudden vision of Donner plying her with chocolate and casually holding her hand as they watched TV together. Of him treating her like Mrs. Isaac Donner, whom he valued with a glorious sort of reverence that she'd revel in. It made her knees weak.

She didn't like being weak. Or wanting something so badly that was so ridiculous.

"No time like the present. The faster we get set up, the faster we can move on Washer."

The truth in that was the only thing that kept her together as she contemplated the faux reality that had just flashed before her eyes.

Yes, she had to move in with Donner, but it was for the job. Always the job. It didn't matter if he treated her like a goddess, it was all for show. She *would not* get swept away in the fantasy of that kind of connection, one she'd always craved but had long ago made peace with the fact that she wouldn't get. She'd become Mrs. Oliver Walken, not the other way around.

Resolute, she steeled herself and stood up with a nod. "No time like the present. Better to be moving in under cover of darkness too. Less eyes that way."

They took separate rides to their respective apartments. Before long, she'd stuffed two suitcases, set them by the door, then slung a full-to-the-brim bag over her shoulder with her favorite blanket wound around the strap. It had taken her less than twenty minutes to pack up her life.

"Efficient," Donner commented as she met him in

front of the precinct to get the keys, as they'd prear-ranged.

"Did you expect anything less?" she returned and checked on the rideshare she'd ordered from the burner phone she always kept on her, which had just arrived.

"I just got the impression you weren't all that thrilled with how fast Agent Colton moved."

"No, it's great," she said with a tight smile. "Like you said, chop-chop. Washer isn't going to come out of hid-ing if he doesn't have a target, and Oliver Walken doesn't exist yet except on paper. We have to get the rest of you in place, and I'm a part of that."

Her reminder spurred Donner to morph back into a cop instantly. He nodded, a snap returning to his gaze that she liked much better than the languid, contem-plative glances he'd been shooting her at dinner, as if he'd like to take a bite out of her rather than what was on his plate.

Back on solid ground, she loaded her stuff into the Uber next to his. Before she could blink, they'd landed at the doorway of their new place. Together.

"Should I carry you over the threshold?" Donner asked with a tiny chuckle, running a hand over his short, silver hair.

Oh, goodness. Did people even do that anymore? The idea should be ludicrous, but for some reason, all she could think about was Donner sweeping her up into his arms without breaking a sweat, gazing into her eyes adoringly as he masterfully introduced her to the real-ity of being Mrs. Isaac Donner. Er, Mrs. Oliver Walken, rather.

Heat broke out across her cheeks, but the last thing

she wanted to do was clue him in that he'd triggered her nerves. "Maybe I should carry you."

That made him laugh for real, which pleased her for some ridiculous reason. The tension vanished—another win in her book. Maybe this wouldn't be so bad.

They crossed the threshold together, which could totally be a prediction of how this partnership would go. If they were both trying to make it work, that went a long way, didn't it?

The condo had a small-but-serviceable kitchen with new appliances and a waist-high bar separating it from the living area. A cute bistro set took up a tiny space in the corner, while a sofa sat against one wall, facing a TV mounted to the other wall with a long hutch underneath it, presumably to hold audio/visual components. Sliding glass doors comprised the entire south wall, which led to a small balcony holding two chairs.

"It's a two-bedroom," Rory told Donner as they simultaneously took in the condo that was way nicer than her walk-up on the Lower East Side. It was a lot bigger as well, but this one had to hold two people—neither of whom were used to being around someone twenty-four seven.

This was never going to work. But it had to.

"I'll let you pick first," he said with a sweeping gesture of his hand toward the back of the condo. "If you have a preference."

Did she? Ashlynn hadn't said much about the place, but maybe one had a better view. As she checked out the bedrooms, she realized one had an en suite bathroom while the other one didn't. The second bathroom lay across the hall, meant to be shared by the occupant and guests.

Rory envisioned taking a shower and then scurrying across the four feet of hardwood floor from bathroom door to bedroom door while wearing nothing but a towel. No. No way.

"I'll take that one," she said, pointing to the en suite bedroom, since he'd given her first choice.

He didn't complain, just nodded and disappeared into the second bedroom to deposit his things, then reappeared empty-handed, a smile on his face. Apparently he either didn't plan to scurry around naked or the thought didn't bother him.

Wait. Did that mean he *would* be scurrying around naked or wearing nothing more than a towel? Her cheeks exploded with heat again, and she ducked her head before he noticed it.

"This is actually great," he said and tapped the bar. "We'll be able to talk shop anytime. Share notes. Keep each other honest."

Rory nodded as she absorbed the implications of being in close quarters day in and day out. At least until they caught Washer. Which hopefully would be sooner rather than later.

"Agreed."

"Speaking of which, we should go over the plan." Donner pulled out one of the chairs from the bistro set, nodding to it as an indicator that she should take it, then crossed to the other chair, sinking into it. He pulled out his phone and swiped his thumb across the screen. "The skating rink mostly plays holiday music this time of year, but I contacted the manager and got him to agree that we can host a week of seventies nights. Lots of Bee Gees coming our way."

Donner waggled his eyebrows appreciatively.

Really? She wrinkled her nose as she slid into the opposing chair. "That sounds terrible."

"What?" Donner slapped his chest in mock affront. "The Bee Gees are classic. Do not tell me you are a disco hater."

"I've never thought about it one way or the other, honestly. I'm not much of a music person."

He side-eyed her as if she'd just admitted to tossing kittens into the Hudson. "We're going to have to do something about that."

"We are. We're hosting a week of seventies nights at the skating rink to lure a serial killer into the open. Let's focus on that," she suggested lightly.

Talking shop, yes. Talking personal details, no. It was going to be hard enough to actually coexist in the same space if they treated each other like cops, never mind diving right into date-night territory where they told each other their likes and dislikes and bonded over shared tastes. And chocolate.

"Yeah, yeah, okay." He perked up. "You know what the other benefit of living together is? You can help me dye my hair."

"I can…what?" Aghast, she stared at him, her gaze flitting to his closely cropped silver hair. "You can't do that on your own?"

"That's what roomies are for," he told her cheerfully. "You said yourself that you were here to be a part of my transformation. I would have done it at my apartment, but I didn't know your cousin was going to be such a mover and shaker. But this is way better. You can see the back, make sure none of it gets missed. We don't want Washer to clue in that it's a dye job, right?"

"Right," she repeated faintly, but why her stomach

had gotten so fluttery at the idea of touching him, she couldn't say.

Not just touching him but sliding her fingers through his hair. On purpose.

Donner dashed to his room and came back holding a small box in his hand with a picture of a guy on the front who looked as if he had been born blond. If the cover model had ever used a dye product in his life, she'd eat the entire box.

"That's what you're using?" she asked, hands on her hips.

"What's wrong with this?" He shoved the box into her hands, and she took it automatically. "Read the directions. It can't be rocket science. Everyone dyes their hair."

"I don't." Hers was the same brown it had always been, and she planned to wear a wig in public.

"That's what makes you so interesting," he said with a wink and opened the flap on the top for her. Then without so much as a by-your-leave, he hooked the collar of his shirt and whipped it off, leaving his chest bare.

Solidly, mouth-wateringly, drool-inducingly bare.

"What are you doing?" she croaked, casting her eyes away from him and focusing on the carpet. "Put your shirt back on."

"I don't want to get dye on it," he said as if this should be obvious and pulled her along with him toward the bathroom. "Come on."

Before she could meep out a protest, he'd swiveled around to lean on the sink, his eyebrows raised expectantly. Maybe with a hint of challenge too.

"Fine." She could do this.

Yanking out the printed instructions, she read through them all twice, with painstaking care—strictly to force him to stand there shirtless. But as far as she could tell, he didn't have the grace to feel even the slightest bit self-conscious. Why would he? Statues had been carved with less care than Isaac Donner. It was criminal how good he looked.

Somehow she managed to get the job done while he bent over the sink, and she only knocked over the bottle of dye twice. Fortunately Donner's hair was so short, she hadn't needed the bit that went down the drain. They waited the requisite amount of time, and then she rinsed off the dye.

Rory toweled off his hair and stepped back. Donner looked completely different with blond hair. A bit younger, more stylish. It was like meeting his brother and thinking how odd it was that they looked alike but had turned out so opposite.

Only she knew that the real Donner lurked underneath. It was like a secret that only the two of them shared. Except she had another secret all her own—she liked the other version better. And she had no business recognizing a preference. This was a job. Only. Not an opportunity to develop a slight crush on the man she'd just moved in with.

But she had a feeling that ship had sailed the moment he'd handed her the flowers earlier.

"Okay, *now* it's time to put your shirt on," she told him.

Chapter 6

Isaac couldn't seem to stop looking at his reflection in the mirror. It shouldn't have been that drastic of a change to go from his natural silver to blond. He already had the blue eyes, for crying out loud.

But that didn't change the fact that a total stranger stared back at him. Oliver Walken. DJ at Rockefeller Center. Husband. None of these things felt right, as if he'd put on someone else's skin.

"Do you hate it?" the detective asked, her gaze seeking out his in the mirror from her position behind him, concern dripping from her expression.

She thought she'd done something wrong. "No, you did a fantastic job. I can barely tell it's fake, and I was here for the whole transformation."

"Well, you do look different."

She busied herself with cleaning up the aftermath of WalkenPocalypse. Even the sink had rivulets of colored gel running down the basin. Hopefully the product hadn't stained the porcelain permanently, but that was a problem for the FBI's cleaning service. He had enough on his plate at the moment—namely that the detective had been off-kilter since the moment he'd picked her up for dinner earlier.

She hadn't even brought the bouquet of flowers he'd given her to their new place, opting to leave them at her apartment, where they'd likely die before she returned. It was telling, but what message he was supposed to take from it, he hadn't worked out yet.

"Detective." He stilled her hands, which were currently balling up the instructions with enough force to turn the paper into a diamond if she kept at it. "Thank you. For helping me with my hair. I couldn't be any more of a target if I tried."

"You fit the profile," she agreed readily. "It's been a long day. We should…you know. Go to sleep. Reconvene in the morning."

He let her escape because honestly he needed some downtime too, which he spent organizing his stuff in the bathroom and then in the closet in his new bedroom.

The mattress on his bed was new and not terribly uncomfortable, so he slept like a rock, his alarm waking him at his normal time of 6:00 am. The little bit of intel he'd done on this building had revealed a huge perk—a gym for the residents, which he planned to take full advantage of while he could. His regular gym around the corner from his apartment would take too long to travel to, plus he couldn't be seen in his undercover getup at his regular haunts.

When he padded into the kitchen in search of coffee, still barefoot, the detective had already beaten him to the punch. She stood by the sink, a mug clasped in both hands, drinking what smelled like the most heavenly substance on Earth.

"You made coffee already?" he asked, wondering if she'd mind if he kissed her in thanks.

And now he was thinking about kissing instead of coffee. This was going to be a long, long assignment.

"Good morning to you too," she shot back smoothly with a laugh that he hoped meant she wasn't actually offended by his lack of manners.

"My apologies," he said with a deep bow. "Good morning, my lovely wife. I trust you slept well?"

"Okay, stop it. I take it back. That's creepy. I prefer it when you're just you."

Well, that was a pleasant early morning confession if he'd ever heard one. He crossed his arms, gripping his biceps hard so he didn't reach out and sweep her into that kiss he'd just imagined. "I prefer it when you're you too. But at the moment, we're Cassandra and Oliver, and Oliver would like some coffee if Cassandra is sharing."

"I made enough for two."

The detective met his gaze over her cup of coffee, something shimmering there that he wished he had the latitude to explore a little bit more. It would have been nice if setting himself up in this undercover marriage had taken a bit of the shine off his fascination with her, but instead, he found himself wondering what kind of wife she would be if this was real life. Would she make coffee for him on a regular basis?

Because he could get used to this. More so than he would have guessed. "Thanks, Detective. And thank Agent Colton for me too."

The FBI didn't mess around. As he poured coffee into the mug he found in the cabinet above the coffee maker, he noted that someone had stocked the place with basics. Not just dishes and silverware, but pots and pans, spatulas, even a cheese grater. When he opened the refrigerator, he found enough food to feed a family of four for a week.

"Ashlynn mentioned that she'd lucked into a place that had already been set up for someone in Witness Protection, but whoever it was backed out of testifying, so it was just sitting here. She had a contact in the US Marshals Service who offered it up."

"That is a lucky break," he commented, but he had a feeling it wasn't luck at all.

If the detective hadn't ponied up her offer to go undercover with him, he had zero illusions about whether these doors would have been opened up to him. It paid to have family in the business.

Not that he would know. Isaac and his father both had *detective* in their job title, but he'd never mistaken what he did with what his father did. Or more to the point, his father had never let him forget that Isaac's career trajectory left much to be desired.

"We should spend the morning going over plans for our first day on the job," the detective said. "You said you already talked to the manager at the rink. When can we start?"

"We have to wait for our documents, just to make it official, but if they come today, I would imagine he'd be fine with it if we started tonight."

She nodded once. "That would be great."

He took a sip of his coffee and nearly had a religious

experience right there in the kitchen. "This is fantastic. What did you do to it?"

"I brewed it in the coffee maker," she said with raised eyebrows that said she found him hilarious. "Maybe you should lay off the Starbucks once in a while. Appreciate something different."

"I'm a cop in New York, Detective," he said with a grin. "Starbucks is what keeps me sane."

But he did not miss the point, namely to appreciate what was in front of him, and, at the moment, he appreciated it all right. The detective had already taken a shower this morning apparently, judging by the slightly damp hair at the base of her neck, which was not an area of the woman he should've been focusing on, but with her severely short cut, it was hard not to. Plus she smelled like something fruity, but he couldn't quite tell what.

Normally in this kind of a situation, he'd move in closer and get a good whiff, nuzzling the areas in question to give himself more clues, maybe hazarding some guesses while getting familiar with the woman's curves. This was not normal by any stretch. But neither did he think the detective was going to react well to any kind of public displays of affection, let alone private ones. That might be the more critical thing to focus on today.

No one had to know that practicing affection in the name of this undercover job fit into his overall agenda. Neither did he plan to apologize for taking full advantage of this situation to indulge his curiosity as to what Detective Colton tasted like. Later though. First things first before he scared the crap out of her.

"There's not much plan to talk about," he said. "Do you eat breakfast?"

"What does that matter?"

"Because I'm going to cook for you, and I would prefer it if you eat."

She watched as he pulled out a heavy nonstick pan from the drawer beneath the stove, then swiveled to extract the eggs he'd spied earlier from the refrigerator. Surely whoever had done the shopping around here had added some type of bread to the mix.

The pantry at the end of the galley-style kitchen revealed the rest of the goods, including a package of English muffins, which he held up triumphantly. Taking two out, he split them with a fork and plopped the halves of the first one into the toaster sitting next to the coffee maker.

"This is fascinating," she murmured. "I have never seen anything like it in my life."

"Breakfast?" he called over his shoulder incredulously as he flipped on a stove burner—electric. Too bad. "You've never seen someone make eggs and toast?"

"A man specifically," she clarified with a laugh. "This is the rare sighting to which I'm referring. My mother did all the cooking, and my father... Well, let's not go there."

"Oh, no, you brought it up. I am learning that in your world, gender roles are firmly in place, and this intrigues me. Spill, Detective." He cracked an egg into the pan with one hand, then threw the shell into the trash can beneath the sink before the runny whites had spread too far. "Your job is to entertain me while I'm feeding you."

"That's not part of the deal." She sipped her coffee with maddening calm, as if she intended to leave him completely hanging. "We're working together, not dating."

Taking a moment to crack a second egg into the pan,

he left them to fry in olive oil as he glanced up at her. "In this case, they're one and the same. We have to get to know each other. Be comfortable with small intimacies. Otherwise we tip off Washer, who is without a doubt watching the rink with eagle eyes even as we speak. We are not going to get a second chance at our first impression. He must think we're married the second we step onto the scene, or this won't work."

She rolled her eyes. "Cassandra comes from a very boring middle-class family with no skeletons in their closet."

"The opposite of Detective Rory Colton, I take it?" he prompted as he flipped the eggs. The first English muffin slices popped up with a beep, so he transferred it to a plate and stuck the other two into the slots.

"How do you talk and cook at the same time?" she asked, and he didn't mistake it for anything other than a diversionary tactic.

She didn't want to talk about her family. Which was odd, considering how much of it she had. Sometimes he thought the entire law enforcement presence of New York City was named Colton. But he could give her a pass for the moment. She was right, after all. He didn't have to know the truth about Rory Colton, only the fictitious background of Cassandra Walken.

He just didn't like it.

"Ancient Donner secret," he advised her, annoyed with himself for being bothered that she'd held back. "My family is Irish. I was born knowing how to cook."

With everything finished, he plated it and handed her one. The detective accepted it without comment and fished two forks out of the drawer behind her, offering him one as if they'd choreographed everything ahead of time. It was nice.

"We're a good team," he told her as they settled into their respective chairs at the bistro table, the same ones from last night. Funny how quickly they'd picked sides of the table.

"My family is Irish too," she said in yet another diversionary tactic. "I don't know how to cook."

This time, he didn't let her get away with it. "Why do you change the subject when I say something you don't want to address?"

"Because I don't want to address it?" she said with a thin edge of sarcasm and shoveled eggs into her mouth, which pleased him far more than it should.

They were eggs. He shouldn't care a whit if she ate them or threw them into the garbage can, but he did. He wanted to do things that made her smile, made her laugh. He wanted to crack her veneer, spilling out whatever lived behind her no-nonsense shell. Get answers to burning questions, like what did she think about when she gazed at him so coolly? Why didn't she want to discuss her father? Why had she seemed so overwhelmed by the simple elements of the dinner he'd taken her to last night?

"Then you say something like *Isaac, shut up*," he advised her. "I have thick skin. I would rather hear something honest from you than to keep playing hopscotch."

"You want honesty?" she asked with raised eyebrows, as if to warn him that he might not like what was coming, and pointed her fork at him. "I'll give you honesty. I am a huge fan of English muffins and an even bigger one of a man in my kitchen slaving over the hot stove. If we make that a thing while we're working this undercover job, you'll get no complaints from me."

Noted. He conceded the battle—but not the war—and stood, collecting both of their empty plates from the inlaid bistro table. "We should go to the grocery store and maybe Home Depot. Target too."

Confusion and suspicion vied for the primary emotion in her expression. "Because why?"

"Because that's what newlyweds do, darling," he told her with a grin. "If Washer is as smart as they say he is, he'll be checking us out. Talking to our neighbors. Spying on us. The more normal we make our lives seem, the better."

She didn't look convinced. "We'll have to wait a few hours until everything is open."

"Perfect. I have to hit the gym anyway."

Later that morning, he found her at the bistro table, neck deep in what looked like case notes. She'd already donned a light brown wig that changed her appearance but not enough that it bothered him. Expecting an argument, he tapped his watch when she glanced up, but she just grabbed her tiny handbag. Shocking.

As they were leaving their new condo, he noted a couple of plainclothes cops at two and six from their front door, well out of sight, but he'd been expecting them based on the thoroughness of the setup thus far. Agent Colton had not disappointed him.

"Looks like we have eyes and ears," he murmured to the detective and she nodded.

"Saw them the moment we stepped outside."

Was there anything sexier than a competent woman? Before becoming fake married to this one, he'd have said yeah. Piles and piles of things. But he couldn't remember what any of them were.

Because he wanted to and he could, he slipped his fingers through hers, and also as expected, she nearly came out of her skin—but in that subtle way of hers where she tamped down on her freak-out in favor of shooting him a sidelong glance.

But he still saw the initial flare in her gaze because he'd been watching for it. Whether she'd reacted in pleasure or revulsion, he couldn't say, and that was what kept him coming back for more again and again.

"Is this really necessary at this point?" she wheezed out under her breath. "Washer isn't watching us right this very minute. He doesn't even know we exist."

He stroked a thumb over her knuckle. Definitely not revulsion. That warmed him dangerously fast, which shouldn't have been a thing given the December snap in the air. "Practice makes perfect."

She rewarded him with an eye roll that made him grin, and nothing could have pulled it off his face for the entire fifteen-minute walk to Times Square. It was a beautiful day in the city—sunny and chilly, with no snow forecast in the ten-day outlook, and the Christmas decorations sparkled in the sunlight. Everything seemed crisper, more vibrant.

And the detective hadn't let go of his hand. If he didn't know better, he might think she enjoyed their early morning walk too.

They stopped into a small market she knew about on the way, calling out to the owner, who was arranging melons in a bin facing the sidewalk. The place was clean and bright, a far cry from the stores in his neighborhood, but this was the tourist district for you. They selected a few ripe bananas, some oranges and an exorbitantly expensive clamshell of blackberries, but since all of it would go on an expense report for Captain Reeves to foot the bill, Isaac didn't worry too much about it.

Just in case the FBI's makeready service wasn't as crackerjack as he'd originally thought, he loaded up on a few more essentials, already planning out some meals he could cook for the detective. She let him carry the groceries to their next destination, which instantly made him suspicious, until he realized he was so loaded down he couldn't hold her hand.

That was when he realized a smart woman might be even sexier than a competent one.

When they got back to their building at Rockefeller Center, he did an automatic scan of the perimeter, noting the security cameras, the position of the plainclothes detail, exits, places a perp could hide, the usual.

Except this wasn't going to be a routine operation. And he had an additional target to consider.

He glanced at the detective as she climbed the stairs to the building entrance, which required a security code as most did, but that wasn't infallible.

Washer was FBI. He had contacts. He had skills. Was he good enough to hack the security cameras? The door code? Or at least good enough to find someone who could? Isaac wasn't used to worrying about that kind of thing—at least not for his own safety.

And he wasn't expressly worried about the detective either. She knew how to do her job. But he felt unsettled. Inside, where he couldn't quite reach or soothe his normal way—with a Jack and Coke or a night with a beautiful woman that he never had to call again.

Of course, that never worked for long and also wasn't appealing for some reason.

"You're still carrying, right?" he asked her once they'd gotten to their condo without incident.

"Always." She glanced at him, brows raised, and lifted her tiny purse to indicate that her weapon lay tucked inside. "Why—did you see something concerning?"

"No, it's just…" How did he explain this feeling inside, one he didn't quite understand himself? "I'm making myself a target voluntarily. You're not."

"I most certainly am," she countered. "I signed up to be your fake wife. That makes me a target automatically."

That didn't help in the slightest. "It shouldn't. You're not Washer's profile victim."

"That doesn't matter. He only kills blond, blue-eyed men in their thirties at landmarks. We have no idea if there are other unsolved murders he's responsible for—people who got in his way or are linked to his victims."

Panic crashed right through the center of his chest as he absorbed her point. She wasn't wrong. He just didn't like it. Nor had he considered the fact that while he'd set himself up as a target at the skating rink, she could be in danger anywhere at any time. Washer's MO wouldn't apply, which made him even more unpredictable.

He let that lie for a bit, processing and considering options as they put away their groceries. At Target, the detective had purchased a lamp with dragonflies flying across the shade, which didn't go with the serviceable, bland condo. Or with the woman herself, but he'd begun to accept that he didn't really know her well enough at all, not as a partner and certainly not enough to sate his fascination with her.

What a fortunate coincidence that diving deeper into knowing the detective also fit his new objective of keeping her safe. Both of which had nothing to do with the job, but he'd take that to his grave before admitting it to anyone, let alone himself.

Chapter 7

Rory felt like she'd been waiting for the courier with their fake documents for a million years. She'd started jumping at every small noise, convinced she'd heard footsteps outside despite the fact that no courier service on the planet could access the building without authorization.

Donner had taken over the table, his laptop and case notes spread out to encompass the majority of the thing, so she'd set up camp on the couch with her own laptop, but she'd barely gotten any work done, thanks to a fine awareness of Donner's presence in the room.

She could feel him as if he'd cozied up next to her on the couch, then slid his fingertips along every inch of her.

"I need to run by the precinct," she announced to Donner, desperate to get out of this holding pattern. And the condo. "I think it's our last opportunity to do anything remotely connected to our regular lives before we start working at the rink. After that, we'll be in deep cover and can't afford the exposure."

"No," he said immediately without looking up from his laptop. "It's already too late. We have no idea where Washer has tentacles. He's been quiet for the last week, but that doesn't mean he's not watching Blackthorn and the rest of the FBI team embedded at the 130th. I'm new and I've been keeping a low profile. He shouldn't know you exist yet, but if you waltz in there, he might."

Ugh. He was right. But she wished he wasn't.

She had to do something besides sit on her hands. This was the longest she'd been away from the action in her entire life, unless the captain forced her to take vacation. Plus, she'd been trapped in this condo with Donner for hours already, and she still hadn't gotten used to his blond hair. Or that lazy smile he shot her sometimes when he noticed that she'd glanced in his direction.

It wasn't like *that*, as if she'd been checking him out. Though it wouldn't surprise her if he thought that. He seemed to have an overinflated sense of his own importance. Or rather, he used to. Since moving into this place, he'd let her pick her bedroom, cooked her breakfast and carried her lamp. She'd have never called him gallant, but that shoe fit for some odd reason.

Okay, he bothered her for reasons she had yet to fully understand, and none of them were the same reasons he'd bothered her originally, back when they'd first become partners.

That was why she had to get out of here.

"Okay, then I need to run by my apartment," she lied. His eyebrow quirked. "Because you suddenly remembered something you have to have that I can't take you somewhere around here to purchase?"

"Yes. The flowers you gave me."

That got his attention in a big way. He closed his laptop lid, focusing every bit of his laser-sharp gaze on her. "I'll go with you."

What? No. The whole point had been to get away from him and his blond hair that wasn't really blond, but only she knew that out of all the people they came in contact with. It was their secret. That knowledge made them a team, and she hadn't been quite prepared for how that made her feel.

As if her skin had been turned inside out, for the record.

"I can go by myself," she insisted. "I'll holster my weapon and wear a coat."

Donner's expression told her how unimpressed he was with that plan. "Oliver doesn't go anywhere without his wife. He loves spending time with Cassandra. He can't get enough of her."

Her eye roll was so exaggerated she nearly sprained something. "It's weird to refer to your fake self in the third person."

"Fine. I can't get enough of you and have no intention of spending even a fraction of a second apart," he murmured, his voice dropping unexpectedly into a sensual register she did not like.

Well, no, scratch that. She liked it too much. What she didn't like was her reaction to it, to the warmth that spread along her nerve endings as she stared at him. He didn't blink, didn't take it back, didn't qualify that he only meant the sentiment to apply to Oliver.

It was almost like the words had come from his heart.

But that was the problem with faking something like being married. It was hard to separate fact from fiction, especially the way Donner did it.

"Never mind," she muttered, training her eyes on her laptop to avoid looking at him. "It's silly either way. People don't actually talk like that. Even newlyweds."

Donner slid out of his seat at the bistro table and did exactly what she'd envisioned a hundred times—he grabbed her laptop and shut the lid, setting it on the coffee table, then dropped into the space next to her, that far-too-perceptive gaze slicing her open and reading the things inside her without her permission.

That was why she'd been trying to leave. So this wouldn't happen. It *couldn't* happen. Feeling things was for suckers.

"I talk like that," he said, contemplating her with a cocked head. "I find it fascinating that a man has never told you he can't get enough of you."

"It's not that interesting." She felt exposed all at once, as if she needed a shield against Isaac Donner. Er, Oliver Walken. Whatever mix of the two he'd conjured up. Would he make a federal case out of it if she plopped her computer back into her lap?

"What's wrong, Detective?" he asked silkily, as if he'd practiced exactly how to caress those syllables with extra innuendo and dark promise.

"Why do you always call me that?" she demanded. Or rather, she'd meant for her tone to come across as authoritative and no-nonsense, but the breathiness kind of ruined that.

"What, you mean Detective?"

"Yeah. The other guys call me Colton or, in the case of my cousins, Rory. It's a perfectly fine name."

In response, he reached out and clasped her hand in his, bringing her fingertips to his mouth in a shudder-inducing move she suddenly couldn't stop watching. Like a car wreck happening in slow motion that you couldn't look away from even though you knew a lot of bad stuff was about to go down.

"You haven't figured that out yet?" he murmured against the ends of her fingers in an almost kiss. "It's who you are, down in your bones where no one can be anything but true to themselves. When I look at you, that's what I see, Detective. And it's what intrigues me the most about you."

Something exploded behind her rib cage, and she very much feared whatever it was would never quite knit back together the right way. *How* did he know exactly the right thing to say to her? "That's the nicest compliment anyone's ever given me."

"Then that's an even bigger shame than no man salivating over you so much that he can't bear to let you out of his sight."

That pulled a half-hearted chuckle from her depths. "I'm not the kind of woman men salivate over. It's practically laughable that you even think that could be a remote possibility."

His gaze burned into hers. "Oliver feels that way about Cassandra."

Right. She blinked to break the weird connection that had sprung up between them, the one he'd accidentally forged with his lovely compliment. Or rather, the one she'd imagined. None of this was real. She hadn't morphed into some kind of siren that Donner couldn't resist, nor did she even want that. The less she cared about anything he said to her, the better.

Then she could stay in her numb little shell and never be affected by anything anyone around her did.

This time, her eye roll was exaggerated to show that she got it. That she could play along with all of this for the sake of the job. "Okay, sure. We'll go with that. Cassandra is equally devoted to Oliver. She thinks it's great that he follows her into the shower."

Something crackled in the space between them as Donner's eyebrows rose. "She does, does she? Oliver happens to be a huge fan of that as well."

"Oh, I didn't mean it like that." Her cheeks burned as the something turned a little darker and far more electric, sizzling across her skin. "I meant because you said Oliver couldn't bear to be apart from Cassandra. So, you know. They'd have to do everything together. Even showers."

"Yeah. That's what I meant too." He closed his eyes with a happy little hum, as if fantasizing about a shower right in that moment. "It's just a happy coincidence that Oliver's favorite thing to do with Cassandra can be done in the shower. Or anywhere he follows her. Coat closet at the skating rink. Kitchen countertop. Bathroom at her parents' house."

Oh, goodness. Now she was thinking about it too. Curse him. "Cassandra's parents are deceased. And even if they weren't, she would never, ever do such a thing."

His grin said otherwise. "I have it on good authority that she would. And does. Oliver has made her a convert of it. That and fondue."

If her cheeks flamed any hotter, she'd incinerate. "Oliver did not convert Cassandra into a fondue lover. She learned how great that is on her own. Also, she is a lady who would not desecrate a kitchen countertop with *that* kind of activity."

Unfortunately, Rory Colton might not have been able to put herself in the same category, because she could envision herself falling prey to a man's pretty words to the point where she'd let him strip her naked in Times Square. Obviously she was that weak. Look how worked up this conversation had gotten her, and it wasn't even real.

"Kissing?" Donner said innocently. "Cassandra thinks it's a desecration to be backed up against the counter and kissed thoroughly? You're kidding."

Kissing? *Really?* She shot him a withering look as he laughed, clearly enjoying himself. "So now you want me to believe that Oliver follows Cassandra into the shower to *kiss* her?"

"What did you think I meant, Detective?" He slapped a hand to his chest as if affronted. "Get your mind out of the gutter, please. I've been talking about kissing this whole time, and you're trying to turn it into some kind of indecent fantasy. I'm shocked, frankly—"

"Knock it off, Donner," she said through gritted teeth. "I'm going to my apartment *without you*, and you can't stop me."

The faster she got out of this place, the better, as a matter of fact.

Donner's gaze went flinty. "Wanna bet?"

"Bet on what? Whether you're coming with me? You're not, by the way."

"Oh, no, Detective. Bet me whether or not I can stop you," he said with more texture in his tone than the twill couch beneath them.

She stood up. So did he, towering over her.

"Is this you threatening me?" she asked with a laugh. "Because I don't feel threatened."

"That's curious," he murmured and reached out to finger a lock of her hair, sweeping it from her forehead. "How do you feel?"

As if his finger had been dipped into a volcano. But she didn't flinch, even as it continued on, tracing a line down her throat, then back to her chin, tipping it up to force her gaze to his.

"Like you're using seduction to get your way," she told him point-blank. "There's no reason I can't go to my apartment alone. You're just being stubborn."

"And why do you think that is?" he challenged her, his thumb coming to rest just below her bottom lip.

"Because you're you," she said, circling her hand to encompass his general self, which happened to be at torso level, reminding her of the perfection that lay just under the sky-blue T-shirt he wore. "I've never met someone so arrogant in all my life. I can take care of myself. I don't need a bodyguard."

"Think of me as your devoted husband, then," he suggested. "Who can't—"

"Bear to let me out your sight." She glared at him. "I heard you the first time. I get it. You don't trust me. That's what this is all about. You're afraid I'm going to scare up a lead on this case and if you're not right there next to me, you'll miss out."

His gaze flickered. Not a lot, but she caught it just the same.

"I'm right," she said smugly. "You've got a competitive streak a mile wide. It goes part and parcel with the arrogance, thinking you deserve to win, so you should. Maybe I'm going to crack this case wide open while you're playing DJ Oliver at Rockefeller Center and there's not a thing you can—"

His mouth landed on hers before she could protest. Throw up a hand. Squeak.

Donner was *kissing her.*

She was so shocked she could scarcely move, let alone shove him away, and then his hand slid around to the back of her head, cradling it, drawing her into the kiss against her better judgment, and then she wasn't thinking at all. Everything melted under his masterful touch.

The flowers. The gallantry. *The washboard abs.* It all swirled together into one big impressionist painting with Isaac Donner's signature scrawled across it in loopy letters, and she craved every one of the colors. She wanted to reach out with both hands and feel each brush stroke, so she did, wrapping herself around him as the kiss deepened, flattening her palms on his glorious back.

He made a sound of pleasure, and it thrilled her that she could illicit such a thing from a man. Except he wasn't a man. She was kissing her *partner.*

Wrenching away, she fled to the kitchen, putting the bar between them. "What was that all about, Donner? Don't do that again."

"I think you meant to call me Oliver," he corrected her, his expression blank. "And I'm not only going to do it again, you are too, Cassandra. This is what we both signed up for."

"I didn't sign up for that kind of kiss," she said, her lips still tingling. "Married people kiss each other good-bye in public, and it lasts for, like, a half a second. That was the kiss of people having a forbidden affair behind a locked door, about to be torn apart by life and circumstance."

Desperate. Needy. Reckless. A lot of other things she had no names for, but the underlying thread had a common denominator: the knowledge that only this man could tame the storm inside.

That didn't describe a fake kiss from a fake husband.

"I thought it was a pretty good kiss too," he admitted. "Exactly the sort that will convince Washer we're legit. As soon as he sees one."

Back to business. She'd been seared from the inside out, and all he could talk about was the job.

As he should. She shook her head. Hard. It didn't clear her Donner-drenched senses, but it did calm her somewhat. She should've been thinking about the job too. That was all this was. Her partner was a great actor, one who could obviously fake a lot more than his name on paperwork. She could take a lesson.

"Point taken," she told him briskly, willing herself to accept that kissing Donner was a part of her job and she did want to succeed. "Public kisses only though. From now on. I mean it."

He grinned. "Wanna bet?"

Chapter 8

Mercifully, their fake documentation came early that afternoon. Isaac made a mental note to send Agent Colton a box of Godiva chocolates and a bottle of excellent champagne for getting him his get-out-of-jail-free card so quickly.

So far, he'd honored the detective's mandate to stick to public kissing only, but not because she'd thrown her weight around.

Because he feared he'd be thoroughly unable to handle a second kiss like the first one.

Well, on second thought, he'd handle it, all right. But not in a way that would be conducive to capturing the Landmark Killer. Spending the afternoon with the detective sprawled out across his bed in various states of undress, sure. And he had no doubt she'd been right there with him on that trajectory during the first kiss, one step away from something they couldn't take back.

All of this over what had started out as a distraction. How else could he keep her from storming out of the door on a solo errand after she'd expressly told him she hadn't wanted him along?

It had worked though, hadn't it? There'd been no more talk of leaving. He'd won the bet and lost the war.

Instead, the detective had shut herself up in her room, leaving him to pace like a caged tiger who'd scented blood on the other side of the bars.

He'd deserved it for letting that kiss get away from him.

And now he held salvation in his hands. One driver's license that swore up and down his name was Oliver Walken. Agent Colton's guy had even doctored the picture to make him blond and altered the lighting so it wasn't immediately obvious that it was fake. She'd unwittingly matched the color the detective had dyed it too. Fate.

Not only did this driver's license mean they could start at the rink tonight, it meant he and the detective would be in public for hours. Also known as the mandated venue for their second kiss, and he intended to take full advantage of it.

When he texted her that the documents had come, she emerged from her room, her expression flat and conveying nothing of her thoughts. That was okay— he knew exactly how to get her flustered and affected.

"We're scheduled to be at the rink by five," he advised her, opting to stick to his all-business mode while in their condo. It was easier that way. "We'll handle the music until the rink closes at midnight."

They spent thirty minutes coordinating with the rest of the team via a quickly spun-up conference call, assigning surveillance spots and opening communication paths based on the work they'd already done in anticipation of this. Isaac texted the manager of the skating rink to double-check that his DJ equipment had been set up and received an affirmative.

"I think we're as prepared as we're going to be," he said. "Let's go."

She nodded and donned her wig, grabbed her purse, extracting the Glock inside to rehome it in the shoulder holster that she covered with a coat. Which was exactly what she'd suggested she would do earlier, when he'd mentioned tagging along with her to her apartment.

He got it. She could take care of herself. She had been for a long time before he came along. But knowing that didn't erase the abject panic that gripped his lungs when he thought about Washer coming after her because she'd aligned herself with Isaac.

Making himself a target, he could handle. Making Rory one, no. Not sitting well with him.

And he was about to take her directly into the line of fire.

The only thing that got his feet moving was the repeated mantra that Washer's MO did not include killing women at landmarks. He wouldn't veer from it. He couldn't, or he wouldn't be the Landmark Killer, and all of the intel pointed to Washer being proud of his "accomplishments," including earning a nickname that would be immortalized in serial killer history.

The second he and Rory hit the street, he turned up his collar against the chilly breeze and slid his fingers through hers, squeezing once.

She glanced at him but didn't pull her hand free. "You don't waste any time."

"Shh. We're in character now," he murmured. "From

now on, I'm Oliver, you're Cassandra. We're legal and everything."

This was it. They were going to be under the microscope each passing minute, especially once they hit the skating rink.

Isaac nodded to the plainclothes cop and then to the random businessman who crossed his path next, playing the part of a friendly resident of this block. His senses sharpened, honing his intake of his surroundings. A dog peeing on the side of the building, his owner facedown in his phone, oblivious. A knot of high school students giggling about something as they passed by. No threats.

That was when he started to believe this would work. He could balance the detective and the case. Look at him holding hands while on the job.

They walked together in perfect sync, a rarity that he enjoyed as they strolled along seemingly without a care in the world. Two lovers in the city on their way to work.

"There it is," the detective said as the enormous lighted tree that presided over the skating rink came into view.

"Cassandra." Nothing. The detective didn't even blink. He tugged on her hand with a laugh, strictly because she was so cute. "That's you, my darling."

She flinched and shot him a look. "I know. It's just weird, okay? I won't slip again."

"Let's make sure," he murmured and pulled her into an impromptu kiss, right there in the middle of the sidewalk.

Couldn't get more public than this.

"Trying to walk here," one of the passersby called with a snarl and then muttered, "Tourists."

Isaac didn't care. He had the detective in his arms

again, and only the word *bliss* could describe how she felt. Her mouth under his. Her hand skimming his jaw, drawing him forward. The crispness of the air stinging his cheeks and her heat warming him.

"Nice," he breathed against her lips, letting his draw up in a smile. "You didn't even sock me."

"Sanctioned," she whispered. "I'll initiate the next one."

Oh, that worked for him and then some. "I appreciate your work ethic, Detective."

"We can't screw this up," she murmured, nuzzling him as if she couldn't get enough, but he knew she was hiding her lips from anyone who might've been watching. "If Washer comes after you and something tips him off, he'll do whatever it takes to give us the slip. Then he won't rest until he finishes the job, and that makes him infinitely more dangerous than the average criminal."

"Sure. But that's an infinite number of chances to nab him the next time," he said into her hair. "It's better than Washer lying low. I'm all for whatever draws him out of hiding."

She nodded. "And I'm all for not blowing our cover. Whatever it takes."

Even kissing him, apparently. He couldn't be offended just because he'd enjoyed their kisses a little more than was expressly necessary to get the job done.

When they got to the rink, skaters already covered the ice like so many ants in a busy colony, all moving in the same direction, but some veering off on their own agenda, then sliding right back into the flow. Two skaters collided as they watched, both going down in a tangle of limbs, but they were laughing, so it must not have been too hard of a crash.

To the right of the Prometheus statue, just under the enormous lighted tree, some busy bees had set up a heated white tent, per the team's instructions. It was the perfect spot for visibility, both ways. The surveillance team could keep an eye on Oliver and Cassandra, and Washer couldn't possibly miss the tent. In fact, it provided a great setting for an ambush, especially when it came to the Landmark Killer. What better location for him to strike than in the shadow of the famous Rockefeller Center Christmas tree?

After checking in with the manager, Isaac led the detective to the tent and ducked inside. As command centers went, it was pretty sweet, with a top-of-the-line laptop preloaded with disco music, a Pioneer controller, microphone and headphones. Everything he'd requested.

The detective stared at the equipment. "You know how to use all that stuff?"

"You doubt me?" He blinked in mock incredulity. "You are looking at the guy who killed it at the Lincoln High prom. Of course I know how to use it."

Granted, that had been a million years and several generations of equipment ago, but the basics never changed.

"Better you than me," she commented and moved one of the chairs right to the edge where she could observe the entire rink at once.

Surveillance. It was exactly what they'd planned. There was no need for a second DJ, and she'd been a cop long enough that he appreciated her eyes on the crowd. But did she have to sit right there in the open where Washer could easily pick her off with a long-range scope?

He texted her on the burner phone she carried for

team communications: Maybe you could move your chair back inside the shelter of the tent?

She glanced at her phone and raised one hand in question, then texted back: I can't see the crowd if I move my chair. You have done surveillance before, right?

He sent her an eye-roll emoji, the one that looked just like her, and typed: It's warm in the tent. Cold at the edge. Plus you're way over there and I miss you already.

She shook her head and deliberately placed her phone facedown in her lap, pointedly ignoring him.

He texted her again: I know you've been chomping at the bit to be a target, but you don't have to paint a bullseye on your chest.

She shot him a withering glare, read the message and texted back: Don't you have a job to do, Oliver??

Isaac counted to ten before he stomped over and moved that chair for her. And then forced himself to count to ten again while reminding himself that they had a plan and it didn't include him having an anxiety attack at the thought of letting the detective do her job.

Meanwhile, she'd taken him to task about his own job, and rightly so. He dove in, rearranging the equipment setup to better suit him, then fired it up so he could familiarize himself with the software the department tech guy had loaded onto the laptop. The laptop had been integrated with the PA system, and he took a moment to make sure all the components could talk to each other, including the microphone, which connected via USB.

It took about twenty minutes to get it all working as

it should. The manager stopped by at the tail end, nervously hovering at the back entrance to the tent.

"Do you need anything?" he asked, his voice cracking as he shifted from foot to foot like a condemned prisoner waiting for the firing squad to finish loading bullets.

The detective glanced over, a scowl on her face as she clued in to the exact issue Isaac had already identified—this guy was a civilian and not at all used to undercover operations. If he didn't relax, he'd blow everything to pieces.

If Washer made them as cops, it would be all over. He might even move on to another landmark, kill someone else and then take credit for it. They'd lose any momentum on this case, and someone else would die because the manager was freaking out.

"Hey, Steve," Isaac called loudly. "Come check out this setup. The music is going to be great!"

The manager's eyes flared wider as he absorbed that he'd been invited to jump right into the lion's den, but he didn't argue and crept over to the table. Maybe he thought Isaac would shoot him if he didn't do as suggested.

Isaac grinned at the manager to show that it was fine, everything was totally cool, or would be as soon as he stopped acting like there was something to be concerned about. As soon as the guy got within earshot, Isaac leaned in and murmured, "Maybe you should think about taking the week off."

Steve shook his head. "I don't have any vacation left this year. Besides, the closer we get to Christmas, the more people pour through the gates. We need all the personnel we can get since we lost people due to all this business."

The manager swirled his hand to encompass the tent and the undercover op as a whole, presumably.

"Yeah, sorry about that," Isaac murmured. "We'll do our best to be out of your hair soon, hopefully without headlines."

Nodding, Steve stared out over the crowd. "That would be great. I'm having nightmares about a bloodbath."

The detective came up on the manager's other side and laid a comforting hand on his shoulder, leaning in to speak softly. "We did a lot of prep for this, and some of the best profilers in the business ran the odds. We wouldn't have put the public in danger if we thought the suspect would open fire during this busy time at an iconic landmark. We're good at what we do, Steve. That's why we're in this tent, separate from the crowd. An easy target."

For whatever reason, her comments seemed to calm Steve. She led the manager from the tent, murmuring to him with an encouraging smile as she diffused the situation expertly.

"Impressive," Isaac told her as she rejoined him at the DJ table. "As a reward for getting that potential hazard under control, I'll let you pick the first song."

She wrinkled her nose as she scanned the song list he'd pointed to on the laptop. "I don't know much about disco music. It's all ancient."

With a grin, he captured her hand in his—because he wanted to and he could, thanks to Steve getting her out of her surveillance chair and within his reach. "Oh, right, how could I have forgotten your hatred of all things disco?"

Glancing at their joined hands, she cocked an eyebrow. "Maybe we'll call it *refined taste* as opposed to *outright hatred.*"

"Let's circle back to that after you've been treated to all of the classics in the next few hours, shall we?" he suggested and pulled her closer to bury his lips in her hair. "Meanwhile, we're in public and we have a job to do."

As he'd hoped, she took that as the opportunity to make good on her promise of earlier, leaning in to plant a tiny kiss on his cheek. "Yes, we do, and that music isn't going to play itself."

And with that she fled for the edge of the tent, leaving him with the reminder that the job sometimes sucked.

Chapter 9

Rory spent the remainder of the night on edge, tense and slightly irritable. A fan of disco music she was not, but there was something super cute about how enthusiastic Donner got about it.

That was what irritated her—Donner was not cute.

And she should not have been thinking about kissing him again. This was a job. Only. Except she had every right to kiss him whenever she felt like it, especially here and now when she could be spontaneous about it.

That was also part of the job, never mind how she couldn't quite reconcile this rabbit hole she'd fallen down where kissing her partner was one of the job requirements.

The kissing was supposed to be fake though. Not an enormous distraction that left her worried she'd miss something. So she'd reneged on her intent to throw Donner for a loop at some point during the night with a well-timed kiss that fried his hair, the way he always did to her. He'd earned it. But she couldn't move from her spot by the edge of the tent, even when her fingers went numb.

If she missed something, people would die—Donner first and foremost. This feeling that she had to single-handedly protect him from Xander Washer? Not a fan of that either.

They had a team for a reason. She wasn't in this alone. But Donner was *her* husband. Fake husband, yes, which did not negate the sense of responsibility she felt toward him in the slightest. There might've been something wrong with her that she couldn't seem to separate fact from fiction.

He didn't seem to have any issues, curse him. He'd never lost his smile once, fielding requests from the skaters via a heavily advertised app that Ashlynn had put together so they could remain distraction free inside the tent.

That had worked out.

When Donner announced the last song of the night, she couldn't decide if she was disappointed or relieved that she'd spent the last six hours on high alert for no reason.

Both. She had to do better.

Donner packed up his stuff, stowing it in the locked storage area Steve had pointed them toward, and called it a night. On the walk home—or rather, to the FBI's condo—the temperature hovered just around seventh level of arctic hell, and she regretted not having taken advantage of the heated tent. Being a cop was not for the weak, so she sucked it up.

"Cold?" Donner asked when she shivered for the third time.

"No, I was just thinking about kissing you again," she shot back, only for Donner to laugh and sling an arm around her, drawing her into his side.

"Get over here and let me warm you up, Mule Head."

"Compliments will get you nowhere," she grumbled, refusing to be charmed once again by his insistence on doing the exact opposite of what she expected, namely something chivalrous and thoughtful.

"I'm pretty much going to call it like I see it," he told her cheerfully. "You act like a mule, you get called one. You didn't have to sit at the edge of the tent the entire time just to spite me."

"I didn't," she countered hotly as they rounded the corner of their building, forcing her to lower her voice just in case. "Your job is music. Mine is paying attention."

Not that she could necessarily claim to have done that. Tomorrow, she'd figure it out and get it right. They wouldn't get a second chance.

Donner didn't seem too impressed with her argument, tsking as he hustled her into the lobby and up to their floor. Never in her life had she been more thrilled to have an elevator to their floor and very much feared she'd gotten spoiled in the short time they'd lived here. How did you go back to a walk-up after this luxury?

She'd actually started to thaw a little bit.

Not enough for Donner though. The moment they'd checked the perimeter and entered the condo, signaling *all clear* to the perimeter detail, Donner shut the door and grabbed the collar of her coat, helping her slide it off.

"I'm not five," she groused, relieved that she hadn't had to bend her fingers, which had started tingling as they warmed up in the heat of the condo. "I can undress myself."

He raised his eyebrows as he tossed her coat onto the loveseat at a right angle to the couch. "Don't mind me. Keep going, then."

"Ha, ha," she said with a saccharine smile. "You know what I meant."

"Yeah, and you're freezing," he said, his expression all melty with concern that she wished she could say was faked, but she'd lost the ability to tell. "Body heat can't be beat to solve that problem."

"Poetry?" she murmured as he stripped off his own coat, then proceeded to ignore all personal boundaries, wrapping her up in his arms.

Dear Lord, he felt good. She wanted to spring away, maybe slap him for being so…caring. But she couldn't do anything but stand there as he warmed her up for no reason other than because he'd noticed she was cold.

"Detective," he murmured, his nose in her ear for the four hundredth time that evening, except it wasn't expressly necessary now that they were behind closed doors. "It's okay if you want to put your arms around me too."

"Are you cold?" she asked automatically, her eyes closed as she rested her head on his shoulder. Just for a second.

"Something like that," he said with a rumbly chuckle she felt against her chest. "Though maybe more to the point, I would like you to."

She felt so floaty and lovely that she did, smoothing her hands along his back until she hit a spot that felt as if it had been made for her palms. Strictly a tit-for-tat kind of situation. He'd done something nice for her; she could return the favor.

He made a noise in his throat that didn't sound like anything to do with heat transfer. Glancing up, she met his gaze. *Mistake.* Concern had been replaced with something else, something dark and full of intense promise. Awareness climbed through her as she went from chilled to feverish in a flash.

Bringing his hands up to cup her cheeks, he feathered both thumbs across them. "You're starting to get some color back."

"You might be too good at this," she muttered.

"Warming you up?"

"Using innocuous activities as seduction methods," she corrected.

"I notice you're still standing here."

Which should have been the catalyst for her to move, but she couldn't, not without making sure she told him exactly how unaffected she was. "Practice makes perfect. The more comfortable I am with your hands on me, the better of a show we put on tomorrow night for Washer, who is most likely now aware of your existence."

The glint in his eye said he didn't believe her excuse, but he released her, stepping away and taking all of his delicious body heat with him. "One day you're going to trip over all of that smugness."

"What's that supposed to mean?"

He contemplated her for an eternity, and she stared back at him coolly, determined not to let him see a blessed thing that was raging around inside her.

"It means that one day you'll run out of excuses and

then you'll have to admit that you like it when my hands are on you."

"Can't admit something that's not true," she told him primly, wiping the lie off her face with what felt like monumental effort. He already wore his arrogance like a second skin, as if it had never occurred to him that a woman could resist him. Well, he had another think coming, didn't he?

They were partners. Not lovers, not married, nothing.

Donner raised his chin. "Wanna bet?"

Ugh, that man. She flounced from the living area to her bedroom, closing the door without slamming it—a feat that should've come with chocolate as a reward—and got ready for bed.

She needed sleep and fuel in that order, but she couldn't seem to drift off. Before even a tiny thought related to Isaac Donner could swirl through her head, she forced herself to go over the layout of the skating rink, looking for vulnerabilities, replaying the traffic patterns of the skaters, visualizing the entry points to the tent.

Washer would be there tomorrow night. She could feel it.

Whether he took a shot at Oliver Walken or not remained to be seen. But he wouldn't succeed at taking out his next victim, not with Rory Colton on the job.

After maybe four hours of sleep, she woke to her alarm and sprang out of bed to throw on some decent clothes instead of venturing out in search of coffee in her pajamas. Not that her matching plaid pants and oversized button-down shirt could be construed as even remotely sexy, but Donner had a habit of turning the tables on her when she least expected it. There was no reason to give him any ideas. Better safe than sorry.

But when she emerged from her room, it turned out that all the ideas would be on her side. Donner had beaten her to the kitchen and stood there shirtless, a pair of gray flannel drawstring pants slung low across his hips, calmly measuring coffee into the machine as if Rory stumbled across the elements of a male boudoir photo shoot every day.

Her mouth went dry as she tried not to stare, but it was hard not to want to feast her eyes on so much perfection doing anything, let alone making coffee.

"Planning to share?" she croaked and cleared her throat, crossing her arms over her quivering midsection.

How was it fair that he looked like *that* after a decade on the force and she looked like…*not* that?

Donner glanced over his shoulder with a grin, that boyish Irish charm spilling off him in waves. "Depends on what you're after, though odds are high I'd be game for whatever you'd like me to share with you."

It should've been illegal for a man to be so sexy this early in the morning. She cleared her throat. "Coffee. Everything else is not a thing."

He raised an eyebrow. "There's a thing, trust me. But for now, coffee. I got you."

"Are you sure you know how to run that machine?" she asked, desperately hoping it didn't sound like as much of a subject change to him as it did to her. "You didn't seem like much of a drip aficionado yesterday."

"I'm a fast learner."

When it beeped, he even poured it for her, and she took it without comment, dumping cream and sugar into the cup as he watched. Then she took a sip and nearly moaned.

"It's good, right?" he asked, nudging her. "Better than yours."

She rolled her eyes. The guy turned everything into a contest. "Not half bad."

"Google-fu to the rescue," he said and snagged his own cup. "You're not going to tell me to get dressed? I wasn't expecting you this early, or I would have thrown a shirt on to ensure your delicate sensibilities wouldn't be offended."

"I work in a mostly male precinct," she advised him with a smirk. "You don't have anything I haven't seen before."

Only because he'd taken his shirt off when she'd dyed his hair, but he didn't have to know that was what she meant. There was no way she was admitting that he might have had the best body of any man she'd ever met. Maybe even among those she hadn't met.

"Great, then I won't worry too much about making a fashion statement behind closed doors."

"Let's worry about Washer," she said with a snap to her tone that he didn't miss.

But in his typical fashion, he seemed more amused than taken to task. "I'm always worried about Washer. My main goal in life is to bring him down."

"Your second goal, you mean?" she corrected him as she let the hot coffee do its job to both warm her and piledrive caffeine straight into her veins. Donner didn't mess around with a coffee scoop, and he'd gotten the stuff strong indeed. "After making my life miserable."

He cocked his head. "Am I making your life miserable?"

Trust him to cut to the chase and never let her get away with a flip comment. She shifted under his intense scrutiny, painfully aware that he seemed to be expecting an honest answer, which threw her for a moment. She opted to laugh it off. "You know you live to antagonize me."

Although it had been a while since he'd baited her to quite the degree that he had at the precinct when they'd merely shared the air between their desks. Now that she thought about it, he'd spent a lot more time lately perfecting his seduction routine. That was why it had been so hard for her to sort out what was happening—he'd teetered her kilter off by switching up his game.

She had to be better at managing whatever he threw at her.

"Come on, Detective," he said with an enigmatic smile. "You never heard the old saying that boys only tease the girls they like?"

Dumbfounded by that revelation, she drained her coffee cup as a number of things that shouldn't have been there swirled around in her chest. But she had to say something, so she blurted out, "Is this a confession?"

He shrugged. "The moment I stop being honest with you is the moment you know you've lost my trust. You're my partner, for better or worse. That's its own kind of marriage, one that frankly has more at stake than the romantic kind. We don't have the latitude of getting it wrong."

That hit her sideways. Warmth, dangerously thick and lovely, spread through her chest, and it wasn't the coffee. It was almost like he'd cracked her open and done a thorough analysis of her psyche, then picked out the one thing he could say that would affect her the most.

"It's always about the job," she murmured. Her love language. He'd known that too, and chosen to be real and honest with her instead of flirty and arrogant. And worse, this discovery meant she'd misjudged him and not by a little bit.

They had much more in common than she'd have guessed.

What was she supposed to do with this?

He nodded once. "It is always about the job. So that's how you know I'm telling you the truth when I say taking down Washer is goal number one. I fully expect you to be right by my side, doing it with me."

The man could not have conceived of a better pep talk. All at once, she felt bulletproof and ready to take on Xander Washer. Which she was pretty sure had been Donner's intent.

The only problem? They had hours until they could leave for the rink. Whatever could they do to pass the time?

She eyed Donner thoughtfully, fairly certain she'd pegged him dead to rights when labeling him as competitive as he was arrogant. Look at how he'd one-upped her coffee game.

"You up for a little wager?" she asked him.

Chapter 10

Rory pulled off her safety glasses and nearly threw them to the ground in frustration, careful to engage the safety on her Glock before she rounded on Donner. He'd smoked her every time, no matter what kind of target had come up. Eight rounds in a row.

"How do you keep beating me?" she squawked, which made him laugh. Obviously he felt quite safe from her wrath now that her weapon couldn't be fired.

"Was I supposed to let you win?" he asked with wide, innocent eyes. "I did not get that memo."

"You were supposed to tell me you're some kind of firing-range savant," she groused, though why she hadn't guessed that would be the case, she'd never know.

The man did nothing poorly, and he'd literally just told her this morning that the job mattered to him more than anything. Of course he'd spent umpteen hours on end practicing at the firing range well before they'd ever met.

"Look at it this way, Detective," he said and holstered his own weapon with the kind of care other men might've taken with a hundred-thousand-dollar sports car. "You're still a winner because you have me for a partner."

There was the arrogant, competitive cop she knew and loathed. Except something had shifted inside because she didn't really hate him, not anymore. But she still didn't intend to feed his ego. "We have different definitions of the word *win*."

He grinned. "You'd rather have a partner who eats a lot of doughnuts and couldn't shoot the broad side of a barn? Let me call the captain right now and see if we can sub John Maloney for a bit. See how you like being undercover with him. Or maybe—"

"I get it, Donner," she said through her teeth. "I'm the luckiest cop on the planet because I landed you as a partner. And best of all, we still have about two hours until we have to be at the skating rink, which is plenty of time to get ready. Let's go."

She'd had more than enough of losing, that was for sure.

Donner waited until they'd slipped through the back entrance to the shooting range in Brooklyn, one they'd picked because it had no police association. He glanced at her. "You'll never get better if you don't compete against the best, you know. That's why I didn't pull any punches either. The last thing anyone needs is a false sense of their own skill. Now you know exactly where you stand, and next time, if you beat me, you'll know you've gotten better."

"Thanks, Obi-Wan, I'll keep that in mind." At least she'd had an opportunity to blow off some steam, and she took some solace in that. "Grab an Uber, and don't forget we have to double back through the Upper East Side to throw off any tails."

Without the distraction of the shooting range to occupy her thoughts, the operation roared back into her head with a vengeance, setting her on edge. So much for suggesting a bit of downtime with a dual purpose—she hadn't had to think about kissing or the Landmark Killer or fake marriages for a while, and she'd had an opportunity to brush up on her short-range skills, for all the good that had done.

When they got back to their condo after a quick stop at the deli on the corner for a late lunch, they spread out on the bistro table, a schematic of the skating rink up on Donner's laptop and Cash and Brennan on FaceTime so they could go over logistics.

They'd ended up treating last night as a trial run by default, since Washer hadn't shown. Tonight he would. She had no doubt, which made this the real deal.

"Let's test the equipment again," Rory suggested, unable to stop her pulse from scattering.

"Alpha," Brennan's voice sounded in her ear as he spoke into his tiny microphone, always ready to be a team player.

"Bravo," Cash said, next in line because they always went alphabetically, and with three of them named Colton, they had to use first names.

"Charlie," Donner said, and Rory heard it twice, in her earpiece and live since he was sitting next to her.

"Delta," she said, wrapping up the test and glancing at Donner, who shot her the thumbs-up. Cash and Brennan repeated it on their ends.

Everything was a go, and no one had said a word about her insistence on doing the drill a dozen times. The twins were used to her style, but Donner wasn't, yet he'd apparently elected to give her a break thus far, which made her suspicious.

She let it pass, too keyed up to force the issue.

"Guys, talk to me about crowd control," she said.

Dutifully, Brennan spoke up, his voice tinny thanks to her ancient iPhone that she refused to give up because learning a new screen layout and interface did not rank high on her list of fun things.

"I'm covering the south entrances, and Cash is covering the north," he repeated without a trace of sarcasm despite this being the fourth time she'd commanded him to walk through it. "We have paramedics from two stations on alert in case we're wrong and Washer goes after a different target."

"We're not wrong," Rory interjected tersely. "He's never hit a target at a landmark who didn't fit the profile. He won't veer from that now, not when we're offering up blond, blue-eyed Oliver as a sacrificial lamb."

Washer picked victims who had first names with beginning letters that spelled *Maeve O'Leary* in order. Five victims thus far, and an *O* name would be next. He'd even left a note with the last victim telling this to the world. Washer reveled in the idea of following in Maeve's footsteps, of having a name as meaningful as hers. She'd been known as the Black Widow Killer, Washer as the Landmark Killer. He wouldn't do anything to jeopardize the lore of his reign of terror.

Rory let all this run through her head as a litany.

Reinforcement. They couldn't afford to be wrong, or people would die. She couldn't live with that, ergo, this would go down as prescribed. No other option.

Finally Donner pulled her to her feet but didn't release her hands. "Let it ride, Detective. There's such a thing as being overprepared."

"Not in my world." What did it say about her that she took comfort from standing with Donner like this, hand in hand? They'd grown closer by living together, sure, but this was something different. They'd become a unit.

Donner raised his chin. "Broaden your horizons. Your instincts are good. Use them."

She let the compliment and the advice flow through her, emboldening her. Assuring her. She was a great cop. It was all she'd ever wanted to be. This was her chance to show everyone that Coltons knew how to get the job done.

Rory grabbed her coat, holstered her weapon, hooked her purse over her arm. All rote activities that should have soothed her but didn't. Because Washer had slipped through the fingers of the best of the best thus far. The responsibility for this collar rested with her. She couldn't fail, or it would be Donner who died this time.

"Don't worry, Detective," he murmured as they left the condo. "We're in this together. Your FBI boys will be there too. We have it covered."

How had he realized consternation still chopped through her chest, beating against her rib cage in taut waves?

Because that was what he did. His observation skills clearly rivaled his shooting abilities. That made him a great cop too. But still very much a target. She couldn't lose another partner.

On the street, he tugged her into his side, slinging an arm around her as they walked. A legit married-people move that she had no call to argue with but wanted to all at once.

Because she got a little mushy when he did that. And that was not kosher.

Stiffening, she tried to walk without touching his side, which only ended up hurting her spine.

"Relax," he murmured. "I can hear your brain on frappe mode from here. You're going to tip off Washer if you keep walking around like you're expecting him to jump out at any moment."

Ugh, yeah, she got it. She knew. It was just like Steve last night, except this wasn't a civilian freaking out, it was her. And not for the reason Donner thought.

Being fake married was part of her job too, and she hated how often she had to remind herself of it. It would surely be a lot easier if she could get back to the place where she hated her partner and wished he would die. That would work splendidly in this situation.

Except she'd never *really* hoped he'd die. And she probably never really hated him either, which would explain why he'd snuck under her guardrails so easily and endeared himself to her when she wasn't looking.

There was no help for it. She relaxed, and the weight of his arm at her waist automatically allowed him to snug her deeper against his side. It was so not terrible that she almost sighed.

Maybe one day, she'd get married for real. It could happen. After she'd logged twenty years on the force and didn't care about accolades or promotions or whether she'd get shot and leave a spouse behind.

"That's my girl," he murmured, and she almost

snapped back that she was neither his nor a girl when she remembered this was all for show.

"If you'd really wanted to distract me, a kiss would have filled that bill better," she said instead and then nearly bit off her tongue as he shot her a glance full of very-difficult-to-misinterpret heat.

"I am nothing if not willing and eager to follow instructions," he said and leaned in to drop a kiss on her temple that had none of the promise from his expression a moment ago.

More disappointed than she knew what to do with, she stared straight ahead and tried not to think about the warm and tingly patch of skin near her eye.

Just when she thought she had the man figured out, he knocked her for a loop once more.

The skating rink was packed again tonight, with a blur of colors and people in all shapes and sizes milling about. Some skated. Some clung to the guardrail around the ice, clearly too timid to let go. Some stood above the rink near the statue of Prometheus, watching the skaters below.

That was where Washer would be. It was the best vantage point, in the shadow of the tree. The enormous evergreen would be what everyone focused on, not a killer with a cold, calculating expression on his face as he targeted yet another male stand-in for his stepfather. Ashlynn had been the one to ferret out that information—Washer's targets all mirrored a man he'd come to loathe growing up.

"Alpha," Brennan said into his microphone, which meant he was in place, hidden from view but still able to see the rink.

"Bravo," Cash called to indicate he'd also moved into his predetermined surveillance spot.

They'd talked about having the two of them pose as skaters, but logistically, that made little sense as they'd be hampered when Washer showed up. Better to have them at street level in the event they made the suspect before he struck.

That was best-case scenario. The one she'd be doubling down on.

"Charlie," Donner murmured as he paused near the entrance to nuzzle her hair. She shot him a surreptitious thumbs-up.

"Delta," she said to him with a smile as if she'd just whispered an endearment, hoping if anyone watching could read lips, it had looked like a whole different word.

They entered the complex with their employee badges and waved to Steve, who looked like he'd eaten bad seafood when he caught sight of them but managed a sick smile. Rory ignored him, her gaze tight on every face she passed, running Washer's official FBI photo in her head next to each one, superimposing them, discarding the individual when it didn't match.

Odds-on, he'd be in disguise anyway. But she couldn't assume anything. Or let down her guard for a millisecond. He could strike anywhere, anytime.

When they reached the tent without incident, she tried to jump-start her lungs as Donner retrieved his DJ toys from the locked closet and spent twenty minutes setting them up. Rory stood at the edge of the tent, hyperaware of every sharp movement from the skaters beyond the barricade. The heat on her back felt good, but she wouldn't be lulled into enveloping herself in it fully.

Donner cued up the first song, announcing it expertly into the microphone as if he'd been born to be a DJ.

"You missed your calling," she told him with a tight smile as the song started playing. She'd learned the first night that she couldn't talk until the red light on his mic blinked out or everyone in the rink would hear her.

"One could argue that I didn't miss it," he said with a laugh. "Since I get to do it on the job after all."

Rory nodded and went back to watching, her spine so rigid that she felt taller already. Exit points. She marked them in her head. Brennan at two o'clock, Cash at nine.

"Is the tide high?" she asked, the phrase they'd decided to use to ask for a status, which was a joke Donner had come up with because washers used Tide to clean clothes.

Rory hadn't found it funny, but she'd been overruled.

"Tide's still low," Cash responded, meaning he hadn't seen Washer.

"No tide here," Brennan chimed in.

The minutes slogged by, each one taking a million years. Only Donner seemed to be rolling with it, less on edge than she'd have assumed. But nothing seemed to bother him, so theoretically, this shouldn't either.

It should've bothered him that Washer hadn't appeared yet. Cash and Brennan checked in every so often, both on red alert. He wouldn't get by them. He couldn't. Unless he'd disguised himself. A distinct possibility.

Movement registered out of the corner of her eye, and she shifted her gaze without moving her head. A figure. Someone had entered the tent. No one was supposed to be in here.

She pivoted. A man, ski hat pulled low, wool scarf

up around his nose. Most importantly, he had a 9 millimeter in his hand pointed at Donner's head.

Washer. No question, despite the winter gear hiding his features. And he had a *gun*.

Isaac. He was in danger. His pupils widened as he slowly lifted his hands, his gaze glued to the gun. The vest he wore would do no good if Washer shot him in the forehead.

And they had no idea how good of a shot the Landmark Killer actually was. She did not want to find out in this horrific of a way.

Panic warred with terror, both jockeying for position in her clogged throat. She couldn't lose Isaac. Immobilized, she fought to get in gear.

Move. Now.

Rory's vision narrowed and her pulse skyrocketed as she leapt into action, karate kicking the gun from Washer's hand. It skittered away, sliding under the table holding the DJ equipment.

Danger eliminated, the iron grip on her lungs eased off a fraction.

Washer glanced up, his shocked gaze meeting hers. Just for a moment. A millisecond suspended in time as she memorized every stitch and detail on his outfit. His face. Man, she had forgotten how young he was. He still looked like a teenager. A dangerous one.

Get him. Zip ties in right pocket. Do it.

Before she could spring toward him, Washer dashed from the tent before either she or Donner could unfreeze themselves. *No, no, no.* He could not get away.

"Suspect on the move," she shouted into her earpiece as she took off after him, running down Washer's identifying characteristics. None of which would matter if he ditched the hat and scarf.

The second she cleared the tent, she ran smack dab into a man the size and consistency of a brick wall. It knocked the air from her lungs, and she wheezed, trying to catch her breath.

"Are you okay?" the man asked, oblivious to the fact that he'd just impeded a police chase.

"Move," she bit out and flung up her hand with her badge clutched in her fingers, dodging the mountain of a man without a backward glance.

Too late. Washer had vanished into the crowd. She cursed, scanning one hundred eighty degrees, pausing far too long on each face in an attempt to match her target. Nothing.

"Tell me you've got a visual," she called into her earpiece, frustration steeling her voice.

"Copy that," Brennan responded. "I see him headed toward 5th."

"On it," Cash said, the slap of his feet hitting cement reverberating through the channel.

"Stayin' Alive" wailed through the speakers as Rory stood at the edge of the ice, her pulse pounding painfully in her throat as she waited for the status update. Everything carried on as if nothing had happened. And to the world, nothing *had* happened. Donner had never stopped playing the part of the DJ to keep his cover safe, leaving the crowd oblivious to the fact that he'd nearly been toast.

"I lost him." Cash cursed, breathing heavily. "Christmas crowds. Everyone is bundled up and in a hurry."

Rory smacked the railing with the heel of her hand and echoed Cash's inventive swear word.

Chapter 11

"He'll try again," Isaac advised the detective as they debriefed in the tent while another ABBA song played over the loudspeaker, drowning out their conversation.

"I know," she shot back tersely. "That's what's concerning me. Next time, he might get a lot luckier. We should have shut him down this time."

Well, he thoroughly agreed with that, especially given his disadvantaged position as the DJ. That was a complexity he'd never factored in.

How was he supposed to avenge Allison and prove to his father he was a good cop if he was stuck in the tent all the time?

Brennan and Cash, who were twins but looked nothing alike, both paced in angry, zigzagged lines. Clearly they were all frustrated by the unexpected turn of events, which he would normally have a lot of compassion for but seemed to be a bit short on this time.

"What went wrong?" he asked the room at large, because the events had been a blur to him.

One second, Washer had had a gun shoved in his direction, the next, the detective had disarmed him in a truly impressive move worthy of Jackie Chan. Before Isaac could unfreeze himself, Washer had fled with the detective in hot pursuit. Which had given him time to get his head together. His pulse had shot into the stratosphere, only to be faced with an empty tent where the threat had been.

He should have been on the other side of the table. The one in pursuit.

But he'd signed up to be the DJ, and a DJ wouldn't chase a guy with a gun. A DJ would stay put and keep up appearances.

"He surprised us," the detective offered grimly. "In spite of every one of us on high alert, no one saw him approach the tent."

"How is that possible?" he barked at the Colton twins. "You guys forget how to do surveillance with those cushy FBI jobs?"

The agents glanced at each other, and Brennan spoke first. "We think he came up from the concourse and hid behind the tent. We literally didn't see him go in. Once Rory tagged him, we got a visual on him leaving, but he cut up through the gardens and it's just—"

"The wrong time of year to be chasing a suspect in a ski hat and scarf," Cash finished for him, his expression hard. "He took advantage of that. We won't get caught out again."

It was an explanation and an apology in one, which Isaac took with as much grace as he could, nodding his thanks. After all, it was his neck on the line, not theirs.

He'd done his job by providing the bait—as much as it chafed to be left out of the action—and they'd failed to do theirs. As much as he hated depending on other people, he sensed that they knew they'd screwed up and it weighed on them.

The detective rubbed her temple. "Did he make you?"

Cash shook his head. "I don't think so. I never got close enough."

"Then our covers are still good," Isaac surmised, relieved that at least that had gone right. "Washer didn't see you chase after him since you ran into that big guy right at the entrance to the tent. That means we can give him another chance to try again. Tomorrow night."

"You don't think he caught a clue after my kung fu move?" the detective asked ruefully, still rubbing her temples. "I saw his face. He couldn't believe it."

"He can join the club," Isaac said and patted his pocket where they'd stashed Washer's gun in a plastic bag to take to evidence as soon as possible. "It was nothing short of spectacular. That's not the first time I've dodged a bullet with my name on it, but it's the first time I wasn't the one responsible for removing the threat."

That was the one bright spot. The detective had his back. As a partner should, but he'd also had his share of bad luck in that department. For the first time ever, he felt like part of a unit.

It was nice.

But she had a point. Washer might have put two and two together after being so successfully disarmed, or he might assume that Cassandra Walken had taken self-defense lessons. Lots of women did, especially ones who lived in New York City. They had to bank on the latter.

Either way, Washer likely had not taken kindly to the detective's interference, and now all bets were off.

She glanced up from her phone. "Captain Reeves ordered our detail to be upped. We've got ten undercover cops coming to do twenty-four seven rounds here at the rink and two more at the condo."

Overkill in Isaac's mind, but he'd take whatever help they could get, assuming it went smoothly from here on out and the new blood didn't take a page from the failed operation here this evening. "Roger that."

They sent the twins away in the event that Washer elected to return to the rink after a few hours' lull. If he did, he'd be furious that the detective had thwarted his deadly plans. Likely irrational as well. They obviously couldn't predict his moves.

And now the detective had a target on her back too.

It was another complexity that Isaac hadn't seen coming and didn't know what to do with.

He spent the rest of the night in tense agony, alert and ready to spring into action himself if Washer threatened the detective, but also grappling with this weird protective bent that had seemingly cropped up overnight. He'd volunteered to be in the line of fire, knew what came along with that. A cop had to rationalize that out in his head every day—that this one could be his last. He accepted it, as long as the bullet stayed aimed in his direction.

The thought of Washer's gun pointed at the detective sat in his gut with an acidic, painful edge.

That, he did not like. Or care to examine.

When he played the last song, his nerves finally

started to relax their hold on his body, which in turn released a mental strain he hadn't quite realized was there. A headache rushed in to replace the tension. Great. That was all he needed to pile on to his current level of misery.

Finally, the nightmare of a night ended, and he didn't even mess around, just ordered an Uber and bundled the detective into it. And yes, he totally intended to expense it. The captain could consider it hazard pay.

The detective didn't argue. She seemed likewise drained, letting her head fall back on the seat.

"Hey," he murmured, mindful of the Uber driver, who likely tuned out everything that happened in his back seat, but they couldn't be too careful. "Are you okay?"

"I should be asking you that," she said with a side-long glance at him. "You always seem unflappable though, so that's why I didn't."

"I'm flapped plenty, trust me," he said, which earned him a small smile. "My life flashed before my eyes, and it's only then that you realize how much you've put off for later, thinking you'll always have time to do the stuff you've been meaning to do."

"Like what?"

Well, he hadn't meant to dive right into the philo-sophical, but he had opened his mouth. "You know, the usual. Climb Mount Everest. Go to the moon. Swim with sharks."

Fall in love. Have a partner for life who always had his back in a way that went beyond the call of duty. Finally let Allison go, to allow her memory to drift up into the ether as a feeling of forgiveness stole over him.

These were dreams he'd never shared with anyone.

Things he'd never have and never expected to have. All of them were out of reach, which he'd known for a long time. It was just difficult to reconcile sometimes that he would likely die in the line of duty without having ticked off any of the items on his secret list.

Her expression was priceless. "These are the things you think about not having done when someone aims a gun in your direction?"

Shrugging, he gave her a small smile in return. "I dream big."

"And I call BS," she said as the lights of 49th Street played over her face, rising and falling more quickly than normal due to the late hour. "That's not what you really think about when facing mortality. You think about the relationships that ended or never began. People you've lost. Regrets."

The fact that she'd basically called him a liar and then told him exactly what was in his head stunned him. Had she dialed into something he'd inadvertently given away, or was it a lucky guess? "Sounds like you're speaking from experience."

Something flashed in her expression, but the lights slid from her face before he could catch it. "Let's just say that I don't need a gun shoved toward me to think about those things."

Which meant she must've considered them on a frequent basis, especially to have spit out that list so quickly. What regrets did she have? Aside from her previous partner, she'd obviously lost someone important to her—who? A lover? A husband? They'd never talked about anything that personal, so he didn't even know if she'd ever been married.

And now he wanted to know.

They arrived at their condo building before he could delve into any of it. She stuck a little closer to him than she normally did, but he couldn't quite figure out the reason behind it. Faking it for the audience, or feeling a little closer to him because of the near miss with Washer?

They weren't necessarily mutually exclusive—which, if that was the case, he didn't mind at all.

Inside their condo, he took a moment to double-check the locks, which gave the detective a chance to flee, and he almost let her. But he grabbed her hand before she could get too far.

"Hey," he murmured, his gaze flicking across her face, glad for the low lights of the condo that allowed him to evaluate her reactions at will. "Are you doing okay?"

"I should be asking you that question." She shrugged lightly. "I'm not the one who almost got shot."

He chuckled. "Neither am I, thanks to my quick-footed partner. But that's not what I meant. Are you okay about everything else?"

Her gaze traveled over his face in kind, a thousand different things floating between them, none of them easily identified. For a half second, he expected her to bring up the vibe that had sprung up since she'd saved him, this weird sense of being a team. Of being totally in sync. And maybe he wanted to hear that she liked it too. That something had shifted between them.

What would he say if she did admit she felt it?

But in the end, she looked away and shook her head, her mouth stretched into a tight, frustrated line. "The fact that we lost him? No. I'm not even a little okay about that."

Of course that was what was bothering her. The job.

It bothered him too, and that was the more important thorn in their sides. The rest of it? Not a thing. Or rather it was a thing, no question, but not one he could focus on at the moment.

No matter how hot the detective was in her element.

Yeah, he'd own it. When she'd kicked that gun away, it had sparked something inside him that would be very difficult to put out. It was useless to pretend otherwise. She'd intrigued him from the first, but throw in everything else there was to like about her? He'd developed a huge crush on his fake wife before he'd even realized she'd snuck under his skin.

Too bad she was also his partner. The timing couldn't be worse to indulge in a mutually satisfying fling, even if everyone in this room thought it would be a great idea to go there—and he could say with absolute certainty that *no one* in this room thought that.

"We're going to get Washer," he promised her. "There's no other option."

Exhausted all at once, Isaac sent the detective off to her own room and didn't think too much about following her, just to see if she'd look at him again with that slightly mushy-eyed expression, as if glad he hadn't ended up bleeding out on the floor of the tent.

Isaac couldn't sleep though. The condo was too quiet. His bed was too empty.

Or at least that had always been the case before when he got this restless. After they closed this case, he'd have to find a no-strings woman to ease this ache inside. And figure out why that didn't sound appealing in the slightest.

A metallic *snick* drove everything else from his head. That sound didn't belong in this condo.

Soundlessly, he rolled from his bed and stabbed his legs through his pants, buttoning them with one hand. He reached for his weapon and disengaged the safety with the other. Then took two seconds to throw on socks so he could avoid announcing his presence on the squeaky hardwood floor.

On cat feet, he crept out of his room, gun plastered to his breastbone, his gaze darting everywhere all at once. The detective's dragonfly lamp cast low light from the corner of the living area, affording him a decent view of the entire condo, from the kitchen to the sliding glass doors that led to the minuscule patio overlooking 48th Street.

The exterior door stood slightly ajar. The source of the snick earlier. Someone had picked the locks. Or had scored a copy of their key somehow.

Washer. With his FBI contacts and resources, either could be true. It had to be him. He was *here*. In the condo.

Isaac expanded his lungs, drawing in air in measured cadence, trying to keep his pulse regulated. He swept the kitchen slowly, training his gaze on each shadowy corner. Nothing.

Where are you, you slimy piece of filth? This place wasn't that big, and Isaac would have passed Washer if he'd gone into his bedr—

A cry from the detective's room propelled him into motion. *Rory.* No!

Bursting into her bedroom, he scarcely had time to register that Washer had his hands around Rory's throat. Instantly, Isaac struck with the butt of his gun, colliding with Washer's temple.

His grip loosened, allowing the detective to launch

her own counterattack, bucking against Washer's hold. That gave Isaac a second to get the guy into a choke-hold and drag him away from the bed. But the slippery killer immediately employed some kind of evasive maneuver, breaking free.

Everything slowed to half speed, as if inside the frame of a movie where the director had taken artistic license to allow the viewer to examine each detail. Washer lunged for the detective again. Her face registered grim determination as she steeled for his attack. Isaac raised the gun and aimed, his pulse beating a rhythm in his throat.

This time, he wasn't behind a table. This time, Washer wouldn't get away. Allison's voice floated through his mind, echoing, as if she'd called out, only to find herself closed in on all sides. Trapped. Begging to be set free. A kill shot, Isaac's aim true, would accomplish that.

The detective made a noise of warning in her throat.

Suddenly, Washer ducked and spun, crashing into Isaac before he could react.

They both went down, and Isaac instinctively flung his arm toward the wall, pointing his gun away from the detective. Washer grabbed his wrist and banged it against the floor, trying to knock his fingers loose from the weapon. Painful pricks stabbed through his hand as the nerve endings hit the wood over and over.

But he didn't let go.

Washer climbed onto his chest, his knees digging into Isaac's forearms. The guy couldn't weigh more than one fifty, but he had insanity and sheer determination on his side, making it difficult for Isaac to dislodge him.

They grappled for a few tense moments, the heel of Isaac's hand jammed up into Washer's throat, Washer's grip on Isaac's gun hand manically tight. Washer wouldn't stay still, continually shifting back and forth, his face a mask of rage.

Rage—because he couldn't kill Oliver Walken in this condo. This wasn't a landmark. It would go against everything the killer had set up thus far.

All at once, Washer broke free and spun, launching himself at the detective.

That was when it dawned on Isaac that he wasn't the one in danger here.

Chapter 12

Rory only had a millisecond to react. As Washer lunged toward her, she flung up her arm to block him.

But he never reached her. Donner jumped onto his back, taking Washer down to the carpet with him. The two men wrestled, both fighting for Donner's weapon again.

Seeing her chance, she pulled out her concealed gun to shoot, but there was no clear line to Washer, not with Donner on top. Her pulse beat so loudly in her temples that it sounded like it bounced off the walls.

Or maybe that was because the walls had started closing in.

She couldn't do nothing. But she couldn't risk hitting Donner.

She could jump into the fray, but she'd almost blown their cover earlier at the rink, when she'd stripped Washer of his gun. Every training move ran through her head, her muscles screaming at her to move, to do something.

But she couldn't figure out what to do that wouldn't alert Washer to the fact that she was a cop. Or worse, that Donner was one too.

Suddenly, Washer got a lucky shot to Donner's face, raking his fingernails down her partner's cheek, drawing blood. Donner grunted but didn't lessen his grip.

Everything sharpened as she sorted options. Lamp. Blunt instrument. Not the weapon of a cop. *Do it, Rory*.

As soon as she stretched toward the bedside table, Washer's attention shifted to her and he rolled, knocking Donner askew. Seeing his opening, Washer kicked Donner in the throat, shoving him off. Donner went down onto his back, hard, coughing.

Washer scrambled to his feet and fled through the bedroom door. The front door slammed, making Rory's decision easy. She grabbed her burner phone and sounded the alarm to all undercover units watching the building to be on the lookout for Washer.

How they'd missed him coming in they'd need to answer for later.

Donner rolled to his feet and wobbled toward the door.

"Not so fast, tough guy," she called out and snagged his hand, leading him in the other direction, back toward her bed, setting him down as gently as possible.

The fact that he didn't argue spoke volumes. The red mark across his throat made her physically ill, and blood still seeped from the gashes on his face.

"I have to…go. Go after…him," Donner rasped, his voice a mess of missed consonants and lack of energy. He tried to stand, but she sat him back down.

"We have a team for that," she reminded him gently. "Let one of the plainclothes guys get him. It's not worth it for you to try and end up back on the ground."

"It's mine though," he slurred, but she got the gist.

"I know. I wanted that feather in my cap too. It's in the blood, I guess, to want to be the one who takes down the suspect," she agreed ruefully, and she did get it. "But you can barely walk. Let me put something on those new holes Washer scratched into your pretty face."

On cue, Donner's hand drifted to his cheek, and he touched the scrape marks. "Sucker had long, sharp fingernails."

"Among other things," she said, glad at least that he was humoring her attempt to keep him talking in case he had a concussion. "I'll call for paramedics in a minute."

He snagged her hand, letting it slide until their fingers nested. "I don't need medical attention. Sit with me."

Since her knees still felt like the consistency of jelly, she accepted the invitation, gingerly wedging herself onto the bed to keep from rocking him too much. "You should at least let me put something on your face."

"Nah." He waved that off, his gaze searching hers with sudden depth, but she had no clue what he was looking for. "I'm already hard on the eyes. A few more scars won't change that. Maybe I'll find a chick who digs scars."

"Maybe," she returned with raised eyebrows. "Or maybe you'll find one who thinks it's ridiculous to let your face bleed when you don't have to."

That made him laugh for some reason, and it was a welcome sound, if a bit soft and still not as on brand for Donner as she'd like.

"Fine," he conceded. "If you have a burning need to play Florence Nightingale, do your worst."

Well, she actually planned to do her best, which wouldn't be up to standard in any way, shape or form, but she'd already had her share of screwups this evening, not the least of which was letting Washer get away. At least she could put some antibiotic ointment on Donner's wounds and make sure he didn't need anything else.

He let her dab the areas with an ointment-covered Q-tip but not very patiently and not without a lot of swearing.

"Hold still," she admonished him for the fourth time, her gut clenching as she cleaned up the angry trails of blood drawn by a serial killer. "You're worse than a little kid."

"How would you know?" he groused, shooting her a wounded look. "You torture a lot of kids this way?"

"No," she shot back point-blank. "None of them consider it torture, and they sit quietly with no complaints like angels. You should take a lesson."

"You're lying, obviously." He sucked in a breath. "If anyone can let you put that stuff on an open wound without flinching, I'll give you a million dollars."

Rory laughed, cursing how shaky she sounded—and she wasn't the injured one. "I didn't say they didn't react. I said they didn't complain. There's a big difference, and besides, you don't have a million dollars."

"I could. You don't know. Please tell me you're done, Nurse Ratched."

Jeez. Men were the worst about getting their war wounds dressed and even bigger babies about pain. "Maybe if you'd won the fight, it would have hurt less."

Okay, she could have gone without saying it quite like *that*.

The atmosphere in the room dropped into the frigid range instantly. "I can't believe he got away again."

She shivered as something dark climbed through Donner's expression. "I know. It's like he turns into smoke and vanishes. He's spent a lot of time inside the FBI. He clearly has picked up a few tips if he's that good at evading capture. I mean, he was right here. In my sights."

"You should have taken him out, Detective." Donner's voice hadn't gained enough strength for her liking, but he did a good job of piercing her with his comment, nonetheless.

She bristled automatically. "I would have, but your fat head was in the way every time I aimed for him."

"Aww, I'm thrilled to learn that you care," he said with a laugh, but it wasn't a joke to her.

"It's not funny, Donner," she said as the emotional wave of the entire night overloaded her all at once.

She'd been genuinely worried about hitting him. About losing him. That was what she got for letting him get under her skin. Beneath her guard. She did care, despite all her mental blocks against it. When had that *happened*?

More to the point, how could she have let it affect her job performance?

Unable to stand so close to him, she dropped the Q-tip into the trash and paced the length of the bedroom, angry with herself. And maybe at Donner too. Why did he have to have such a daredevil personality? The man never hesitated to jump straight into the volcano.

"Hey," he said quietly and snagged her hand again, a move he'd made more often than she could count. It worked to slow her down but not to decrease her agitation. "I'm teasing, Detective. I'm a fan of your being concerned about hitting my fat head with your bullet. I don't need a second target on my back. And I'm pretty sure you're a better shot than Washer."

The compliment shouldn't have pleased her or even registered, but he obviously knew exactly how to sweet-talk her. "I'm glad one of us thinks so. If that was the case, I wouldn't have been so concerned about whether I could take out the suspect instead of my partner."

His fingers laced through hers, squeezing tightly, his thumb rubbing an absent pattern across the skin of her hand. But he didn't speak, a rarity, and the lack of a wisecrack or a snarky comment lent a strange weight to the conversation.

Finally, he glanced up at her, his lashes heavy. "That's the first time you've called me your partner. I wasn't sure we'd gotten to that place yet."

"I'm afraid so," she said with mock gravity, desperate to lighten the mood but not at all certain she'd be able to. "If I lose you, I have to break in yet another one, and I cannot—"

"It's okay to care, Detective," he murmured. "If we didn't care, we wouldn't be on the job. We'd work at a big-box store or take tickets at the zoo."

No. That was wrong. Caring didn't work for her. Caring about people led to losing them. Or to them making horrible decisions in the name of love, like her father had. She still couldn't quite look Sinead in the eye because how did you apologize for something like what their father had done?

It was bad enough to lose someone to an untimely death, but when they chose to walk away, leaving a family broken? Unforgivable. And that was the way most people did things, throwing away everything, including relationships, when they stopped working.

"Caring just leads to pain," she muttered and then immediately wished she'd kept her big mouth shut.

"I disagree," Donner said, and when she tried to yank her hand from his, he didn't let her. "Caring is what makes life bearable. When you have someone who matters, that's when everything starts to make sense. It's the reason you act, the reason you get out of bed in the morning. The reason you don't curl up in a ball in the corner when things don't go as planned."

"The job is why I do all of that," she advised him flatly. "I get out of bed because I have sworn to uphold the law, to wear my badge with honor. The job never disappoints me. The job never does anything I don't expect."

All at once, he stood, towering over her, his body big and solid, with heat radiating from it. Case in point. People often did the most unpredictable things, things she didn't want them to do. But she couldn't stop them from doing them anyway.

Donner's gaze sought hers, held, sucked her in as she drowned in his blue eyes. Her insides quaked as the significance of the moment intensified. "Can the job touch you like this?"

He raised a hand to her face, letting his fingertips graze her cheekbone, then slide down to cup her jaw. Her skin caught fire, burning at the place where his flesh covered hers. Powerless to stop it, she stood there, her knees doing their jelly impersonation again but for a wholly different reason this time.

"Can the job make you feel like this?" he murmured, both hands to her jaw, tilting it up to meet his, his mouth millimeters from hers.

And then he kissed her. No audience. No playacting. No reason to be here with him like this other than the obvious one—because they both wanted it.

Instantly, the kiss deepened, fusing them together until she didn't think she could step away from him at gunpoint.

She should answer him. Tell him the job couldn't make her feel like this. Nothing could. Except Isaac Donner. Only she couldn't explain how he made her feel. She didn't have words that would adequately convey how her entire body had turned into flame, how he'd woven himself into her very fiber so that she couldn't quite sort where she ended and he began.

It was more than a kiss.

It was a celebration. Of life, of experiences shared, both bad and good, of partnership. Partnership in a way she'd never known before. And she craved this.

Connection had long been her Achilles' heel. She wanted it, wanted to be with a man like this, but only this one. He made her feel safe, as if he truly got the things inside her and would never leave her as a result of it. He knew she couldn't handle losing him. It was okay. He'd stop setting himself up as bait, stop painting a target on his back.

That was when reality crashed over her, and she wrenched away, her chest heaving. She fled for the bathroom, locking the door. Barricading herself inside. Because she trusted herself that little.

So much for only kissing in public. That was what she should have done—thrown down that rule and flounced away. But she hadn't.

Sinking to the cold, hard tile, she rested her head against the vanity, letting the wood bite into her skin. She needed the grounding, obviously. Donner wasn't the type to let a stupid kiss affect him the way it had her. What was wrong with her? Thinking Donner would stop being Donner just because he'd kissed her. Insanity. She'd let herself forget what happened when she let her guard down, and she'd done it willingly this time. As if she had nothing to lose.

When in reality, she had everything to lose. Including her job. This case. The Landmark Killer. He'd already gotten away twice because she'd allowed Donner to distract her. Because she'd let him into her head where rainbows and unicorns frolicked, apparently.

What a disaster.

And she called herself a cop. It was inexcusable.

"Detective." Donner rapped on the door. "Normally I would leave a woman alone who has shut herself up in the bathroom after I kissed her. But Blackthorn just texted me on my burner phone. One of the plainclothes is down."

Oh, dear God, no. Scrambling, she yanked open the door to be immediately confronted with Donner's grave expression. "Tell me it's not Carlson."

"It's not Carlson," Donner confirmed with a nod. "It's Banker, but don't worry. He's banged up but on his way to the hospital. Washer introduced him to the business end of a lead pipe. Could've been a lot worse, but at least that was the only cop he took out on his way to you."

She flinched reflexively. "To me? You mean to get into the building?"

The look he gave her sat funny on her nerves. "No, Detective, I meant what I said. Washer was here for you. Not me."

"What are you talking about? I'm not a target. Wrong gender, wrong name, wrong location." She ticked each point off on her fingertips as she listed them.

"Correct on all counts. Which is why he didn't come after me here," he told her with more gentleness than she would have expected. Or would have thought was warranted. "The only reason he tangled with me just now is because I got in his way. Deliberately. Tonight was retribution for earlier. At the rink."

"When I kicked his gun away." Her stomach rolled and splatted to the ground.

Isaac had jumped into the fray in the condo to save her. Not because he lived on the edge or had a death wish. Because Washer's last bullet had had her name on it, not Oliver Walken's.

And Willy Banker's skull had an extra concave spot thanks to her too.

Wanting to hear the answer herself, she pulled out her phone and texted Sergeant Blackthorn herself to ask after Banker's status, willing the news to be positive. An eternity later, Blackthorn confirmed what Donner had told her, that Washer had whacked the plainclothes cop who had been covering the east entrance to the building in the head, rendering him unconscious. But Banker was alive, his vitals strong enough that the ER doctor hadn't sent him to the ICU.

"Thank God," she breathed. "Everyone is okay."

For now. But for how long?

"For the record, I'm not okay," Donner said with a rueful grin and fingered his throat. "Washer must be working out during his downtime between victims. That sucker can kick."

"I'm sorry," she murmured, guilt souring the back of her throat. While she'd been busy freaking out about this situation surfacing all these feelings she had no idea what to do with, Donner had been quietly suffering. "We need to debrief everyone and then sleep for a million years."

"Copy that," Donner agreed. "I already gave Blackthorn a rundown, but he wants your formal report in the morning. You should update the captain before she hears about it from someone else."

Rory nodded, her fingers flying over her phone's screen. "Did you order an APB on Washer already?"

"Blackthorn did. All units. But poof—our boy is gone again. So much smoke in the streets of the city with the largest population density in America." Donner kissed his fingers and made an exploding motion, his mouth set in a grim line. "He won't get near you again. Don't worry."

That wasn't what she was worried about. The thing foremost in her head was how perfectly shaped Donner's lips were and how easily he shifted her attention from the case to his mouth with nothing more than a gesture. It was ridiculous, and she could no more fight her body's reaction to whatever stimuli he put in front of it than she could conjure up Washer out of thin air.

She had to clear her head, or very bad things would start happening.

Chapter 13

While Isaac fully understood the point of having an official phone number, one that was registered to the department and readily found on the web, he did not enjoy the fact that Xander Washer was using that number to taunt him.

"This is the third text this morning," he complained to the detective over a soggy bowl of corn flakes that should have stayed crunchy according to the box. But apparently that promise didn't cover the length of time it had taken him to get one of the precinct's tech geeks on standby to try to triangulate the sender's location.

"He's sent me two," the detective commented with a wry twist of her lips as she munched her own corn flakes. "I guess I should expect another one soon."

"This is what he does?" Isaac asked, baffled at the logic of it—or lack thereof. "Like, this whole time, before I joined the team? He's sent these kind of texts to everyone?"

The detective shrugged. "Yeah, pretty much. What does yours say?"

By way of answer, Isaac tapped up the messages and slid his phone across the table so she could read it for herself: Are all new guys as dumb as you?

"What does that even mean?" he asked. "As far as he knows, I might have a hundred leads on his location."

But he didn't. Which Washer probably knew, hence the text. That was the problem with someone smart and slippery *and* FBI on top of that.

Washer hadn't figured out that he'd sent these texts to Oliver Walken though. At least their undercover gig hadn't been blown to pieces, not yet anyway, if he was still sending texts to their department phones, clearly not realizing they were the same people he'd been trying to kill. And that meant he had another chance to catch the Landmark Killer. Another chance to silence Allison's ghost.

With each step, she got a little fainter. Unfortunately, that allowed the very-much-alive specter of Isaac's father to take her place, his deep baritone filling the silence, telling him he wasn't good enough. Isaac didn't need a punk killer adding his own spin on the mix.

"The message doesn't mean anything other than something he thinks will get under your skin," Rory said with a grimace. "Try not to give him the satisfaction."

Isaac did a double take. "I notice you're not particularly bothered by the texts. What do yours say?"

The detective scowled and kept munching her cereal. "That's not relevant."

Oh, what have we here? "That's what someone says when it's highly relevant. What do the texts say?"

"If I wanted to share them, I would."

Crossing his arms, Isaac contemplated her, cluing in that the hard set of her mouth meant she'd gone into Mule Mode. He hadn't seen it that much lately, but ever since he'd kissed her last night—the real one, the behind-closed-doors one, the only one that counted—the detective's back had been up. Shame. That had been one stellar kiss. Ill-advised timing, sure. But that didn't detract from the fact that he'd gone after something he wanted and had been richly rewarded—until something had reversed course in her head.

Probably it was for the best. The detective had been warming up to him slowly, and yes, he had immensely enjoyed reeling her in, but the case came first. He couldn't afford to mess up the partnership that seemed to be on the right track at last.

"Is this because of last night?" he asked.

"What?" Full-blown panic raced across her expression. "What *about* last night? It's fine. Everything is fine. I'm not… I mean, it was a kiss, Donner. We've kissed each other before. It's part of the cover. Don't read into it. I'm not reading into it. We're all good here."

Amused, Isaac watched as her face turned the color of Christmas cranberries. He'd meant because Washer had gotten away—twice. But he could totally go with this direction. "Just so I can be sure I'm on the right page here, what would I be reading into that kiss that I'm not supposed to be reading into it?"

"You know exactly what I mean," she countered fiercely while trying to bolt her coffee, which must have gone down the wrong way.

She started coughing and sputtering, and since he never shied away from a reason to touch her, he circled the table and whacked her on the back a couple of times while murmuring nonsense words designed to calm her down.

It didn't work. If anything, she got more agitated, flinching away from the place where her shoulder had grazed his stomach. Yeah, the contact had zinged him too.

"Whoa, Detective," he said and raised his hands in the air so she could see them, hopefully registering that he'd stopped with the unwanted touching. Also a shame. She smelled like something clean and slightly nutty, as if she'd washed her hair in almond milk, and it was so her to not smell like a perfume factory that his knees went a little weak.

Great. Now he'd started cataloging his favorite things about her. And noticing them did even more zingy shenanigans to his insides.

"Why do you always do that?" she demanded, her eyes watering.

"You're going to have to be more specific."

He'd own that he liked touching her, if that was the behavior being called on the carpet, but since she'd misinterpreted basically everything he'd said since asking to see her text messages, he wasn't going to assume anything.

"You twist things around, making them sound vaguely suggestive, and force me to talk about things that are out of my comfort zone."

"If I'm still under oath, Counselor, I'd like to remind the court that you're the one who started talking about kissing," he said, faint amusement coloring his tone that he should've totally tempered but didn't have the energy to. It was going to take every ounce of what energy he did have after a very late night to keep up here, obviously. "If you didn't want to talk about it, why did you bring it up?"

"Because…" Her mule face made a reappearance. "It's the elephant in the room. We need to be clear about what is and isn't happening here."

"Well, that's the first time I've been accused of kissing like an elephant, but I'll take the performance review under advisement."

"See, that's what I mean." She jabbed her spoon in his direction. "You twist everything. Next you'll be telling me that I enjoyed the kiss and we should do it again."

His eyebrows shot up as he processed that. "Well, now that you mention it, Mrs. Pot-Calling-the-Kettle-Black, I will remind you that you were into the kiss, but I can take a hint. When a woman barricades herself in the bathroom, I'm pretty capable of figuring out that suggesting a repeat of the thing that pushed her in there would not go well for me. But I find it curious that you're suggesting it in the same breath as accusing me of being the one to twist things. Maybe we should settle this truth-or-dare style."

"What?" she snapped, outright wariness replacing the stubborn mule face of a moment ago. "Did I teleport back into high school when I wasn't looking? Adults don't play truth or dare, at least not sober."

Isaac's phone buzzed, but he ignored it. It was probably Blackthorn reminding them they had a conference call to attend that started in a few minutes. But this was more important.

"You heard me." He jerked his chin. "Since you started this tango, let's finish it. Tell me the truth about what's in those texts, or I'm going to kiss you again. Which one is more objectionable, I wonder."

"Are you insane? I'm not doing either one. You don't get to dictate my choices."

The cereal had completely lost the detective's attention, and he did not mind it being squarely on him instead. Her green eyes snapped with fire that lit up her whole face, and he'd never been more attracted to a woman in his life.

"Fine. You choose. Truth or dare."

"This is literally the stupidest game I have ever heard of. What do I win?"

He grinned. "That depends on what dare you pick. Mine would have landed you back in my arms for round two of what we started last night. I would call that a win all day long."

"You're completely insufferable." She rolled her eyes and shoved her phone in his direction. "I cannot believe that's how you goaded me into showing you these texts."

So she wasn't going to play. He'd actually thought she'd use the opportunity to kiss him. He'd given her the perfect out. She didn't even have to own the fact that she wanted to. He must've been slipping.

More disappointed than he had a right to be, he took her phone and read the texts himself, whistling. "Wow. Washer knows how to cut to the bone, doesn't he?"

The first one read, Too bad about poor Uncle Mike. If you were a better cop, you could stop all the killing.

The second one read, Maybe you should call your sister and commiserate. Oh, that's right. She hates you.

The detective sniffed. "I'm not letting it get under my skin, remember?"

Except she totally was. That was why she'd been so adamantly in Mule Mode. But she'd showed him the texts; that meant the content was fair game. And he had a case to solve with a partner he clearly didn't understand well enough.

"What's this reference to Uncle Mike?" he asked.

For a moment, he didn't think she was going to tell him. She busied herself with clearing the breakfast dishes, grabbing his as well, which was a domestic move that he wouldn't have bet she realized she'd adopted. Far be it from him to mention it. Or the fact that he kind of liked the idea of having a partner outside of the job. Someone who did things like clear the breakfast table occasionally and maybe hung a shirt on the back of the door while he took a shower because she'd noticed he'd forgotten to grab clothes again before stepping into the spray.

He'd never had anything like that, but he remembered his mom doing it for his father sometimes. Not that he thought the detective would be even remotely right for the permanent partner position that had started jockeying for space in his head.

Besides, the detective had her own job to do. More likely he'd be hanging a shirt on the door for her instead of the other way around. You know, if mules started flying and something a bit more personal came out of this fake marriage than a killer behind bars.

She came out of the kitchen and rested both hands on the table, leaning into it, her gaze troubled. "Uncle Mike was Ashlynn's father. Died at the hands of a serial killer. A beat cop. We were never sure if he'd been targeted specifically or if he stumbled into the line of fire during the case. But how Washer knows that's such an open wound for me, I haven't yet figured out."

"He's sent texts like this directly to Agent Colton?"

She nodded. "Yeah, though it affected all of us. You comment all the time that so many Coltons are in law enforcement. Uncle Mike is why."

That definitely filled in a few blanks. And infuriated him that Washer would use something so personal to taunt them. It was one thing to send a couple of neener-neener texts to the new guy mocking Isaac for not being able to catch a killer, but it was another thing entirely to poke at deep wounds.

"I'm sorry," he told her quietly. "For teasing you about the texts. And for Uncle Mike."

She shrugged it off. "I'm more sensitive about it than I guess I wanted to admit to either one of us."

A smile tugged at his lips. "You don't say. What about the other one? Your sister hates you? What's that all about?"

The detective scrubbed at her face, fatigue lining her eyes in a way he didn't like, but she'd had just as late of a night as he had. And as much trauma, at least emotionally. Physically, she'd escaped Washer's rage, but he knew it haunted her that he'd gotten away, same as it did him.

He should've probably felt worse about how he'd lured her into this conversation. Maybe later he would, but for now, he sensed her opening up in a way she hadn't before, and he was here for it.

"Sinead doesn't hate me. Probably," the detective muttered. "You haven't heard the gossip at the water cooler? I'm shocked."

"Well, I didn't say that," he corrected carefully. "I always keep my ears open, but regardless of what's been passed around down at the precinct, we're not there right now. I'm more interested in what *you* have to say about it."

The expression on the detective's face did really nice things to his insides. Apparently she didn't have a lot of people in her life who came to the source instead of believing everything that came out of some yokel's mouth. And she clearly appreciated it. Whether she'd give him any credit for it remained to be seen, but regardless, he did like being ahead of everyone else pretty much always.

"Isn't there a conference call in, like, five minutes?" she said with a head jerk as if she'd just remembered.

"Not so fast," he said with a tsk and crossed his arms. "Blackthorn can't start without us, so I say that means we dictate when it begins. Not the clock."

She sighed. "Your middle name is Bullheaded, I take it."

"Takes a mule to know one," he agreed cheerfully. "I'm not letting this go. You're upset, and I want to know why."

Among other things. He also had a burning desire to be the one she turned to, the one who'd risen up above the rest of the playing field to *matter* to her. Where that had come from, he had no idea. But that didn't change the facts, and he wanted to win this challenge at all costs.

"*Why* do you want to know, Donner?" she cried, her gaze tortured and twisting with darkness he felt helpless to stop but wished he could with everything inside him. "This is not story hour. We are not doing this thing where we bond over Washer's ability to rub salt straight into the wound. We're detectives, not a married couple. The sooner we get that through our heads, the better."

"I wasn't confused, Detective," he murmured and crossed the small dining area to tip up her chin so he could speak to her without the barrier of space between them. "When I kissed you last night, it wasn't because I needed the practice. You fascinate me. You have from the beginning. I couldn't help but want to explore you a little bit more. Then and now. Every little piece that you share with me feels like the equivalent of being handed a bag full of gold. None of that has to do with the case, by the way. I would feel like this even if we'd caught Washer last night and we literally had no reason to be in the same room except for the obvious one."

Her expression softened as she contemplated him. "What reason is that?"

"Because we can't stand to be apart."

Chapter 14

Rory felt like all the oxygen had been sucked from the room as she stared up at Donner, desperately searching for a flicker of truth, something that would tell her he was lying. Spinning words into fairy tales seemed to be one of his many talents.

He didn't flinch or look away, unabashedly allowing her to peruse her fill. Forcing her to own the awareness rippling between them like an energy current on high.

"It's time for our conference call," she told him and held up her hand to ward off the protest she assumed was coming. But she couldn't do this. Not now. Maybe not ever.

She could not be attracted to her partner. It was not happening. This stupid undercover assignment was messing with her brain. Her heart.

Distractions would get someone killed, that was a given. She had to be better than this.

The real question was why he was working so hard to be a distraction. There was no way he meant what he said, not the way her insides wanted to interpret it. Sure, he'd thrown down some pretty words about how much she intrigued him, but that was probably because she didn't fawn at his feet like a teenager at a Harry Styles concert. Not because it was true.

"We'll play it your way, Detective," he finally said as he banked some of the fire in his gaze. "But this is not over."

Donner released her without taking a pound of her flesh with him, but how, she couldn't fathom when it had felt like his hand had fused to her chin, as if he'd taken a blow torch to the area in question and turned up the heat.

Scrambling to recover from what had been at its core nothing more than a conversation about some text messages sent to them by a deranged killer, she whumped into her seat at the table and set up her laptop. But instead of sliding into his own seat on the opposite side of the table, where there would be a yard of wood between them, Donner dragged his chair over to her side and cozied right up to her elbow.

When she glanced at him with what should have amounted to an epic glare warning him from his current course of action, he just grinned. "No reason we can't share, is there? We're calling into the same conference. It would be all echoey and stuff if I log in on a computer that's five feet away."

Harrumphing, she shook her head but didn't tell him to go away because that would be childish. Though she felt like being childish. Among other things.

Okay, what she really wanted was to go back in time

and take Donner's dare. The kissing one. Instead of sharing Washer's texts. Now he had the equivalent of a dorsal fin on his back, and that look on his face very much resembled a shark who had scented blood.

Of course, if she'd kissed him, then he would have figured out how much she'd wanted to. And that wouldn't have worked either.

Thank goodness for Sergeant Wells Blackthorn, who had provided a much-needed breather in the form of a conference call, which was really going to be a dressing down, which she sorely deserved.

But when Wells's face materialized on her screen, with Cash and Brennan closely following behind in their own outlined squares, no one looked mad. They all wore identical expressions of concern.

"I got your report, Detective Colton," Wells said by way of greeting, which she appreciated because it meant he planned to get down to business immediately. Good. She needed the distraction.

And the fact that she'd just labeled work as the distraction in this equation rankled. Before she'd met Isaac Donner, nothing had mattered more than the job. She'd been a cop for a third of her life and had never wanted to do anything else. Why did it take a call with her boss to get her mind off the broad range of possible scenarios that could occur behind these closed doors when all bets were off? When she didn't have the shield of only kissing Donner in public?

That was where she'd gone wrong. She should reinstitute that rule immediately. Donner would honor it. Or rather she'd make him. He'd thrown it out the window last night, but to be fair, she hadn't protested. As long as she set clear boundaries, everything would be fine.

The heat burning her elbow where Donner's chest lay not a millimeter away contradicted that with huge capital letters.

"The report is accurate, sir," she told Wells and cleared her throat.

It felt weird all of a sudden to be so formal with her sister's husband. But he hadn't been Sinead's husband for more than a spot in time. He'd been Rory's sergeant a lot longer and the lead on this case since the beginning.

Besides, she and Sinead weren't close. They weren't as distant as they had been, not since they'd both started working on this case. It was…different. Nice.

Funny how things changed in the blink of an eye. She and Wells had a connection that hadn't existed before. Now it did. Same between her and Sinead. She couldn't change that any more than she could ask the sky to stop being blue. Had something changed between her and Donner that also couldn't be reversed?

She shook her head. The distraction from the distraction obviously hadn't worked either. What in the world was she going to have to do to clear her head, for crying out loud?

"The report is factual, yes," Wells returned. "But you left out a critical piece in your report that did manage to rank a mention in Detective Donner's report. Are you not of the same opinion that Washer now considers you a target?"

She glanced at Donner, a huge mistake. He was too close, and she very much feared her face reflected the sudden spike inside as she registered the way he was watching her. A video call with her colleagues was not the place to start allowing her body to broadcast things without her permission. Actually, there was no good time for her body to be doing anything she didn't expressly allow.

Turning her attention pointedly away from the overwhelming masculine presence at her elbow, she shook her head. "I don't disagree with Detective Donner's assessment. I just didn't consider it relevant for the report. The important aspect of this situation is that Xander Washer broke into Cassandra and Oliver's home and attacked them both. And then he fled. The question we should be asking is why. If Cassandra is truly a target, he would have finished the job at all costs. What are we missing that we need to know?"

Donner shifted, and she hated that she had such a fine awareness of such a simple thing as his straightening up in his chair.

"I can answer that," he said. "He realized he was outmatched. His primary agenda is killing Oliver Walken at Rockefeller Center. If he'd continued to fight with me, he would have eventually lost, and he knew it. I saw the exact moment it occurred to him. That's when he cut his losses."

Rory absorbed that and nodded. "That gels."

Wells's gaze darted between her and Donner. "The two of you didn't compare notes before you submitted your reports?"

She let that hang there for a moment while she scrambled to figure out how to respond that she'd been too busy avoiding Donner to do her job. It was inexcusable, and it was even more so that her boss had to point it out.

"Donner was hurt," she blurted and pointed over her shoulder at the scratches on his face. "It was more important to ensure he received adequate medical care, sir. I made that call. You can put that in your official report."

"I'm not looking for someone to take a fall, Detective Colton," Wells said somewhat wearily. "We're trying to catch an elusive, disturbed serial killer. Missing elements from a report are not conducive and make the job harder. Next time, make sure you're on the same page, or there's no reason for the department to foot the bill for this very expensive undercover operation."

Rory blinked. He was saying they should act more like a married couple? Was that the implication here? Because she and Donner lived in the same house, their reports should automatically match? That didn't even make sense.

She let it ride since she had no comment and couldn't very well argue with her boss in front of her colleagues. They talked through the incidents, both at the rink and later in the condo, including additional work done by the plainclothes detail to find evidence against Washer for the assault on Officer Banker. Nothing had turned up, another frustrating failure.

A second team would take over that investigation while the primary team managed the initial one of keeping both undercover detectives alive while tracking the man determined to kill them both.

Finally Wells seemed satisfied and let them all go.

Except the silence in the condo weighed on her, and she put her head in her hands. She couldn't even claim to be surprised when she felt Donner's fingers on her shoulder. What did it say that she'd been expecting it?

"It's okay, Detective," he murmured. "I'm not going to hold you to the deal. If you don't want to talk about Sinead, it's cool. It's more important that you trust me as your partner than whether or not you trust me as a friend. And after what I just heard, I'm not sure either is happening."

"You don't get it," she told him. "I didn't leave out the part about Washer targeting me because I don't trust your assessment. It was because—"

She bit that off. How was she supposed to explain that she'd brushed it off? Her safety was irrelevant. Oliver was the target of note here, the one who mattered.

If she told him that, he'd read into it. Correctly, no doubt, that she'd already started to care, despite what she'd told him to the contrary. If she lost another partner...

"I do get it," he said quietly, and his fingers slipped from her shoulder. "You're stuck with me against your will. I turn everything into a competition, and you just want to do your job. We're oil and water, and the events of last night highlighted that."

His heat vanished in an instant as he left the room, his door clicking shut. Great. She'd driven him away, flipping the script from last night. This time, he'd been the one to flee the situation.

Good. They *were* oil and water. It made no sense for them to be skating so close to the personal line. There should be nothing but business between them. A professional distance that they might occasionally cross in public due to the parameters of the job they'd both agreed to do.

It was just that she'd never had to work so hard to separate business from personal. Especially not when it came to intimate things like living together and kissing her fake husband, neither of which felt as business-oriented as they should.

And she'd do well to put that out of her mind. Spend

some time focusing on the case. Go over notes to be sure she hadn't missed anything, especially given her current level of preoccupation.

Busying herself with opening files on her laptop, she shoved everything out of her head and started at the first report. Within four seconds, her attention drifted, and she frowned.

Last night, she'd fled the room because he'd struck a nerve when he'd kissed her. Was that why Donner had left today? Because he'd been wholly unable to handle the situation a second longer?

She shut her eyes in search of fortification that never came.

Wells expected them to be on the same page. That was never going to happen if she ignored the big warning signs he'd flashed at her during that call.

Before she could change her mind, she slid out of the chair and crossed the room, standing before Donner's bedroom door, palm against the wood as if that would somehow communicate the state of mind of the man on the other side of it via osmosis.

Maybe it would be more to the point to wish it could communicate her own state of mind. She shouldn't be here. She shouldn't care whether she'd hurt his feelings or created some kind of hostile work environment. But she did. And not because of the job, though all signs pointed to that being the number one reason she *should* care.

"Donner," she called and whacked the door with the heel of her hand. "I'm sorry."

The door opened after a beat. He stood there contemplating her, his expression blank and as difficult to read as a dead laptop. "For what?"

He was going to make her say it. She nearly groaned. "For everything. For pretending like I don't care, when I do. That's why I left out the part about me being a target in my report. Because I need everyone to focus on you. You're the one we need to protect. Not me. I can't stand the thought of losing you."

"Now, that wasn't so hard, was it?" he asked softly.

His gaze caught fire as he sucked her into it, drowning her with sudden and fierce emotion she didn't understand. He hadn't moved, but she felt his presence wash over her as clearly as if he'd reached out to touch her. Awareness spiked, pulling strings inside her that she had no idea could be plucked in quite that way.

"For the record," he murmured, "we need to protect you too. For the same reason."

"Because you don't want to break in a new partner either?"

He smiled, and she had the feeling he'd seen right through her. "Because I care too."

Chapter 15

A siren blared in the sudden silence, rushing by on the street below. Neither of them so much as flinched, though Isaac would bet the detective had a similar reaction to his when she heard a random siren—he always pictured a beat cop hot on the trail of a B&E suspect, adrenaline high as he or she sped to the scene. Sometimes he experienced a flash of jealousy that he didn't work the street any longer.

Then he'd go back to his files and remember that being a detective had its great moments too. Out of the blue one day, he'd come across the Landmark Killer case in a random city-wide plea for information, back when the team had been trying to figure out the suspect's identity. A ripple had swept down his spine, one that meant this was something he should pay attention to. A premonition he'd known better than to ignore.

This case would be the one.

Except it hadn't gelled for him quite the way he'd expected. At his old precinct, he'd had a reputation that he'd built from the ground up, earning respect the old-fashioned way, by closing difficult cases. None of them had been splashy enough to flaunt in his father's face. Solid work, yes. Worthy of gaining the respect of Chief Donner, no.

Ironic, right? The only person Isaac wanted to acknowledge his accomplishments never had.

But the Landmark Killer... Man, it was the case of a lifetime. If anything could get his father's attention, Xander Washer fit that bill. Losing the guy twice in a row had rubbed Isaac raw, as if he'd put on his skin inside out, and not just because he hoped to shove the accomplishment in his father's face. Allison sat there in that invisible motivator seat too, reminding him why his father never acknowledged his son's successes—he hadn't earned the ultimate approval yet.

As he stood there in the doorway of his bedroom, the detective's sweet body within arm's length, another ripple rocked him to the core, and with it came the realization that he'd been meant to work this case but for a wholly different reason than he'd assumed.

If he hadn't, he'd never have met Rory Colton, and that would have been a tragedy indeed.

They'd been born to work together, that much he believed wholeheartedly. The way her mind worked, her sharp wit, her dedication. Never would he have bet those qualities would find their way onto his list of must-haves in a woman. Frankly, he'd spent a lot of time cultivating a preference for women who excelled at leaving—or at least didn't whine about it when he did.

This was the first time he'd ever thought about what

"One Minute" Survey

You get up to **FOUR** books <u>and</u> a Mystery Gift...

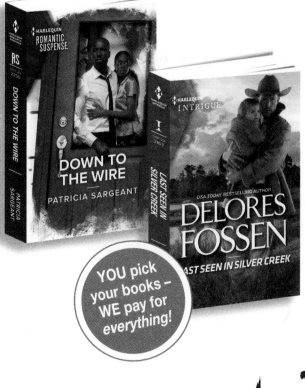

YOU pick your books –
WE pay for everything.
You get up to FOUR new books and a Mystery Gift…
absolutely FREE!
Total retail value: Over $20!

Dear Reader,

Your opinions are important to us. So if you'll participate in our fast and free "One Minute" Survey, YOU can pick up to four wonderful books that WE pay for when you try the Harlequin Reader Service!

As a leading publisher of women's fiction, we'd love to hear from you. That's why we promise to reward you for completing our survey.

IMPORTANT: Please complete the survey and return it. We'll send your Free Books and a Free Mystery Gift right away. And we pay for shipping and handling too! ← *We pay for EVERYTHING!*

Try **Harlequin® Romantic Suspense** and get 2 books featuring heart-racing page-turners with unexpected plot twists and irresistible chemistry that will keep you guessing to the very end.

Try **Harlequin Intrigue® Larger-Print** and get 2 books featuring action-packed stories that will keep you on the edge of your seat. Solve the crime and deliver justice at all costs.

Or TRY BOTH!

Thank you again for participating in our "One Minute" Survey. It really takes just a minute (or less) to complete the survey… and your free books and gift will be well worth it!

If you continue with your subscription, you can look forward to curated monthly shipments of brand-new books from your selected series, always at a discount off the cover price! Plus you can cancel any time. So don't miss out, return your One Minute Survey today to get your Free books.

Pam Powers

"One Minute" Survey

GET YOUR FREE BOOKS AND A FREE GIFT!

✓ Complete this Survey ✓ Return this survey

1 Do you try to find time to read every day?

☐ YES ☐ NO

2 Do you prefer stories with suspensful storylines?

☐ YES ☐ NO

3 Do you enjoy having books delivered to your home?

☐ YES ☐ NO

4 Do you share your favorite books with friends?

☐ YES ☐ NO

YES! I have completed the above "One Minute" Survey. Please send me my Free Books and a Free Mystery Gift (worth over $20 retail). I understand that I am under no obligation to buy anything, as explained on the back of this card.

☐ **Harlequin® Romantic Suspense**
240/340 CTI G2AD

☐ **Harlequin Intrigue® Larger-Print**
199/399 CTI G2AD

☐ **BOTH**
240/340 & 199/399 CTI G2AE

FIRST NAME

LAST NAME

ADDRESS

APT.# CITY

STATE/PROV. ZIP/POSTAL CODE

EMAIL ☐ Please check this box if you would like to receive newsletters and promotional emails from Harlequin Enterprises ULC and its affiliates. You can unsubscribe anytime.

HI/HRS-1123-OM

HARLEQUIN Reader Service **—Here's how it works:**

Accepting your 2 free books and free gift (gift valued at approximately $10.00 retail) places you under no obligation to buy anything. You may keep the books and gift and return the shipping statement marked "cancel." If you do not cancel, approximately one month later we'll send you more books from the series you have chosen, and bill you at our low, subscribers-only discount price. Harlequin® Romantic Suspense books consist of 4 books each month and cost just $5.99 each in the U.S. or $6.74 each in Canada, a savings of at least 8% off the cover price. Harlequin Intrigue® Larger-Print books consist of 6 books each month and cost just $6.99 each in the U.S. or $7.49 each in Canada, a savings of at least 10% off the cover price. It's quite a bargain! Shipping and handling is just 50¢ per book in the U.S. and $1.25 per book in Canada*. You may return any shipment at our expense and cancel at any time by contacting customer service — or you may continue to receive monthly shipments at our low, subscribers-only discount price plus shipping and handling.

▲ If offer card is missing write to: Harlequin Reader Service, P.O. Box 1341, Buffalo, NY 14240-8531 or visit www.ReaderService.com ▲

BUSINESS REPLY MAIL
FIRST-CLASS MAIL   PERMIT NO. 717   BUFFALO, NY

POSTAGE WILL BE PAID BY ADDRESSEE

HARLEQUIN READER SERVICE
PO BOX 1341
BUFFALO NY 14240-8571

NO POSTAGE
NECESSARY
IF MAILED
IN THE
UNITED STATES

made up a woman he'd be proud to stand next to for an extended period of time. Maybe it was the fake marriage talking, but the detective might've actually been the full package. Beautiful, strong, principled and first and foremost, unaffected by his charm.

That might've been her most attractive quality.

It was almost as if she'd studied the fastest way to get his attention and then done it but didn't care that she'd snagged him, wholly unconcerned that she'd begun leading him around by the nose. He might as well have had a sign on his back: Lost Puppy Needs a Good Home.

Isaac did love a good challenge. And here stood the most important one he'd ever faced, and that included the Landmark Killer. Which was saying something.

"You're still standing here," he murmured, as if this might've been news to her.

But honestly, he'd started to wonder if she did understand the implications of bearding a man in his den, so to speak. You didn't knock on the door to a man's bedroom unless you wanted to see the inside of it.

On the flip side, it wouldn't surprise him if she'd never even considered the move provocative. She did seem a bit of a tomboy, the buddy of all, totally unaware of her own beauty in a way that a lot of men overlooked as quickly as she'd friend-zoned them.

Isaac wasn't a lot of men. And there was nothing friendly about the way the detective made him feel.

"I'm still standing here because you deserve to be treated like an equal partner in this relationship," she said quietly. "We do need to trust each other. Especially since we literally hold each other's lives in our hands. It's Partnership 101. I'm sorry I've been screwing it up."

His insides went a little soft and squishy, and he cleared his throat, which had suddenly gotten tight for some unknown reason. "I like the sound of that. Having a good partnership means we work better together, and that's what's going to land Washer behind bars."

"Agreed." She nodded once. "The job is important. But understanding each other is important too. Maybe we could talk for a while."

And he had to swallow again. This was more than an apology. More than an offer to work on strengthening their partnership. And he was here for it. "You're in luck. I happen to have an open slot in my schedule for the day."

"Can we go somewhere? A coffee shop?" she suggested.

"No. We cannot." He eyed her, struck by the odd dichotomy of the detective, who was so fearless when it came to facing down a maniac with a gun but shied away from real intimacy with a man. "A coffee shop is in public. That's where we act like married people. This conversation warrants a venue where neither of us can hide behind the roles we've fallen into. Make it real, or else forget about it."

Her eyes widened. "Did you seriously just quote that Santana–Rob Thomas song to me?"

He crossed his arms so he didn't immediately yank her into his embrace, but dang, was that a tall order. Any woman who recognized a song reference got his motor running in a huge way. "That depends on whether you like the song or not."

"How can you not like it? That's literally one of the catchiest songs ever recorded."

"Good answer."

Except it meant she knew exactly what line came before the one he'd said. *Give me your heart.*

He let it stand without qualification, even though he hadn't intended for it to be any kind of declaration. She could interpret it however she wanted, as long as she didn't clam up again. They were on the verge of something great, whatever that ended up being. A stronger partnership. A better cover as two married people who were really into each other. Something more.

All of the above.

"Do you often listen to classic rock, or is that an anomaly?" she asked, seeming to be genuinely curious.

"Oh, did we start the conversation already? Okay, hold on a sec."

If they were going to do this, they would be doing it right. First, he brewed an entire pot of fresh coffee, then hit the linen closet for two blankets, settling the detective onto the couch, where he opened the vertical blinds on the patio to reveal the view of 48th Street and beyond. His own apartment overlooked an alley that featured not one but two dumpsters for double the garbage stench in the summer. He'd enjoy the million-dollar upgrade while he could.

"Better than a coffee shop," he told the detective as he handed her a mug full of the fragrant drip variety that had come with the condo, another upgrade he'd been enjoying.

Of course that one was easily remedied with a trip to Target after this case was over. A drip brewer couldn't be more than fifty or sixty dollars, and it would be worth it to continue this coffee bliss.

The thought of returning to his normal life did not settle into his chest well. This was the first time he'd actually thought about what it would feel like to return to his apartment that suddenly seemed lonely and sad. And not because of the garbage. Because the detective wouldn't be there.

She took the mug and sipped. "We agree on that. Much better than takeout coffee."

"Then why in the world would you suggest such an awful place to have our first heart-to-heart?"

The spot he took next to her on the couch was too far away for his taste, but if he'd read the room right, that might not be a factor for long.

She was softening toward him. Hallelujah.

"I have a feeling you know why," she said ruefully. "You have this uncanny ability to read between my lines."

"There's a lot there worth paying attention to," he advised her with raised eyebrows as he purposefully dragged his gaze down to the place where the blanket he'd draped over her covered her bottom half. "But to be fair, that skill is what makes me an excellent detective. Let's see how good I am. You suggested it because you wanted the relative safety of a crowd, where it would be impossible for you to ravish me once you realized I am in fact insanely hot."

She laughed as he'd intended and finally relaxed, which he'd hoped for, but with her, it was never a given that she'd react even remotely how he wished she would.

"I'd like to say that's ridiculous, but I'm pretty sure you'd see through that too," she commented.

He bobbled his coffee, nearly spilling it on his leg. "Wait. What?"

That was actually the right answer? He shook his head

hard, but she didn't take it back, just sat there watching him with a slight smile.

"Being in public works for me on many levels. It's where we do things like hold hands," she admitted readily, which did nothing to change the speed of his rapidly accelerating pulse. "You always walk on the outside of the curb, ensuring I'm on the inside, away from traffic. Twice you've steered me around stuff on the sidewalk— a bicycle and a cardboard box. It's your inherent protective instinct. I'm not even sure you register that you're doing it, but I notice. It's nice."

"I...uh... You're welcome?" he offered, too befuddled to come up with a better response. "You like holding hands?"

She laughed again, and it bloomed inside him like a warm glow. "That's the thing you picked out of my speech to comment on? Yeah. I like it. Shocking, I know."

It totally was. Not that she liked holding hands; he'd already figured that part out. But for her to vocalize it on purpose... He definitely hadn't made enough coffee. More caffeine needed, stat.

"What else do you like about being in public?" he asked, back to being the puppy, begging for scraps of her attention, but who could blame him? This conversation was shaping up to be full of revelations.

"Is that your coy way of trying to get me to say I like kissing you?" she asked point-blank and sipped her coffee with maddening leisure. "If I may be honest, no, that is not one of the reasons I like being in public."

Deflated, he sat back against the cushion. "I always want you to be honest."

She nodded. "I started thinking about how it would

feel to be on the other side of this. You're pretty transparent with me, and I've done nothing but hold up a stop sign."

Yeah, because she didn't know how to reach out. It was something he'd noticed from the first. She yearned to connect but seemed wholly unable to figure out how it was supposed to be done.

"Put it down," he advised her bluntly. "You're off traffic duty, Detective. Tell me what you're thinking right now. No holds barred. No filter. No judgment. Lay it on me."

Her eyebrows shot up and she lifted her mug. "I was just thinking that I was going to have to hire you to come to my apartment and make coffee each morning because this is fantastic."

"I learned how to make it from you, doofus. Try again."

She chuckled. "I was thinking how horrible it was going to be to go back to my apartment where I have no one to badger me into hanging out on the couch in the morning instead of working. This is nice."

"Much better," he murmured and eased his hand over to cover hers, sliding their fingers together. "We can hold hands inside too."

"I know. It just has a lot more implications the moment we cross the threshold."

That it did. And the fact that she hadn't shied away from mentioning it felt like progress. "Tell me about Sinead."

She didn't pull her fingers free, which also had implications. Instead she stared through the glass between them and the rest of the world. He didn't mind a bit that his back was to the outside view. The inside view was better.

"My mom was a home-wrecker," she said, without apology. "Or at least that's what I heard Sinead's mom call her that time she showed up at our house. I was little, but the yelling... I still remember it to this day. You know what's total BS? They don't have a word for it when a man is the one who does the wrecking. My mother didn't know he was married. But that doesn't matter. Sinead grew up without a father because of me. My father left them when my mom told him she was pregnant."

Wow. Isaac absorbed that, forcing himself to sip his cooling coffee so she could continue at her own pace.

"It's strange that Sinead and I didn't grow up together but we both ended up in law enforcement. Shaped by the same event in that Brooklyn neighborhood all those many years ago, when Uncle Mike died. Do you think that means we have other things in common?" she asked him out of the blue.

"I'm sure you do. Cops are born, not bred," he said. "Lots of people lose someone they care about to homicide, and almost none of them react by putting themselves in that same line of fire. You and Sinead both ran toward justice instead of away from trauma. That means at your core, you're the same."

Rory's eyes grew shiny. "Thank you—that's a lovely way to put it. Is that why you became a cop? To balance the scales?"

"Yes," he said immediately, despite never having answered that question honestly before. "My father is chief of police in the town where I grew up. That's what he thought I would do too. Surprise. I needed to put killers behind bars, not help elderly ladies find missing cats."

"You lost someone close to you in a homicide." Her

keen gaze never left his, and he had a feeling she might rival him in the reading-between-the-lines department.

Slowly, he acknowledged the point with a nod. "Allison. My high school girlfriend. It was the first homicide in our town in twenty years. My father landed the case. He was totally unprepared for it, had no clue how to manage what rapidly became a cold case. Her killer was never caught."

"And you keep hoping each case you solve will bring you closer to absolution," she finished for him.

That was the exact moment when he felt the first fissure in his Allison shell, the one that had encased his heart when she'd died. No one had ever come close to piercing that shell before. It didn't shock him that the detective had been the one to penetrate it, but jeez—how had she done it so fast?

"That's right," he murmured. "It's why I need to get Washer. Why I can't lose him again. Why I need for us to gel so badly, so you can be the other half of my brain. Two heads are better than one."

The detective set her coffee cup on the end table behind her with a click as if happy to be getting rid of it. When she faced him again, something new lit her features, something he couldn't stop drinking in. It was almost as if she'd finally taken his advice and plunked down her stop sign along with the cup. Then picked up a huge flashing green light.

"Can I tell you a secret?" she whispered and beckoned him closer, which he could not comply with fast enough.

The scent of her shampoo, almondy and clean, filled his senses until he couldn't think about anything in the nut family without the detective being inescapably en-

twined. Including himself, because *nuts* perfectly described his current state of mind. "I will always be first
in line to learn your secrets."

"I don't like kissing you in public. I much prefer to
do it in private."

Chapter 16

And now she'd gone and done it. Rory had finally said the one thing she'd promised herself she wouldn't. The one thing she couldn't take back, mostly because Donner would never let her.

True to form, his gaze darkened with all the luscious heat she'd anticipated, and she tried really hard to be sorry she'd crossed that line. But she wasn't sorry. She was tired.

Tired of pretending she didn't crave Donner's touch. Absolutely fatigued with the idea of hiding her blooming attraction to him for a second longer. Bone weary of feigning a lack of interest in the simple connection they shared, when it would be so much easier to give in.

That was the beauty of something so effortless. It just worked. She and Donner meshed. Somehow. It was as baffling as it was comforting.

He got her. And she got him. Almost without even

trying, as if these discoveries had been here all along, like precious diamonds strewn along their path that they could bend down and pick up any time they came across one.

Donner shifted closer, into her space. She might have met him halfway, a tiny bit drunk on the emotional elixir of a man paying such careful attention to her. Blanket. Coffee. Conversation. Soul bearing.

She wanted more.

But she had no idea how to take the next step. The fresh gashes on his face stood out in stark relief, reminding her of the stakes. He'd gotten those defending her.

It was paramount that she and Donner make this partnership work, and somehow he'd convinced her that letting down her guard would lead to that. Her brain still worked—too well. It continually reminded her that opening herself up to Donner would lead to pain in her immediate future, probably sooner than she could possibly fathom. For this to work, she needed to shut down that stupid part of her brain.

"Your wheels are turning so fast there's smoke coming out of your ears," he murmured as he nuzzled the place where her ear met her throat.

A warm, honeyed feeling weighed down her limbs pleasantly, turning her thoughts hazy.

"You're doing a good job of shutting down the factory in my brain," she told him. "Do it some more."

Maybe that was the key. Let him employ all his seductive techniques until she couldn't remember why it was such a bad idea to be opening herself up to him. Why she shouldn't lay herself bare on the altar of hope.

All at once, he drew back, taking all his lovely heat with him. She frowned. "Where are you going?"

"Nowhere, apparently. Not until we get it clear that you can't cop out on this, Detective. If you want me, say so. I'm not pressing my advantage so you can avoid owning this decision. That's not how this works."

She eyed him. "What exactly are you accusing me of?"

He didn't blink, his gaze skewering her. "Letting me do all the work so you can lie to yourself later that I coerced you. You had no choice in the matter. You lost your head over some pretty words, and now you regret everything—let's go back to circling each other, why don't we."

"I'm not going to say that."

"Dang straight," he growled. "Instead you're going to say, *I want you, Isaac. Put your hands on me. Kiss me like you mean it. Like it's real and the fake marriage doesn't exist.*"

"I have never called you Isaac," she said, his name tumbling out of her mouth as if it had always been there on the tip of her tongue, begging to be voiced exactly that way. Slightly needy. Throaty. A tad desperate.

"Which is a shame, Detective," he murmured. "I like it when you call me Isaac. It's like you just whispered a secret to me and now we're the only two people on the planet who know it."

It felt that way to her too. *Isaac.* It was so intimate. Delicious. As if she'd crossed a threshold into some inner sanctum that he'd never let anyone else enter. What did it say about her that she'd become so greedy to feel like this?

"I can't call you Isaac when you're still Detective-ing me," she protested, which was not at all what she'd meant to say, but her mouth had ceased obeying her right around the time she'd knocked on his bedroom door.

"You haven't figured that out yet, Detective?" he murmured, the back of his hand grazing her cheek as he lit her on fire with nothing more than that small bit of contact. "It's an endearment. Calling you something so banal as *darling* would never suit you. *Detective* has far more color. Far more impact, because laced through it is how I feel about you."

Wow. Something a lot bigger than heat blasted through her as the implications registered. "You told me you called me that because it's who I am. Like a title."

Which she'd appreciated at the time. Had worn with a lot of pride. Because he'd nailed that sentiment perfectly. She was a detective at her core.

But now he was telling her it meant so much more than that, and she didn't know what to do with this revelation.

"That's exactly what I mean," he said, his hand traveling down the side of her throat, the backs of his knuckles exploring the place where her shirt gaped, then flipping to run his fingertips across her skin as if he'd lost his sight and had to memorize her shape through feel alone. "You're strong, capable, the embodiment of the job, and I'm so hopelessly attracted to you because of it. It's like the very word *detective* has become synonymous with the image I have of you in my head."

"Is this the part where I should state my wishes?" she murmured, her eyelids fluttering closed as so many things washed through her. "Because I will spontaneously combust if you don't kiss me right this second. *Isaac.*"

He did. Without hesitation. Without apology. Just covered her mouth with his and flung them both into the stratosphere where nothing existed but light and heat and a myriad of dancing colors that sang through her body.

She'd been kissed by other men before. Supposedly. But after being treated to the perfection of Isaac Donner's mouth, every other man on the planet needed to write a letter of apology to women as a whole. And take some lessons. Maybe practice on each other first before they came to any female, hat in hand, to ask for another shot.

Because this man had ruined her. Never had she felt a kiss in every molecule of her body. Never had she realized that was how it should work. Never would she have expected her insides to be crying with relief, to finally feel like everything aligned.

"Still with me, Detective?" he murmured as her mouth cooled instantly.

Man, would she ever get used to hearing that new edge to his voice when he called her that? Hopefully not.

She nodded, nuzzling her cheek against his, appreciating that he was giving her a chance to back out, if that was indeed where her head was at. There was something super sexy about his insistence on being deliberate. It meant there was no question, on either side. She knew he was present in this moment, no holds barred. No agenda. Isaac was here with her because he wanted to be.

And she could give him the same affirmation. "I want you to touch me, Isaac."

"Yes, ma'am," he growled. "But there are many ways to do that. Help me understand the parameters, just so I'm clear. Because I'm here for whatever happens between us. No matter what. I just don't want to rush you."

The plea was so sweet and so easy to answer. She stood and held out her hand to him. "I want to check out the mattress on your bed. If it's better than mine, I'm going to be having a long conversation with the FBI."

The wolfish grin on his face fluttered in her stomach. He grasped her outstretched hand, but instead of letting her pull him to his feet, he yanked her into his lap. She collapsed against him with a startled laugh that she immediately swallowed as he picked her up, cradling her in his arms as he carried her to his bedroom. Though how he could be doing that when she'd melted into a puddle of woman, she'd never know.

When he dropped her onto the bed and stood over her, worshipping her with his eyes, she had the very distinct feeling that what was about to happen would change everything. But no longer did she think that would be a bad thing. He'd forced her to embrace her own desires, and it was heady. Addicting. She couldn't hide behind their fake relationship and pretend she didn't want him any longer.

"I was afraid of this," she said with mock dismay, and he cocked his head, wariness springing into his gaze. "Your mattress is better than mine."

He laughed and crawled onto it, sweeping her into his embrace, and then spent an eternity showing her what a good decision she'd made. Physically. Emotionally. He made love the way he did everything—extremely well.

She'd needed this, far more than she had fully acknowledged. The man knew exactly how to make her feel cherished, exactly how to love her. It was magical and yet grounding at the same time, as if he'd single-handedly erased all the rules of the universe with this one act.

Later, they lay entwined with each other, both satiated and comfortable with it, until the sun shifted past the horizon. Shadows dropped over the room, and for whatever reason, that jump-started Rory's brain. Holy crud, how had it gotten so late? She sprang from Isaac's bed, holding up a finger when he tried to follow her.

"I need some time to get my head screwed back on," she told him with a laugh that might have sounded a teeny bit desperate—which he'd likely picked up on, dang it. "We're due at the rink in less than two hours, and you've turned my bones into dust."

The expression on his face did delicious things to her insides. Things she had to resist. Things she had no business wishing she could ask him to make good on.

"We could take a shower together," he suggested with a wink that would have been smarmy on anyone else.

"No, we can't," she corrected him, still sounding desperate to get out of this room. Unaccompanied. "That's the opposite of letting me decompress. Let me get my wits about me, please. I can't be a cop right now, and I need to be after the last twenty-four hours of disaster."

Ugh, hopefully he didn't take offense. She hadn't meant the part that included being in his bed. At least not consciously. But now that it was out there...

Folding his arms over his chest, he frowned like a little boy denied his toys. "That's what I'm afraid of. If I give you a minute to think, you'll be back on the other side of the table, warily watching me with those green eyes instead of being with me in here where we make sense together."

Since that exact point might have had more to do with her post-lovemaking flight than anything, she stumbled for a second. *How* did he see through her so easily?

"That's not going to happen," she lied and grabbed her clothes, exiting before he could make his case again.

Because he would, and she'd let herself be seduced by his uncanny way with words, his charisma and extremely talented mouth. She already didn't recognize this woman who romped around in bed with a man in the middle of the day.

When she returned to her room, a text message flashed on her phone. From Sinead. Blinking, she tapped it up: I heard about the attack. I hope you're okay.

She texted her back: I'm fine. Thank you for asking.

It wasn't much. But it was something. A little formal maybe. Would they ever be at a place where they were friends? Was that what she wanted?

Yes. If she was being honest. She craved these types of connections. Donner had done nothing but cater to that, as if he'd figured out her Achilles' heel without even breaking a sweat.

Look what had happened to Achilles though.

As she stood under the spray in her own bathroom, door locked just in case Donner was the type to make an unexpected visit to her inner sanctum while she was naked, the whole thing crashed down on her with a vengeance.

Regret coated her throat. And that sucked. She'd forced herself to let go, to indulge in something wonderful for once, and Donner had more than exceeded her expectations. But…

They had to go back to real life. To their jobs. Where they were fake married. She'd have to kiss him in public. Hold hands. Catch his gaze, which would surely reflect the same heat she'd just witnessed over and over again in a very different environment. They'd shared a million secrets with each other, most of them nonverbal. She knew what the curve of his waist looked like. The shade of his skin along his shoulder. What happened to his eyes when she did something that pleased him.

And in the middle of all of that, an unhinged serial killer would almost certainly strike.

She groaned. What had she done? Complicated everything.

This was a disaster. She should never have let herself indulge in this…whatever it was. Fling? Ugh, that sounded vaguely dirty, as if she'd picked up some guy in a bar. Which would have been cleaner all the way around, ironically, because at least she wouldn't have to see a bar hookup again.

She not only had to see Donner again, she had to work with him. Undercover, no less. While worried about him being killed by Washer.

Great, she really hadn't thought that through either. Because before she'd gotten so intimate with Donner, she'd been pretty freaked out about losing her partner. It was a given that sleeping with him would amplify her feelings, ballooning them into something a lot more difficult to quantify and a lot more difficult to manage.

She had to shut that down. No question. She could not do her job and have feelings for Donner. Not happening. Caring led to loss.

But as the steam from the shower filled the stall and she had yet to pick up the shampoo bottle, the sinking sensation inside told her that ship might have already sailed.

Chapter 17

Isaac didn't have to wait long for the detective to shrug on a distinct coolness toward him after leaving his bed. Disappointing. But not totally unanticipated.

He got it. They had a job to do, and mixing business with pleasure certainly wasn't his typical MO. This was uncharted ground, probably for her too. Frankly, he had no idea how this was supposed to work when all he wanted to do was phone in his resignation to Captain Reeves, then spend the rest of his life luring the detective back between the sheets.

Madness. He'd lost a lot more than his focus when he'd started playing this game with her, determined to win at all costs. Well, it had ended up being frightfully expensive, all right. He could hardly concentrate, and the tension between them could blanket the entire city.

"It's time to go to the rink," he called out from the

kitchen after eating a very plain sandwich by himself. If the detective had eaten, he certainly wasn't informed. Or even meant to be concerned about it, apparently.

The detective rolled into the kitchen, her expression blank, which only reminded him of the last time he'd seen her face, when she'd been in the throes of responding to him as a man. That, he liked. This, he did not.

"I'm ready," she announced and showed him that she was wearing her vest, likely because she knew he'd ask.

"No," he countered, arms crossed. "I don't think you are."

She rolled her eyes. "Don't do this, Donner."

Back to *Donner*, were they? He shook his head. "The whole point of earlier was to get more comfortable with each other, not less."

"I thought the point was to scratch an itch."

Wow. Okay. Not on his side, but clearly, he'd missed a few cues on hers. Never had he met a woman so in need of connecting with someone. And he'd given her that. It had been good for him too. Only to be told he didn't know his own mind and the whole scene had been orchestrated as some kind of primitive mating ritual designed to slake a mutual thirst.

"Yeah, that's what it was," he muttered and scrubbed a hand over his face, weary all at once. "Let's go. Time to give Washer his due attention since that's what he so desperately wants."

"You think that's one of his motivators?" she asked, brightening enough at the subject change that his chest hurt just a little.

"What else could it be?" he said, falling easily into shop talk as he engaged the new biometric lock the

FBI's crew had installed early this morning on the front door to their condo.

No one wanted to be surprised again. The gashes in his face still stung, but not as much as his pride, so he sucked it up and followed the detective to the elevator.

"Glory," she said once the doors shut behind them and they knew they could converse without being overheard by other occupants. "It's no secret that he worships Maeve O'Leary, and I'm convinced at least ninety-nine percent of his fascination with her is that she'll live in infamy."

"He'll get his wish on all counts," Isaac told her grimly. "He will definitely live in infamy, but he'll be doing it behind bars where the prison guards will be very happy to pay attention to him for the rest of his life."

"I'm looking forward to providing that opportunity for him." She smiled, and it kicked him right in the gut. Apparently she'd forgotten to play icicle with him.

Once they hit the street, he automatically reached for her hand, sliding his fingers through hers, half expecting her to flinch or jerk back as if he'd burned her. But she didn't, her thumb resting comfortably in the hollow near his as if they'd done this a million times after spending the day in bed together.

If he lived to be a hundred, he would never understand women.

Nor would he ever get used to being so intensely aware of his surroundings, especially when she was a part of them. Half of him was tensed to leap to her rescue if Washer struck again, and the other half was tensed to drag her into an alcove so he could remind himself what she tasted like.

They walked companionably to the rink, or at least

he put up a fair showing of it, waving at Steve and the rest of the crew as they fell into the rhythm of the night crowd at the center. The app he'd set up to allow people to request songs seemed to be a hit, and it worked to keep people clear of the tent.

The detective took up her usual spot near the entrance, diligently surveying the skaters, surreptitiously checking in with both Colton agents who had again taken up their perimeter surveillance spots.

Just like old times. Only Isaac had a fine awareness of what had happened the previous evening, which had him on edge. He was waiting for Washer to materialize inside the tent again, another length of steel in his hands pointed at Isaac's throat.

But this time, he'd be ready for him.

Washer wouldn't get the drop on him again. It wasn't a thing.

Unfortunately another thing that wasn't a thing— Washer didn't show. And that edge never waned, which left Isaac exhausted by midnight, the end of their shift when the rink closed.

"That was brutal," he confessed to the detective when they finally hit the elevator of their condo building again. "I kept looking up, expecting to see Washer in the tent again. With a different color hat this time. New gun. Same diabolical smile."

"Me too," she murmured and rubbed the small of her back. "I don't think I relaxed an iota that whole night."

Once he closed the door behind them and reengaged the biometric locks, he snagged the detective's hand before she could bolt off. "Sit on the couch, and let me take care of you for a minute."

She eyed him suspiciously. "It's late for a cup of coffee."

"It's not going to be *exactly* like earlier," he told her with a laugh and led her to the spot where he wanted her. He noted she didn't protest when he sat on the arm of the couch so he could dig into her back with his thumbs.

The groan that rumbled from her throat spiked through him instantly, flopping his stomach over like a dog that wanted a treat.

"I had no idea that spot hurt so badly," she said and rolled her neck. "Though it's no shock you realized it. I swear I must have a celestial hand scrawling my innermost secrets on my forehead with a Sharpie so you can read them."

The compliment threw a grin on his face wide enough to crack his jaw, but he didn't care since she couldn't see him. "That's exactly how it works. It's like a Twitter feed up there—Rory's tired. Rory's back hurts. Rory needs you to feed her."

She froze so suddenly that he got concerned he'd hit a nerve or something in her back that had messed her up, like a pause button. But then she said, "You called me Rory."

"No, I said that's what would be written on your forehead. Because that's what anyone else would call you. I'm the only one who gets to call you Detective. It's special."

The silence stretched for so long, he thought he'd lost her. But then she said, "You can't say stuff like that. Not anymore."

"Not anymore since we slept together?" he asked with more calm than he actually felt because *what*? "I have news for you. That makes us more intimate. Not less."

"It can't, Donner. We're back to business. We have to be."

Yeah. That didn't make it any easier to do—or like—especially not when it didn't seem to be causing an ounce of pain on her side. "We still have to pretend to be married."

She flipped a hand up in question. "At what point did we fail to maintain our cover tonight? That's what the roll in the sheets was about anyway. We need to work together, and we need to fake being married. We needed to let off some steam. We managed all of that and then some. Now we're back to being partners who are in sync. Right?"

"Right. It's fine," he muttered. The heaviness in his chest started to annoy him. "I'm fine. Our cover is fine."

"Yup. It's all good. We got it out of our systems, and now we can focus on Washer. Like we need to."

Her phone buzzed with a text message, and she flinched.

"What's wrong?" he asked automatically, braced for something not good.

"That's my department phone. There's only one person using that number right now."

Washer.

She slipped from underneath his hands, and he hated how empty they felt. What he needed was a good, hard workout at the gym. He hadn't been by his regular one in several days now, and obviously he needed an attitude adjustment. The one in the building wasn't cutting it.

The detective held up her phone, her expression grim as she nodded to confirm. "Our mutual friend. I hate that guy."

The message read, Miss me yet?

"That's good though," he said. "It means our cover is still in place if he's still taunting us like nothing has changed. He doesn't suspect a thing."

"If he's back to taunting us, we may not see him for a couple of days. Hungry?" she called as she sailed toward the kitchen, apparently bent on making a midnight snack. Once she'd pulled out some crackers and cheese, she stacked them and shoved it whole into her mouth.

He followed her into the kitchen and took a cracker, even though it tasted like sawdust in his mouth. "We need to file a report."

"To say that Washer didn't show and I got a text message?" Her expression told him exactly what she thought about that suggestion. "It can wait."

"It's protocol." Why he was pushing it, he had no clue, but she'd gotten him off-kilter and he was having a devil of a time reorienting.

"I know that, Donner," she shot back. "I wrote the book on following the letter of the law. I think we get a pass on that while we're undercover. I'll get to it tomorrow."

"You'll forgive me if I do mine tonight," he said and marched over to his laptop, making a big show of opening it, then sitting down at the table.

See? He could play it cool too. Nothing to see here. *Everything is fine.*

The detective rolled her eyes and hefted herself up onto the counter to sit there finishing her snack, legs swinging freely as if she hadn't a care in the world.

Irritated at himself and the situation and Steve Jobs— God rest his soul—for making it so hard to log into a computer when you couldn't see straight to type. Isaac finally got the login prompt to recognize his password without having to resort to burned offerings.

The report, as previously pointed out by his partner, had almost nothing in it, so it took, like, four seconds to type up and another four seconds to route to Blackthorn via the electronic submission system.

He'd bet money Blackthorn wasn't sitting on the other end of the digital highway waiting on it either. The man was a newlywed and likely indulging in everything that had to offer. The black emotion currently coloring Isaac's mood might've been more properly called jealousy, but he'd shoot himself in the foot before admitting that, even to himself in his own head.

Because it was stupid. Jealous? Of what? This situation with the detective was perfect. He liked a woman who knew when to back off. Isaac hadn't even had to say a word about it either. What more could he want from life?

A repeat. A repeat to the repeat. That woman from earlier in his bed, longer than five minutes. Not this tension between him and the detective. He liked it a lot better when he'd felt like he could flirt with her and say something suggestive, which would put a gleam in her eyes that meant he'd affected her. When he could use the fake marriage as a springboard to get physical with her, kiss her when he felt like it.

Well, why couldn't he? In the name of their undercover assignment, of course.

His gaze narrowed at the name *Blackthorn* on his screen. Who was married to the detective's sister.

She wanted this to be about the job? He could get on board with that.

"You know what we should do? Have dinner with

Blackthorn and Sinead," he called out to her casually. "We can talk about the case since your sister did the profile. Get some brownie points."

All about the job. She couldn't say no to that, even though technically it would be a double date. He crossed his arms. Two could play this game.

How Donner had gotten Rory into a dress still baffled her. But one minute she'd been processing the idea that he'd arranged to go to the rink late so they could have dinner with her sister, and the next, Donner had invaded her closet to review the options, discarding a perfectly nice pair of Ann Taylor slacks in charcoal.

"You don't want to show up for dinner in these, only to find out Sinead is wearing a dress, do you?" he'd tsked and pulled out a navy shirtdress that she usually wore over leggings, but she'd forgotten those at home in her haste to pack.

Oh, man. Would her sister be wearing a dress? And would she think Rory was weird if she wore pants? Would it be like a test and Sinead would be disappointed that Rory hadn't passed?

She was so nervous, she plopped down onto the bed and thought seriously about taking up yoga. They didn't have to be at Wells and Sinead's brownstone for over an hour. That was more than enough time to master some zen moves that would calm her, right?

"Come on," he said and motioned her over with two fingers. "Put this on, and let's see if this will work."

Dutifully, she snatched it from his hand and dashed to the bathroom to slip on the dress, buttoning it up with shaking fingers. *It's dinner*, she told herself. *Not the Spanish Inquisition.*

It was just…she and Sinead weren't "having dinner together" sisters. She still didn't know if Sinead had been thrilled with the idea or had only said yes because Donner had suggested it as a working session to brainstorm on the case.

Yet…her sister had texted her. Reached out. Surely dinner could only help them move toward the friendship Rory had secretly started to want.

When she came out of the bathroom, Donner whistled. Which made her blush. *Blush*, for crying out loud. The man had seen her naked, and *this* embarrassed her?

"Perfect," he told her. "I am a fan of this dress."

His eyes were on her legs, and her fears about being cold at some point this evening went out the window. There was nothing but pure heat in his gaze. It warmed her up plenty, and she couldn't quite make herself tell him to stop. Even though she totally should've.

Things between them were status quo. Or as quo as they could be when Donner was looking at her like that.

Donner paired the dress with her black boots and threw a belt around the waist like she'd inherited her own Tim Gunn somewhere along the way, then hustled her into an Uber that he insisted on paying for.

Off-kilter in more ways than one, she settled into the seat of the rideshare trying to figure out what angle Donner was trying to play here—because there was one, no doubt.

"Explain to me again why me wearing a dress has anything to do with earning brownie points with Blackthorn?" she muttered as the Uber swung up 47th to go the long way around Manhattan where they would switch to another car in case Washer had a bead on them.

The last thing they needed was to blow their cover

by fraternizing with a sergeant from the 130th and an FBI profiler, both of whom Washer had more than a passing familiarity with.

"Oh, it doesn't," Donner told her cheerfully. "That was strictly for my benefit."

She rolled her eyes. "I should have known you'd wait to confess that once it was too late for me to change back."

"It's like you're reading my mind. What am I thinking about now?"

She whacked his arm. "Something you shouldn't be thinking about, that's a given."

Donner pointedly stared at the place where she'd voluntarily touched him. "Hard not to when you're flirting with me like this. It's shameless. I like it. Do it some more."

"I'm not flirting with you, Donner," she told him firmly. "If I was, you'd know it."

"I'm not sure I would. Why don't you try it, and I'll guess whether you're flirting or simply being handsy with me because you can't stand how good I look in these pants."

She couldn't help it. She laughed. Even though she'd sworn she wouldn't do anything at dinner other than focus on Sinead. Their relationship had been rocky, though she'd like to think they'd bridged the gap over the last few months as they'd worked together on the Landmark Killer case. Did Sinead think that? Was that the genesis of the text message?

"Hey," Donner murmured and laced their fingers together to hold her hand tight. "It's going to be great. I'll be right here."

Stunned, she stared at him. "How did you know I'm quietly freaking out over here?"

Dumb question—he always knew. Next time, she'd think twice about getting involved with a detective who'd earned his stripes noticing details.

"*A*, because you're not being quiet about it at all," he said with a laugh. "And *B*, because you told me you're worried that Sinead hates you. Things are not as they should be between you. This is a chance to work through some of that. It's why I suggested it."

Not for brownie points with Wells? Donner *did* have an angle, but never would she have guessed that he'd put her at the core of it. That he'd suggested dinner as a way for her to connect with Sinead that wasn't too obviously a setup and did mesh with their common goal of catching Washer. It was...perfect.

The man was too perceptive.

That was the number one reason she shouldn't have slept with him and then tried to act like they could go back to being just partners—he'd probably already sniffed out that she wasn't doing so hot at staying neutral. And not because he did look spectacular in his dress clothes.

Because he cared. He'd told her he did. And then she'd brushed him off after letting him rock her world, yet here they were in the back of an Uber holding hands—yes, she should have pulled free and lambasted him about keeping things businesslike, but dang it, she *needed* his strength right now.

He was infusing her with it, all right. Just by being there. What was she going to do with him?

Chapter 18

Rory forced herself to put the strange state of her relationship with Donner on the back burner in favor of focusing on the immediate issue—Sinead. And Wells. Her boss.

That was one of the factors in this she hadn't quite considered. For someone who had always excelled at keeping the job and her personal life separate, she'd fallen down superbly on that front. No one else seemed bothered by it though, so she vowed to get over herself for once.

Donner knocked on the door of Wells and Sinead's brownstone, one of the cuter ones in Soho that he'd inherited from his family. Sinead pulled open the heavy wooden door, her smile on the politer side but genuine.

Okay, you can do this.

"Rory, it's lovely to see you," Sinead said, her green eyes a mirror of Rory's, which was certainly not new

information, but after Donner had told her that she and
Sinead must've surely been the same at their cores, it
struck a chord.

They shared blood. It meant something.

"Thank you for having us. Sorry to be invading you
like this," Rory said sincerely. "It would have been difficult to host you at our condo when it's almost definitely being watched."

"Of course, it's no trouble," Sinead said immediately.
"Wells is beside himself to have guests in the house we
created together. We hired a teenager down the block to
watch Harry for us for a few hours, and she was thrilled
to make the extra money."

Oh dear, Rory had forgotten all about the baby. Wells's
brother and sister-in-law had been killed in an accident,
leaving their infant son behind. Wells had mentioned it
a few times, but it hadn't crossed her mind that Sinead
had chosen to be baby Harry's mother when she'd agreed
to marry Wells.

Instant family. It sounded…nice.

"Isaac." Sinead shifted her attention to Donner. "It's
nice to meet you face-to-face. I've heard a lot about you
from Wells."

"Mrs. Blackthorn," he said with deference and then
murmured, "Sinead" when she insisted he drop the *Mrs.
Blackthorn* with a wrinkled nose.

She let them in and secured the door behind her,
leading them into the one-story unit that had been lov-
ingly renovated into a cozy apartment with a spacious
kitchen that featured a dining area, set with a modern-
style table that would fit four people comfortably but no
more. The downside of living in an expensive, crowded

city. Dinner parties were always on the small side or else hosted at a restaurant.

The couple had wedged a tasteful Christmas tree into the corner and adorned it with glass bulbs in pastels. Beneath it sat a selection of wrapped packages in matching paper. Two red candles sat on the table, both surrounded by bright greens with berries. It was festive without being overdone and served as an immediate indictment of Rory's own living space, which contained not one element to mark the season. Which made her sad.

Wells stood in the living room, a beer in hand. "Donner, Rory. Glad you could make it."

"After we invited ourselves, it would be poor form to skip out," Donner said with a laugh. "Thanks for hosting. We'll reciprocate if there's a point in the future when it's possible."

There was no *if*. *When* they caught Washer. Then it would be safe to have Wells and Sinead over to their condo. She started to correct him.

Except it wasn't their condo. It belonged to the FBI via the US Marshals Service. And once Washer was behind bars, she and Donner wouldn't be living together any longer. They certainly wouldn't be inviting people over for a party.

The sobering thought clammed her up. In the end she didn't say anything. Which made it slightly awkward, but Wells just smiled at her and offered her and Donner a beer, which she took strictly to have something to do with her hands.

"We ordered takeout from the Indian place around the corner," Sinead told them. "It should be here soon. I'm still trying to learn how to use this kitchen, so I hope you'll forgive me for not cooking."

"Curry is my favorite," Donner said cheerfully, and Rory did a double take.

It was? Since when? Or was he just being nice? Suddenly, it occurred to her that she might not know Donner as well as she could. Was that a problem?

"It seems like you're settling in well though," she told Sinead and made a show of glancing around the place. "This is a great location, and you've done a lot with it already for having just moved in."

Sinead and Wells exchanged glances full of hidden meaning and secret sauce that only they knew how to describe. The kind of look only a couple who were deeply in love could share.

It made Rory's throat hurt to witness it. How would it feel to be at that place with someone? Where you trusted each other with intimacy on an ongoing basis?

"It's been a lot of fun," Sinead confessed softly. "More than I would have expected. You hear about how couples fight all the time over design choices and spending money and who knows what. That just hasn't been the case with us. We're always on the same wavelength."

Donner settled into the spot on the couch that Wells indicated, sipping his beer. There was nowhere else for Rory to sit but on the same couch. Next to Donner. It was almost like it had been planned out ahead of time. But by whom, she wasn't clear, and she didn't want to upset the apple cart.

She sat in the exact center of the cushion, not too close to her fake husband and not too far away as to cause comment. Except no one had told Donner to stop pouring out all that masculine heat. It rolled from him in waves, and the spicy scent of his aftershave sucked all the air from her lungs.

"Congrats on the marriage," Donner said, "by the way. You're not going on a honeymoon?"

Wells shrugged. "It's the wrong time. We couldn't wait to get married, but we have the rest of our lives to take a honeymoon. After we close the Landmark Killer case, then we can consider it."

That was the kind of thinking Rory could get behind. The job came first. Everything else was secondary.

Except they had gone ahead with getting married. It was a curious callout, one that sat funny with her. If the job came first, then why risk losing focus in such a major way? Because surely being a newlywed came with a million distractions. Look how hard it had been for Rory to focus after one round of checking out Donner's mattress.

Actually, if she wanted to be completely honest, she'd been distracted by him long before he'd seduced her into his bed. Sleeping with him had just amplified it.

"Maybe you could help us," Donner suggested in a tenor that Rory recognized a mile away. It was his *Everything's cool, but I have something up my sleeve* tone. "We're doing this fake-marriage thing, but sometimes it feels like we're trying too hard or not doing enough. Rory is convinced that married people don't kiss each other in public except for simple goodbye kisses. Is that legit?"

Sure, call her out with a big flaming arrow pointed at her head, why didn't he? And tack on her name to boot. It was like he knew that every time she heard him say her first name, it set off a round of disappointment that he'd opted for the non-nuclear option, the one that did nothing to her insides. *Detective*, on the other hand… that she liked to hear far too much.

Calling her Rory was better. Totally fine. Better than fine. It was good that he stuck with the business-only name.

Wells and Sinead glanced at each other again, not even bothering to hide their smirks, and Wells said, "I can't speak for other married people, but we definitely do a lot of kissing in public that has nothing to do with saying goodbye."

"Huh," Donner said and took a sip of his beer. He didn't glance in Rory's direction, but she could feel the *Told you so* burning through the air between them.

Her face on fire, Rory crossed her arms and then remembered she had a beer in her own hand. She took a sip, promptly forgetting how to swallow, which resulted in a fit of coughing. Clearly concerned, Donner slid over and rubbed her back, which felt far nicer than a rescue operation should.

Sinead's eyebrows lifted as she drank in the cozy scene that was literally nothing more than a partner looking out for the other one. Except Donner didn't slide back to his own seat when she recovered. He sat there with his arm slung across the back of the couch, which meant she couldn't quite sit back without her head grazing his elbow.

All for the job, she reminded herself and ignored the perfect abs on the man sitting less than two inches from her. "So on that note, the issue is that we need to keep convincing *Washer* that we're married, not each other. I think Donner is too hung up on practicing."

"Name one time you were not on board with practicing," Donner murmured, his blue eyes flinty as he offered up a lazy smile that flipped her stomach over and back.

"I'm always on board with practicing," she shot back, ordering her insides to behave. "This job is too important to mess up something as easy as pretending to be married."

"Now it's easy?" Wells interjected, and Rory glanced at him, wondering what it meant that she'd forgotten he was standing there. "Did something change?"

Okay, she'd only thought her face had been on fire earlier. The curse of the Irish wasn't a temper but fair skin that turned her into a walking advertisement for embarrassing moments. Like this one.

"We took your advice, Blackthorn," Donner said with his maddening cheerfulness. "I think it's safe to say we're on the same page now."

"Glad to hear it," Wells said with a nod, but Sinead wasn't having any of it.

"Why do I feel like everyone in this room is talking in cipher but forgot to give me the key?" she asked, her fascinated gaze flitting between the three of them as Rory studiously inspected the painting on the wall over the couch, a lovely Frida Kahlo print.

"It's nothing, darling," Wells said and tilted his beer in Donner and Rory's direction. "Small misunderstanding with a report."

Rory took the opportunity to flee the room by asking Sinead to direct her to the bathroom, where she leaned on the door and pressed her beer bottle to her face. In the entire history of law enforcement, had there ever been a more difficult situation than the one she'd plunked herself into?

On the list of things she never wanted to admit to her boss, a lapse in protocol would be number one. And she had a pretty good idea that sleeping with your partner ranked high on the naughty list. It was unprofessional at best and against department policy at worst. She'd never had a reason to find out before.

She stayed hidden as long as she dared and then finally forced herself to leave the relative safety of the bathroom. But as soon as she cleared the door, she saw Sinead hovering in the hallway, as if waiting her turn.

"Sorry for hogging the bathroom," she said, undoing all the good she'd done to erase the color from her face.

Sinead shook her head and gave her a small smile. "I was waiting for you. I wanted to make sure you were okay. Those clowns might think they're being charming, but I could tell the comments upset you for some reason."

Oh. Well, that was unexpected. And above the call of duty. It was something a sister might do, not that Rory had a lot to draw from in that respect. Her chest got a little tight as Sinead stood there extending another olive branch, this one far more meaningful than the text message.

"Thanks," Rory rasped, emotion clogging her throat. "You didn't have to check on me. I appreciate that you did though."

Sinead tucked her long blond hair behind one ear. The last time Rory had seen her sister, she'd worn it up in a ponytail, a much more professional look. This softer hairstyle suited her and highlighted her delicate beauty, which Sinead had definitely gotten from her mother. Rory looked like their father, with dark hair and his nose.

Hesitating, Sinead finally nodded. "I'm glad you came to dinner, Rory. We haven't ever socialized before. Maybe it's time to change that."

Something bright flooded a lot of dark places inside, and the power of it pricked at Rory's eyelids. "Really?" she whispered and couldn't get anything else past the lump in her throat.

Pathetic. Her sister hadn't done anything but comment that maybe they should get together sometime. No big deal. She was the one who had turned it into Something Meaningful.

"I mean, that would be fine," Rory said in a much less affected tone of voice so her sister wouldn't figure out that the overture had meant everything to her.

"Good." Sinead's smile reached her eyes this time. "I spent a lot of years upset with our father, and Wells finally helped me realize that forgiveness is free but carrying around pain and bitterness is expensive. I'm afraid I let some of that extend to you and that none of it was your fault. I'm sorry I did that. Can we be friends?"

Rory nodded, not trusting herself to speak. Friends. Exactly as she'd hoped. It sounded wonderful. Maybe eventually in time they could become more like sisters, but at the moment, she could use a friend more.

"Now that we've got that settled, if you want some advice on how to act like a doting wife, I'm happy to help," Sinead offered.

That tipped the floodgates, and a tear splashed down Rory's face. "I'm not sure I need a lot of help with that. If you have advice on how to *stop* acting like a doting wife, I'd be all ears."

Sinead's eyebrows rose. "You have it bad for Isaac, don't you."

It wasn't a question, and Rory didn't bother to do a lot of soul searching for the answer when it was already on the tip of her tongue. "So bad. It's terrible. Please tell me you used your womanly intuition to figure that out and it's not, like, tattooed on my forehead."

Sinead laughed. "I'm sorry to be the bearer of hard to hear news, but you should tell your face to behave when you look at him. I realized the second you stepped through my door that something had happened between you. I take it things are not going well?"

"Sinead, I slept with my partner!" she whispered hotly. "Things can't get any more unwell than that. It's not something I'm proud of. I'm mortified to think that Wells might have figured it out. Do you think he knows?"

Dumb question. Obviously she was going around advertising the fact that she and Donner had done a lot more than get on the same page. And it wasn't like she could ask Sinead to keep it from her husband. Everyone would know before too long one way or the other.

"Doubtful. He's observant, of course, but more focused on the proposed reason for the evening's events, the Landmark Killer. He's head down constantly, worried about his team, worried about missing something. He was really excited about brainstorming with you guys tonight." Sinead cocked her head. "Why would you be worried about him finding out?"

"It's unprofessional," she moaned. "Not to mention a distraction from the case. If he finds out, he's going to fire me. And should. I'm so compromised, I don't even know how to act like proper backup because all I want to do is take apart anyone who so much as looks at Isaac crossways, let alone tries to hurt him." Sinead started laughing in the middle of Rory's impassioned speech, and she lost her place. "What?"

"If Wells so much as breathes a word about protocol

or unprofessionalism, you can remind him that he married the FBI profiler assigned to the Landmark Killer case. Don't worry." She rolled her eyes, still filled with mirth. "You're good."

Feeling as if a balloon had been popped inside, Rory stared at her sister. "I guess I didn't think about it like that. You guys seem so perfect together that it didn't occur to me that you might have been struggling with the same issue."

"But we're not struggling," Sinead reminded her. "We're married. Happy. This is what makes the long hours and the difficult cases fade at the end of the day, Rory. Not standing on principle because you work together—which I don't think is a rule, by the way. If it matters to you, then transfer. Or ask him to. These things can be managed if the man is worth it."

That set Rory's head buzzing with unanswered questions. Was Donner worth it? Would she give up the Landmark Killer case for a chance to be with him without compromising her integrity or her focus? Would *he*?

She had a feeling she knew the answer to that. *No.* Not when he had something to prove. Someone to avenge. Someone to best, a contest to win. These things were much more important to him than a temporary fling with the woman he'd been assigned to pretend was his wife.

Where did that leave them?

"I'm glad you're happy with Wells," she told her sister sincerely despite the sting of jealousy in the back of her throat.

They did make it look easy. As if it was as simple as deciding that the obstacles didn't exist and all that mattered was being together. As simple as admitting that's what she wanted too.

"Maybe one day—not now—but some day you can tell me about our father," Sinead said, her expression a little more stark than Rory liked. "It's hard for me to ask, but I feel like I'd like to learn more about him. He's a part of me, and you are too. I can't think of anything I'd like more than to connect with you in that way."

Rory nodded, suddenly happy she didn't wear makeup because surely her mascara would be a mess by now. "I'd like that too. And for the record, I'm not a huge fan of our father either."

"No?" Sinead asked, curiosity edging out the pain that had come along with her request.

How did you explain what it felt like to realize you were the reason another family had been destroyed? And that the man responsible for making that decision was the same one who picked you up from school and sat across from you at the dinner table?

You didn't explain, that's how. "I hate what he did to you and your mother."

And she hated that secrecy and pretense comprised her model for what a relationship looked like. No wonder she'd gravitated toward her own version of that, glomming on to a fake marriage because nothing had ever seemed real in her own life.

"*Hate* is a strong word," Sinead told her mildly. "Just know that we're okay—my mom and me. We survived. We're strong. He missed out on something wonderful."

Yeah, on both counts. Choosing Rory and her mother hadn't won him any points, and she'd never felt like she could depend on her father. Their relationship remained strained to this day.

But she and Sinead had connected anyway, despite their separate painful experiences. It was more than she'd expected and more than she would have offered had their positions been reversed. A sobering thought. Her past was forming her future whether she'd realized it or not. The real question was whether she had the ability to take a page from Sinead and course correct or if she'd keep letting her fears drive the bus.

Chapter 19

"I think we should decorate for Christmas," the detective announced just as Isaac reached into the toaster to pull out a bagel.

"You do?" he responded evenly despite having no clue how to play this unexpected declaration.

They'd left the Blackthorn residence last night and dashed straight to the ice-skating rink where they'd endured yet another uneventful night of DJing and stressing about whether Washer would make an appearance.

Spoiler alert: he hadn't. Nor had he texted anyone. It was a deliberate ploy to confuse them, to keep them off guard. Isaac hated waiting on tenterhooks like one of those wooden ducks with a big bull's-eye painted on its side, set in motion by a carnie for anyone to take a shot at who was feeling lucky.

But this was the job and he would do it until the day he died.

Which could be tomorrow if Washer had his way. Or next week. Or in June of 2065 as Isaac shuffled to the dining hall of the nursing home. That was the problem. He had no idea what was on the horizon, and it made him antsy.

The good news: Washer hadn't come after the detective again. Which worked for Isaac and then some. The less he had to worry about her, the better. Maybe the Landmark Killer had regained his focus on Oliver Walken and forgotten about Cassandra.

The detective calmly sipped her coffee as if this wasn't the first time she'd spoken to him since last night and nodded. "Like Sinead and Wells. Their tree was cute, don't you think?"

Isaac cracked his neck, bagel forgotten as he warmed up to jump straight into this new game the detective had cooked up. Because he did not plan to lose, whatever it was. "The cutest. Why do we want to decorate for Christmas? You didn't get enough jolliness by dressing up as an elf?"

She made a face. "Thanks for reminding me. I had almost forgotten about that."

"I have many pictures on my phone if you would like some additional reminders," he informed her cheekily. Most of them he'd taken when she hadn't been paying attention as a souvenir for his trouble. But he'd happily expose his contraband if it got him deeper into the battlefield.

But she just shook her head. "No, thanks. That's better left in the past. But it's the Christmas season now and our condo is dreary."

She waved a hand at the rather beige living area beyond the bistro set, as if he'd forgotten that they lived in the most sterile environment imaginable. The FBI's stager had zero imagination and might've been color-blind. But this was temporary housing with a means to an end. It was a little shocking that the detective had even noticed the lack of decor, and he certainly wouldn't have pegged her as being the one to point it out. Or fix it.

The concept had *domestic bliss* written all over it. And he was here for it.

Did this mean she was wavering on whatever had created this huge gulf between them?

"I one thousand percent agree," he told her. "You want a tree? I'll get you one."

"No, we have to do it together. As Oliver and Cassandra," she clarified. "It's something married people do. Obviously. That's the whole reason we went over to Sinead and Wells's house, so we could generate some kind of forward momentum on the case. That's what made me think of it."

"Oh. Okay."

Why it disappointed him that she'd only suggested it as a married-couple activity worthy of parading in front of Washer, he couldn't say. Or rather, he wouldn't. Because it was lame to be so envious of Sinead and Wells. Telling himself that didn't make it stop, sadly.

"You don't want to decorate?" She zeroed in on him as if trying to decipher hieroglyphs, and he didn't like being scrutinized to such a degree. She might see something he didn't want her to.

"I didn't say that. I said okay," he reminded her and whipped out his phone to look for a Christmas tree lot. "It's fine. I want to decorate. There's a place that sells trees near Pier 88. Let's go."

The moment they stepped outside, Isaac reached for

the detective's hand, only to discover she'd slipped on a pair of gloves. He frowned. It wasn't that cold outside, and she'd never worn gloves before.

This distance she'd insisted on putting between them sucked. He hated it. Worse, he understood it. They needed to focus, to eliminate distractions. They'd worked through their differences—first at the captain's behest and then because Blackthorn had told them point-blank to stop screwing up.

Besides, he should've been cheering over the space. He loved space. Especially when he didn't have to do anything to create it.

There was nothing more to do here—except Isaac wasn't done. Not by a long shot.

"Not a fan of the gloves," he murmured as they headed down 48th Street toward the Hudson, dodging tourists who were perennially in this area holding printed maps or gawking at the iconic buildings and sites that comprised the beginning of Broadway and Times Square.

"I like them," she murmured back. "They were a Christmas gift from Sin—a *friend*."

Great. Way to make him feel petty and uncomplimentary of something her sister had given her. "It's not Christmas yet. You're going to get into serious trouble with Santa for opening a gift early."

The detective shrugged. "She asked me to open the present last night before I left. Sue me."

Because they were still supposed to be acting like a married couple, Isaac opted to sling his arm around her, which ended up feeling a lot more like they were participating in a potato sack race/obstacle course mashup rather than anything intimate. Finally, he gave up and hoped Washer thought they were fighting if he was indeed even watching them.

Funny, it didn't feel too much like Washer would be wrong if he drew that conclusion.

After a brisk twenty-five-minute walk that should have taken twenty and would have if they'd gone undercover anywhere else in the city, they found the tree lot, which seemed to have slim pickings this late into December.

"That one," the detective said decisively as she pointed at a Douglas fir that had to be at least ten feet tall.

"I hate to break it to you, darling, but that tree wouldn't even fit in the elevator, let alone in our living room," he told her gently. "Unless you want to bust a hole in the ceiling and blame it on rats."

She made a face. "Sinea—*our friends* have those lovely vaulted ceilings. I bet it would have fit in their living room."

"Our friends live in a brownstone. That's a much different animal than a condo building. If you want a house like that, we'll put it on the twenty-year plan and start saving our pennies."

The look she shot him said she'd love to break character but knew better than to call him out on his comment. Washer could've been standing behind them, disguised and listening, at any given moment.

Being part of the job didn't make it any easier to say something like that and not wonder what kind of house they would be buying if they were newlyweds like Sinead and Wells. For instance, he'd just learned that she preferred big Christmas trees and vaulted ceilings instead of the clinical sterility of a million-dollar condo in the center of Tourist-ville. Which worked for him and then some.

"Let's try this one, darling," he said and guided her toward a tree that wasn't much taller than him but had a nice shape. Plus the two of them could carry it back home and avoid paying for delivery.

"Okay," she agreed readily, which frankly shocked him since he'd been prepared for a fight.

Not one to look a gift horse in the mouth, he paid the attendant and helped thread the tree through the netting device that scrunched down all the boughs for easy transport.

Easy being relative. Carrying a six-foot tree through Manhattan would be difficult at 2:00 a.m., let alone midmorning. The tree was heavy, and he'd taken the cut end in order to allow the detective to take the top, which was the lighter, smaller end. But she was a stellar trooper, and they eventually made it back with only two stops for her to readjust her grip.

They set the tree in the center of the living area and flopped onto the couch. The detective stripped off her gloves—finally—and blew out a breath, wafting wilted hair from her forehead.

"So glad I took a shower. I need another one now. I could have done without this coat," she said, which must have reminded her she was still wearing it. She eased out of it and threw the serviceable puffy jacket onto the chair at a right angle to the couch. "Thanks, Donner. I like the tree."

"You're welcome," he murmured as he registered how much it pleased him to make her happy. "You know we have to get ornaments and a stand now, right?"

"Yeah, yeah," she said airily. "Logistics. At least we

have the tree and made a big show of it. If Washer is watching, he'll think that's the most married thing ever. He probably wondered why we didn't have one when he broke in here."

That was a dark subject he'd rather have left at the door. He scowled. "I hope he's thinking about how I'm going to kill him if he tries that again."

"Get in line," she said flippantly and laughed. "You'll have to come through me to get to Washer. I have a score to settle."

"It's not funny, Detective," he growled, and this distance between them needed to vanish like yesterday. Too bad if she had other plans. "He could have killed you. That's not a laughing matter. I can't lose you either."

She stared at him, suddenly cluing in that the light-hearted banter of the Christmas tree excursion had been replaced by something else. And no, he didn't know what either. All he knew was that he needed to touch her. Badly. He thought his lungs might explode if he didn't.

Not the slightest bit tentatively, he reached out and spread his fingers along her jawline, tipping up her face so he could drink her in. "That's better."

"What are you doing?" she asked. "We're not in public."

"No. No, we are not. If I recall, you prefer me to kiss you here, behind closed doors. I thought it was high time to indulge you in that."

Indulge them both. She didn't protest either, which made his heart sing as he claimed her mouth in a kiss that could only be described as *feral*. It wasn't his normal MO. But he wasn't feeling all that gentle, and as she opened under his onslaught, it seemed as if the urgency worked for her too.

She made a noise in her throat, her fingers digging into his back, and it was heady. Finally, finally, she was back in his arms, and he questioned his sanity in ever allowing her to leave.

But before things got too out of hand, he turned his head, breaking the kiss. "Detective, if you have a fundamental objection to my checking out your mattress, now would be the time to say so."

She blinked. "Just to be clear, will I be checking it out with you?"

The missing oxygen in his lungs rushed in as he laughed. "Oh, yes. You will. I'm not sure how we got to the place where you thought it was okay to push me away, but we're done with that now. Just making that clear too. Okay?"

She nodded. "I got that when you kissed me."

"Good," he rumbled. "Because I'm not scratching an itch. It's not working for me to pretend I'm a one-and-done kind of guy. I'm not."

Not with her anyway. Never would he have envisioned a scenario where he'd be arguing the point with a woman, but here they were.

"I'm not really like that either," she admitted, her fingers grazing his cheek where the gashes had mostly healed but were definitely still visible. "What I am is scared."

The acknowledgment humbled him. Cooled his jets— a little. He took one of her hands and held it to his mouth, molding his lips to the ridge of her knuckle. "Don't worry. I'm right here."

"That's what scares me, Donner. Isaac." She caught

his gaze, and the emotion there did a number on his gut. "What happens when you're not here? You of all people should be shying away from something this strong. You know what happens when you let your guard down. When you start to hope that connecting with someone won't lead to loss."

He did know. He got it. All of that was true. "What can I say? You're worth taking that risk. I could no more stop the way I feel about you than I could order the sky to turn purple."

"Which is exactly what color it turns right before dark," she told him with a frown that he felt utterly compelled to turn upside down.

"All of the best things happen after dark," he murmured and feathered a thumb across her lips, teasing the curve of her chin, loving the feel of her under his skin. "Loss is a part of life. It doesn't make it easier to live if you cut yourself off from something wonderful while it lasts. If you'll let me, I'll do my best to make it worth your while, at least for a little while."

She didn't have to know that in his head, he planned to make this last as long as he could. If it made her feel better to think he meant they could play married couple behind closed doors for the rest of this assignment, great. Whatever got her this close to him and pliant in his arms.

"This is a job, Isaac," she reminded him, indecision stamped across her features. "That scares me too, to think about jumping in with both feet. How can we be effective cops if we're constantly worried about each other? Or actively wondering if we're ever going to get naked again?"

His eyebrows shot up. "If you haven't already been wondering that, I must not be as good as I think I am."

She smacked him on the arm. "Your ego is staggering—and I can't believe I'm about to feed it even more—but yeah, I've been horribly distracted by wondering when."

That widened his grin. "Allow me to fix that problem for you. It's now."

Sated didn't begin to describe Isaac's state of mind and, as a plus, when the detective had tried to shut things down again after they'd had enough bliss to kill a regular man, he'd pulled her back into bed and convinced her to forget about fleeing.

So far, it had worked.

But eventually, duty called and they were due at the rink. He let her slip from his arms with enormous reluctance, bracing for more shenanigans and regrets, like what had happened last time.

Shockingly, the detective seemed to have turned some kind of decision corner and even stopped him on the way out of the condo to indulge in a very sexy kiss against the back of the door that dissolved his desire to play DJ for the next seven hours.

"What was that for?" he murmured as she waltzed away.

He tried to guide her back into his arms, only to have his hopes and dreams of a tardy arrival to the rink crushed under her cruel heel as she shoved him out the door.

"Because I wanted to and I can," she told him saucily. "I'm trying on this new normal where we're both aware everything could come crashing down tomorrow and owning it and still doing this thing anyway. No fear.

Devil may care, and no regrets. I'm living large in the moment, so don't ruin it."

The false note of gaiety in her tone sat on his nerves sideways. He could tell she didn't fully buy into what she'd said, and honestly, it sounded awful to him too. But what should he do, confess to her this wasn't just fun and games to him?

Admit that he'd started falling for her?

He barely recognized himself in this scenario, and it was doing a lot more than grating on his nerves to be this into a woman, especially one he should've been cajoling to help him practice self-defense moves or take back to the shooting range. Anything that would help the case. Instead, he was spending hours worshipping her body and mind in a much more hands-on way.

Pathetic.

"That's right," he muttered. "No regrets. Live in the moment."

Funny how every time he slept with the detective, he ended up lying to her afterward. And not like the regular jerk kind of lie, the kind designed to disentangle himself from her. The opposite. It was getting old.

But he also knew the job mattered to her. It was one of the reasons he got such an ache in his chest when he looked at her—she cared about being an excellent cop, the best she could be. And she considered her feelings for him a liability. She'd told him as much, but even if she hadn't, it was carved into her every action and reaction. So here he was, the chump who went along with *no regrets* because he had no choice.

The detective slipped her hand into his, no questions asked, clearly comfortable with it, her green eyes bright as they walked along 48th Street to Rockefeller Center.

He brooded about it and had enough energy left over to be annoyed with himself.

Until a whine and a *plink* drove everything out of his head. He froze.

A bullet.

He reacted instantly, jerking the detective behind him as the second one hit the metal mailbox affixed to the sidewalk in front of them. Right where she'd been standing.

Someone was shooting at Cassandra.

Chapter 20

"Get down," Donner shouted.

Rory ducked reflexively because she trusted him. But she still didn't know what was happening.

A woman in a trench coat screamed and dropped her purse, curling into a ball right there on the sidewalk as several other passersby figured out something was happening and fled down 48th.

Another *thunk*, and the metallic sound rang out near Rory's head.

Bullet.

Her entire body blipped into high alert as she scuttled backward, but there wasn't a whole lot of room to hide on the sidewalk. This was a tourist area that the city actually kept pretty clean and clear.

She had to protect herself, but the woman in the trench coat was in the line of fire.

In a flash, Rory stood and ran, flinging herself over

the woman, her body a shield. She had a bulletproof vest. The innocent bystander did not.

"Stay down," she told her.

Donner didn't hesitate to veto that.

"Get off the sidewalk," he barked and yanked them both to their feet. "The shots are coming from the balcony at my two o'clock."

They ran as a unit to the nearest business as a bullet buried itself in the concrete five feet behind them. Donner pushed both of them inside the door and shut it in Rory's face.

"Stay here," he mouthed and pointed at the interior, a bank lobby. They were in the vestibule with the ATM.

"As if," she shot back and pushed on the door, but Donner had it held shut, as if that would keep her inside once he took off.

He was going after the shooter—Washer, unquestionably. There was no way she'd let him take on a killer by himself, but Donner seemed to be operating under some delusion that she'd sit tight.

The moment he shoved away from the door, she yanked it open to follow him, but another shot hit the ground directly in front of her.

Dang, Washer was a crap shot, but better than she'd have expected. Cursing, she ducked back inside behind the bulletproof glass, foiled. There was no way she could follow Donner, not if she wanted to live. And she did, but she also wanted to be the one to make the collar.

The pedestrian, a woman in her midforties, cowered in the corner away from harm.

"You'll be fine—he's not after you," Rory told the woman in a clipped tone, though she had no assurances of the sort. Washer might care nothing about collateral damage as long as he eliminated Cassandra Walken, since apparently he still intended to take her out.

Trapped and frustrated, Rory stood there glowering, hating life, hating that Donner had charged straight into the eye of the storm. If he found Washer, their cover would be blown for sure this time. No DJ went after an active shooter.

It was the wrong call. Donner should have ducked into the vestibule with them.

But he hadn't because Donner's blood had been infused with Kamikaze genes. He'd never sideline himself like that, and she'd be a fool to ever assume he'd change.

Her throat ached as she envisioned Donner grappling with Washer the way he had at their condo. Washer was fast, and crazy to boot. He could hurt Oliver Walken as badly as he wished yet leave him alive to be killed later at the center. They had no guarantees for Donner's safety just because they weren't at a landmark.

There was more than one way to lose this battle.

She had to save Donner from himself.

She waited thirty seconds. In another thirty, she'd try to exit again. Maybe she could make it across the street before Washer got a bead on her.

Her phone buzzed with a text message, and it was her burner. She glanced at the message, emotion clogging her throat as she saw Donner's name on the screen.

Donner: He's gone.

"It's safe to leave now," she informed the woman. "I'll walk out with you to make sure. I'm a cop."

She flashed her badge to assure her vestibule-mate, as the woman's face dissolved into relief. "Oh, thank you so much—you saved my life. You're a hero."

Rory ducked her head. "It was my partner's quick

thinking that got us in here and out of the shooter's range. He just let me know it's all clear."

"Your partner isn't the one who acted like a human shield out on the sidewalk," the woman corrected her wryly and then hugged her, which marked the first time anyone had shown gratitude for Rory just doing her job.

"You're welcome," she said and patted the woman's back awkwardly.

They exchanged contact information so Rory could get her statement later. As they exited to the street, Rory picked up the woman's purse from the sidewalk, which, thanks to the active-shooter situation, remained intact—a true miracle on 48th Street. The woman took it and hurried on her way, leaving Rory to hightail it after Donner.

She found him on the balcony of the office building across from the bank. It was an old-school smoking area for the workers, largely abandoned in this day and age when so many had quit tobacco for a myriad of reasons and most places didn't allow smoking anyway. The perfect out-of-the-way spot for a shooter to lie in wait, especially if Washer had been watching them for several days, a very likely probability.

Wow. She'd never expected to get such an affirmation that all of their public playacting hadn't been for naught.

Donner stood to the side, his expression troubled as she stepped out onto the balcony, four stories from the street. Wind whipped through the area, bringing a cold chill with it. He met her gaze and didn't flinch, taking the ire she blasted in his direction without hesitation.

"How dare you take off like that?" she snapped. "He could have killed you."

Donner shrugged. *Shrugged*, like his life mattered to no one. "I had a reasonable doubt."

Ire shifted to white-hot anger in an instant.

"This is not a court of law, Donner. We're not trying to decide someone's guilt or innocence. It doesn't matter if this isn't a landmark. There are other blue-eyed blond men in the world with *O* names. If you die, he just has to move on to another victim, but I—"

She choked on it. *I won't move on.*

Oh, man, she was going to cry. She *never* cried.

"Hold up there, Detective," he murmured and, all at once, he'd pulled her into his arms, holding her tight, infusing her with warmth she had no clue she'd needed.

Ugh, she was still so mad at him, but he was so... everything. She should step away. Keep yelling at him. Make him see that this whole situation *sucked*. But she couldn't do a thing other than stand there and soak him up.

"I'm sorry," he whispered somewhere in the vicinity of her ear.

She pulled back to eye him, tears forgotten. "Did you just apologize to me?"

"Maybe." His expression lightened. "If you repeat that to anyone, I will deny it."

"It's too late—I have it on a loop in my head. I can hear it again anytime I want." She closed her eyes and let a small smile fly. "Ooh, there it is again. Donner apologizing. Because he was wrong."

"I didn't say that." He chuckled. "I was totally right to go after him. He was shooting at you."

His warm lips found her temple, brushing it, lingering. Saying so much more than his voice had. Yeah, she wasn't in any hurry to remove herself from his embrace either.

It had been a near miss. Too close. And she got it. She'd been the target. He'd gone after Washer not because it was Washer but because he'd been threatening *her*.

"We're a team," she whispered, her fingers tight against his back as if holding him like this could ensure nothing would ever happen to him. "Don't forget that."

What she meant was *Stop putting yourself in danger.* Because she needed him. But she couldn't say that.

His laugh was not amused this time. "It's not something I can easily forget when you were about to storm in alongside me. Thankfully you stayed put like you should have."

The ire returned with a vengeance, and that was when she tore free from his embrace, letting all the coldness in the world swirl between them. "You can't keep me behind glass, Donner. I have a job to do too."

"Don't I know it," he returned, scrubbing at his jaw. "That's what makes this situation so impossible. We're both targets, and you're even worse about putting yourself in danger than I am."

"Worse?" she squawked. "How am I worse? I don't charge into every situation, ready to die for the cause. I didn't give myself an *O* name and offer myself up as a sacrificial lamb."

"Didn't you?" He raised his eyebrows, his blue eyes steely. "The vestibule was right there, and you could have ducked in there immediately, but instead you played the superhero, throwing yourself on that woman as if your head had magically turned into a bullet-resistant Frisbee."

"There were civilians," she insisted, though why she had to point that out was beyond her. "It's part of the code. You protect them at all costs, even at the expense of your own life."

It wasn't negotiable. All cops pledged the same, and to assume she'd renege on that because her own life was in danger was an insult. It was totally different than his careless disregard for her intense desire not to lose him.

"Just because you're right doesn't make it okay!" he shouted and seemed to realize he'd become agitated and visibly calmed himself with deep breaths.

"Same goes," she said, also somewhat more mildly, though her gut churned with consternation. "I called it in. Brennan and Cash will be here in less than ten minutes."

"Don't change the subject," Donner said and lowered his voice, which she appreciated in case the twins showed up earlier than advertised. "You matter to me, and I'm done apologizing for that."

Her heart clenched as emotion spilled through his expression. "You can't change the rules midflight. This is a fling, a mechanism to ensure we're in sync, and it's working. Don't screw with that."

"Keep telling yourself that," he advised, and she glared at him.

"What would I tell myself instead? That this is going to end well? That you'll stop throwing yourself in front of every high-speed train that comes along?" She sneered, too distraught to pull any punches. "Sure. The moment you stop taking unnecessary chances is the moment you stop being an effective cop. That's the irony in all of this. The job matters more than I ever will."

He started to say something, then swore, his gaze

locked on something over her shoulder. "Remember where we are. We're picking up this conversation in exactly this same place later."

She turned to see her cousin Patrick bolting through the glass door, Kyra Patel a step behind him, almost keeping pace with his long-legged stride. They were a striking couple with Patrick's Irish complexion and reddish hair a strong contrast to Kyra's long dark hair and pretty brown skin. Anyone with eyes could see they were a unit that went far beyond their jobs with CSI.

"Wells call you in?" Rory asked Patrick, who nodded, then she smiled at her cousin's girlfriend. "Hi, Kyra. Nice to see you again. How's the baby?"

Kyra smiled in return and gave her a thumbs-up. "Growing like a weed. You got anything for us here?"

"Gum wrapper," Donner piped up, and Rory shook her head. Of course he'd left that out while yelling at her about something she hadn't even done.

He'd been the one to dash off to his death without concern. He was the one who knew how she felt about losing him, and it didn't even register with him that he'd done the exact opposite of playing it safe.

That was the problem when you fell for a cop. There was always going to be the next case, the next bullet, the next civilian. The better thing to do would be to go back in time and erase all those small moments where she'd bargained with herself that this would turn out okay.

It was not okay.

And she didn't know how to do a fling properly, obviously. Maybe she should just admit that she'd fallen for him—out loud—and leave it at that. No amount of stuffing would put that genie back into the bottle.

So why fight it? If she told him he mattered, would he change his spots?

It might be worth it to find out. Doing it the other way certainly wasn't working.

Cash and Brennan arrived, not the slightest bit out of breath from jogging up the stairs. After being briefed, they elected to help collect evidence from the street level and vanished again.

She watched as Patrick and Kyra canvassed the entire balcony area, while she ran interference with the few curious onlookers who had wandered from the interior of the building to see what exciting things were unfolding outside their windows. She excelled at keeping people at bay, which was probably the more prudent lesson to take from today, instead of confessing a bunch of feelings to Donner, who would just take it the wrong way.

Finally, the CSI team had done their due diligence, bagging the gum wrapper and a couple of other potential pieces of evidence that could've been fragments from Washer's clothing. Thorough testing would tell the tale—a slow, agonizing process that Rory despised, but Patrick had never wanted to do anything else.

Funny how the Coltons had gone into such different areas of law enforcement. She'd never thought about it as much as she had lately. The wounds of the past shaped the future, but it wasn't a given what that future would look like. Especially with different personalities involved.

"I think this is going to be solid evidence," Patrick told her with uncharacteristic optimism. Kyra had really turned his attitude around. "If it was Washer, we've got his DNA now and can haul him in for attempted."

"If we can find him," Donner cut in shortly. "This is the first time he's tried long range, and in a city like this one, odds are not on our side. He could be on top of any building at any time, even at the skating rink."

Worry lines popped up around his eyes, and her heart twisted. She was so compromised it couldn't even be quantified. Telling him her feelings for him had gone way beyond partnership into uncharted territory might make the difference.

Or it might be the first strike that caused this house of cards to come tumbling down.

Chapter 21

Isaac bided his time, waiting until after he and the detective picked up a few decorations from Target and started hanging them on the tree to bring up the elephant in the room—next steps on the case.

"We have to talk about this," he said, struggling to keep his tone even. "My plan is going to work. We have to try it."

Washer hadn't struck last night. Not so much as a peep during the entire tense seven hours they'd spent at the rink. The Colton twins had jumped at every tiny movement, signaling false alarms until even the detective had told them to chill.

When the queen of not-chill called you on your over-anxiety, it was time for a different strategy.

"Nothing to talk about," she said now, her face a blank slate as she hung a silver ball on the tree.

"Actually, there's plenty to talk about. The case is all

there is, Detective," he corrected her bluntly. "You and I have too much invested to wimp out now."

Even framing it like that didn't seem to thaw the ice that had grown between them the moment he'd suggested his plan: to draw out Washer by staging a costume contest that Isaac would judge out on the ice. He couldn't be a good target for a long-range weapon inside a tent. It made perfect sense for him to exit the tent and highlight the target on his back.

Perfect sense to anyone on the planet unless you were a mule, like the detective.

"It's not wimping out to take standard precautions," she insisted again, her voice wooden.

That was the other thing that was bothering him. Not only had she rejected the costume contest idea, she'd thrown up that stop sign again. He hadn't tried to broach it again today, but suffice to say, the excursion to Target had been silent and edged with the distance he'd grown to hate.

It meant she'd backed off in her head and he'd have to work extra hard to engage her heart, because that was when she forgot about the stuff swirling around in her logic center. And how fun was that to be the guy who had to make the woman he was involved with forget about thinking. He'd rather she thought a lot about them and had arrived at a conclusion more favorable to spending another day in bed. He certainly had.

"Washer is on the ropes," he said gruffly, forcing his attention back to the more important subject at hand. The thing he'd just told her was the most important, which was true, yet also an excuse to talk to her. "He got sloppy. Even though he's not an agent, he has the intelligence to be one, and for him to have left a gum wrapper is a sign."

"Maybe it's a sign that someone else left it," she reminded him mildly as if they were discussing the weather. "We don't have the results back from the CSI lab. It's too soon to be making assumptions about Washer's state of mind."

"Not making assumptions," he grumbled. "It's perfectly obvious he's rattled. He never expected to have two targets, and it's chafing at his serial killer status to have gone this long without a landmark victim. But at the same time, he wants to punish you for stopping him the first time. He's going to strike at the rink soon. Maybe tonight. It's been twenty-four hours since the botched bank shooting. He's bound to be antsy."

"Then you shouldn't be so eager to leave me alone in the tent, should you?" she said so sweetly that he almost did a double take.

It was a neat trap. One he hadn't seen coming, and that was saying something. He scrubbed at the short hairs on the back of his neck, flat handed, too frustrated to form a good argument.

Because she wasn't wrong. What would he counter that with? *Agents Colton and Colton will have your back*? Even family couldn't stop a madman bent on revenge, no matter how good they were at being agents.

This was it though. The final push. They'd had so many near misses. Surely everything would be on their side this time, even if he didn't push Washer into making another mistake.

"Fine," he bit out. "I'll scrap the costume contest idea."

She nodded once and hung another ball on the tree. "You can help me decorate, if you want."

"Sure." If nothing else, it gave him a reason to stand in her orbit, and he did like that, even if the temperature left a lot to be desired. "Now that we have that cleared up, maybe you'd be willing to switch subjects back to the one that was interrupted by the CSI team."

She froze for a second, and he'd have preferred if he hadn't noticed it. But it would have been difficult given how carefully he'd been studying her.

"Also a subject with nothing to talk about," she said with zero inflection. "We're partners working on a case. Anything that gets that case closed is fair game. I've made my peace with that, but until we have Washer behind bars, my mental focus needs to be on him. The job."

Isaac absorbed that, unprepared for how the stark concept made him feel. *Cheap*, in a word. As if he'd offered himself up on the altar of justice, his emotional stake nothing but collateral damage that the detective considered completely appropriate.

He hung a red ball on the tree, stretching to reach a bare spot near the detective's right leg. She shifted slightly so that he wouldn't accidently touch her.

Cold was the other word. As in his insides burned with the frostbite she'd just given him.

But that was okay. The deep-freeze act fired up his competitive streak. This was nothing more than another contest, one he had every intention of winning. The detective likely had no idea she was the prize, so he'd keep that in his hip pocket. But it was a huge incentive to him. He didn't need any such arbitrary deadline as Washer behind bars to know his own mind—and the detective was it for him.

His heart had her name on it. He'd offered it up. And he meant to figure out a way to get her to accept it.

"We should do the last one together," he said smoothly as he plucked the final green ball from the paper tray that reminded him of an egg carton and held it out to her. "It can be like a tradition."

She shot him a suspicious look. "Because we're going to be trimming a tree every year?"

Biting his lip, he held out the ornament. "Humor me. Traditions are important to the Irish. Your people would be proud."

Her eye roll nearly came with its own soundtrack it was so loud. But she didn't argue—*Will wonders never cease?*—and gripped the green hook just below his fingers so they could hang it on the tree together.

Once it caught, he tangled his fingers around hers and brought them to his lips, kissing her knuckle while watching her over it. "Merry Christmas, Detective."

Rory fled for the relative safety of her room after they hung all the decorations on the tree. What did it say about her life that it had been such a bittersweet experience?

She'd decorated the tree at home with her mother lots of times, but her father had never taken an interest. When she'd suggested to Donner that he could help, she'd expected his face to screw up in disgust, not for him to take her up on it.

Joke was on her. He'd turned it into something meaningful and sweet, and she hated the idea of going back to her drab, colorless apartment where she had no tree and no Isaac Donner taking up all the extra space in the room, in her life, in her head. Even her heart felt fuller when he was around.

That was why she couldn't be in the same room with him. It confused her.

But being in her bedroom didn't help when her sheets

still smelled like him. She should wash them. The condo had its own washer/dryer combo—another luxury she'd mourn the loss of once this case was over.

And it would be over soon. He wasn't wrong about that. Washer was getting antsy. She could feel it too. That was how she'd closed nearly every other case—having a sense of how it would unfold. She suspected Donner's mind worked much the same way or he wouldn't have had the reputation that he did.

If both of them thought he'd strike again soon, it was practically a fact.

And that also meant Donner could be dead before dawn.

It was a sobering thought, one that had her second-guessing everything, whether telling him about her growing feelings was a great idea or the worst. Hopefully she'd bought herself some time with her point about waiting until after to have that conversation. It wouldn't be that long to wait, theoretically, but she needed that time.

Before she'd gotten even close to mentally ready for the evening, Donner knocked on her door to remind her it was time to go. She slid her feet into her boots, the lace-up ones that wouldn't flop if she had to run—and she assumed she would be running at some point this evening. Probably after Washer had shot Donner, then fled the tent, forcing her to leave her partner behind in favor of chasing the suspect.

That was how it worked, and she'd done herself no favors to have developed all these stupid feelings that would make it ten times harder to do her job.

And now her heart felt like an anvil, weighing down her chest so heavily that she almost couldn't breathe.

There wasn't anything else but the job. She had to suppress everything else.

When she emerged from her room, Donner didn't say a word about her vanishing act, just smiled, crinkling up the corners of his eyes in a way that meant the smile was genuine, but it didn't quite light up his insides the way it normally did. Instead, sadness floated around in his depths, and that nearly killed her.

"I'm ready," she murmured, wishing they had the kind of relationship where she could fall into his arms and beg him not to go tonight.

But it was his job too, and she couldn't imagine a scenario where he'd stop and take a minute to think through whether he should try something different than charging straight into the fire like he had burn-proof skin.

Kamikaze was his middle name and would be until the day he died.

Which might be sooner rather than later, and stupid, unhelpful tears pricked at her eyelids.

She blinked them away and slung her purse over her body crossways, then holstered her gun in her shoulder strap, resolute. This was happening whether she liked it or not.

"Would you like a hug, Detective?" Donner asked, his tone mildly amused, which snapped her out of her mood, dang it. How was he so good at that?

"Not from you," she shot back. "I wouldn't put it past you to use it as a way to get busy five minutes before we have to be on site, and then I'd be all distracted and sated and drooling over your biceps—and never mind about that."

Okay, she could have totally made her point without stroking his enormous ego in quite that way, but it was too late now. And sure enough, her comment had stuck a big grin on his face.

"It's like you can read my mind," he said even as she shoved him out the door. "But that's fine. We can pick that up right where we left it when we get home later. I'm all about patience when it comes to letting you drool over my manliness."

"Yes, later," she said with false brightness. Whatever got him going. Before she broke down and dragged him into a kiss that would guarantee they'd be late.

Heck, maybe she could keep him in bed all night instead of letting him out into the open where he'd be a sitting duck. There was a stellar idea. Except then she wouldn't be doing her job either, and that wouldn't fly.

Impossible situation. All her fault too, and it sucked.

Before she could tug on her gloves, Donner slid his fingers into hers, warming them instantly—a fact she appreciated since it had started snowing since the last time she'd glanced outside.

Perfect. They'd have a slushy mess on their hands in a few hours. Exactly the kind of weather that made chasing perps miserable.

It was, however, great weather for staying inside and letting Donner make good on the promise of picking up where they'd left off, never mind that she hadn't let the moment devolve right then and there. It was looking more and more like the worst decision ever.

Best decision. *Best.*

They weren't a couple, and as soon as this case was over, they'd go their separate ways—you know, assuming he wasn't lying on a slab at the morgue. She hadn't asked him, but surely he planned to go back to his old precinct if he survived.

He'd transferred specifically for the Landmark Killer case. It wasn't rocket science. No Washer, no reason to be working out of the 130th. They'd have no reason to see each other. Right?

But when she glanced over, he wasn't enjoying the Christmas wonderland swirling around them the way she'd expected. He was watching her.

Donner squeezed her hand. "Smoke is going to start pouring out of your ears soon, Detective. What's got you so wound up? Sorry you didn't take me up on that offer of a hug?"

"Pretty much. Yeah," she told him, shocking them both with her candor.

His gaze registered his surprise for only a second, and then his lips turned up in a soft smile. "Plenty of time for that soon enough. Let's get this guy and then celebrate for two days straight. I'll take you to Miami for the weekend. How does that sound?"

Fabulous. Awful. Everything in between.

Because if he did that, it Meant Something. Something big and scary, and she had no idea how she felt about it. But she did know that saying yes meant she couldn't hide behind the case any longer. She couldn't convince herself that he wasn't serious when he said things like *You matter to me*.

"I guess it sounds like a good way to make you speechless," he muttered and shook his head. "Forget I mentioned it."

She nodded because what else was she supposed to say?

When they got to the rink, her head felt like it was

full of cotton. And she sincerely thought she might cry at any second.

This was ridiculous. She'd never been so out of the game before. And over what? Isaac Donner, whom she hadn't even known existed before she'd landed this case. No matter what happened, when the case was over, she'd go on. That was what she did. One foot in front of the other, same as she had after losing Holleran.

Except she hadn't been in love with Holleran.

What. A. Disaster. Neither did she care to dwell on that, thanks.

Donner set up the DJ equipment, same as he had every other night, but she couldn't stop sneaking side-long glances at him, strictly when he wouldn't catch her. He was a beautiful man—that much she couldn't deny—lithe, graceful, a tad on the lean side, which she would never have claimed as a preference, but she apparently had one. And he was it.

He cued up the first song, a Donna Summer number that she immediately recognized because that was a thing now. She knew disco songs from the first note.

The night wore on, each second lasting a hundred years. The tent got a little stifling with the heat or, maybe more to the point, because she'd created the tense atmosphere inside it, but what was she supposed to do? Rush over to Donner and declare her undying love?

Life didn't work like that. Sinead's mother had probably done something similar at one point, only to wind up alone and broken-hearted. Good grief. Even her own mother had cried a lot over her father.

Rory had double the reason to assume that would likewise happen to her—either Donner would die or he'd wander off once he found something better. That was what men did.

The edge of the tent rustled.

Everything drained from her mind at once. *Washer*.

The one time she'd chosen to sit back away from the opening. The one time she'd elected not to sit where she could survey everything. The *one time*.

But then a head full of long dark hair poked into the tent. "Can I make a request?"

"You should use the app," Rory told the girl, who couldn't have been more than sixteen. A girl that age should've been clamoring to use something on her phone.

Rory made a shooing motion. The teenager couldn't be in here. It was dangerous. That was the whole reason the app existed, which the event people had heavily advertised.

The girl blinked, clearly not getting the point. With a sigh, Rory herded her through the tent opening, cold air slapping her face. "Use the app."

The teenager nodded and dashed away. Rory turned and stepped back inside the tent.

An arm clotheslined across her throat from behind, and metal jammed into her temple.

"Hello, Cassandra."

Washer. She froze. And in that instant, she met Donner's stricken gaze and saw exactly how this was going to play out. Washer couldn't have conceived of a better way to get Donner to throw himself right in front of a bullet.

Chapter 22

Washer pressed the gun deeper into the detective's temple. The cold, hard rage building behind Isaac's breastbone climbed into his throat, nearly choking him.

He swallowed the bile. Ignored it.

Nothing mattered but the next few seconds.

He tracked the killer's tiniest movements, working to anticipate what Washer would do next. The flex of his index finger on the trigger. The slightest tick of his eyelid.

Isaac's own gun lay uselessly beneath his light jacket, which he'd worn strictly to hide it. Bad move. By the time he slid a hand beneath the fabric, Washer would figure out exactly what Isaac intended to do, and…that would be it. Washer would put a bullet through the detective's brain.

And then aim his gun in Oliver's direction.

Though rationally, odds-on, Washer wouldn't actually kill the detective. Not here at the landmark. Isaac knew that. This was a ploy to throw Oliver off guard.

But then Washer's left foot twitched. Lifted. He was making his move. Backing up. Through the tent opening. *He was dragging the detective away from the scene.*

Isaac's vision blacked out. Clarified. Black again. He couldn't process. Washer had slipped by every set of eyes on this tent *again*. This was not supposed to be happening. If Washer took the detective away from the scene, he could kill her and would. The murder wouldn't happen at Rockefeller Center, and his Landmark Killer status would be intact.

No, no, no. Isaac leaped into motion, dashing after Washer and the detective, myriad half-formed prayers falling from his lips.

Washer was still backing away, towing the detective with him. Her gaze widened as she caught sight of Isaac clearing the corner of the tent, her slight head shake nearly imperceptible. Warning him off.

No. She wanted him to retreat. Not happening. It was like she didn't know him at all.

Washer kept going, taking the detective around the far corner of the tent, closer to the statue of Prometheus. Closer to the street. Where he could get away.

Or worse—shove her into a waiting car. In a city this size, she'd become a ghost. Neither dead nor alive because he'd never find her. Never know what had happened.

"The tide is high," he muttered into his earpiece.

At least Colton and Colton could get eyes on the situation from their vantage points. Not that it would do any good if Washer managed to drag the detective out of their view. It was nighttime. The lights of the center only went so far.

He had to stop this nightmare from unfolding.

But as he flew around the tent corner, Washer had sped up and people around him had started to clue in that something was going on. Two teenagers screamed and ran straight toward Isaac, not realizing they were blocking his line of sight.

"Move!" he ground out curtly. They did.

Not fast enough. Washer had gained another five yards, his gaze on Isaac as his lips curled up in the semblance of a smile. Or what likely passed as one in his head. The cruel edge to it told Isaac everything he needed to know—the man was a killer and would not hesitate to continue his path of destruction and carnage.

Isaac took another step toward Washer in this dance of insanity that he'd been locked into. Washer backed up three steps, his gaze swinging around wildly as he looked for his exit point.

Snowflakes swirled in dizzy patterns, drifting to land on the detective's hat, on her eyelashes. Details he could clearly see because he was so focused on her face, the features growing more precious with each passing second.

So it came down to this. A contest of wills between him and Washer. One final competition to see who would come out the winner.

Washer had oatmeal for brains if he thought Isaac would back down now.

But just as Isaac sped up his own forward momentum, Washer lunged to the side, hauling the detective with him. Too late, Isaac realized that Washer had dropped behind a row of trees, where the light didn't reach.

He'd vanished, taking his hostage with him.

He'd dropped out of everyone's range. Including the Colton agents, who were shouting into Isaac's earpiece that they were trapped on the far side of the rink thanks to the stampede of skaters fleeing the area.

Isaac swore and broke into a dead run, his gaze dialed in on the small space where Washer and the detective had just vanished into the vegetation. This was his rodeo to lose. No matter what, he had to save her.

If God had any mercy, He'd see fit to let Isaac trade himself for the detective. Washer could have his *O*-name victim if only he'd give up his other agenda to make Oliver's wife pay.

Make it happen.

Just as he was about to use his momentum to crash through the trees, he wheeled up short. The detective's voice chattered away at him inside his own head as he imagined what she would say. *Stop taking unnecessary chances.*

If Washer stood on the other side, his gun pointed at the opening in a sucker's ambush, Isaac would take a bullet to the head. No time to duck. He'd be dead before he hit the ground.

For the first time in his life, he second-guessed himself.

The detective would hate it if he died trying to save her. Regardless of his noble intentions, she'd be upset. Angry. Devastated. She'd already lost one partner this year. And did he really want to make it a second one?

She craved connection, and he wanted to be the one on the other side of that, giving her what she wanted. For the rest of their lives. He couldn't do that if he died tonight.

He stepped back. He had to be smart about this for once. Consider someone else, or everything he'd been spouting to the detective about how she mattered to him would be a lie.

Cautiously, he crept along the tree line until he could peer around it from a different vantage point. Empty. The spot Washer had squeezed through with the detective was *empty*.

Washer was gone.

Cursing, Isaac sprang around the tree line at full speed, giving futile chase. He couldn't even see a glimpse of the detective's knit hat. Black. No decoration. Her coat: black. Just like everyone else in New York at night.

He'd lost them. He threw in another curse for good measure. He'd held back, like the detective had asked him to, and Washer had beaten him anyway. It had all been for nothing.

Weary, he almost crumpled to the pavement, but that wouldn't help this situation either. She could be anywhere. Washer could have killed her and dumped her body in an alleyway by now. And it would be his fault.

Funny how he hadn't even registered that he'd also lost Washer.

His original goal—gone. No chance to avenge Allison. Certainly no accolade to point to so his father would finally realize that Isaac was a good cop. He'd failed on every level. And he didn't care.

The only thing he could think about was the detective. If he never saw her again, his life would be over.

If there had ever been a question in Rory's mind about Washer's sanity, the Landmark Killer had eliminated all possibility of his mental state being anything else other than unhinged in the first two minutes of this hostage situation.

"Cassandra, we're going to have a lot of fun together, you and I," he singsonged to her as he held her in front of him, hiding the gun he'd shoved up beneath her vest, aimed at a ninety-degree angle, which might or might not have been the right slant to hit a vital organ.

She didn't want to test it. Plus, he could easily incapacitate her with a nonlethal shot and turn his gun on a civilian. Or worse—Donner. She had no illusions about whether he was tracking them. Frankly, she was shocked he hadn't already leaped out of the shadows to wrestle Washer for the gun.

"You and I define *fun* differently," she muttered to Washer as the angle of the gun shifted slightly when he yanked her to the right to go around a group of women dressed in sparkly clothes, as if they'd just come from a party.

"Oh, I think you'll find that we are more in agreement than you might think," he corrected, and she could hear the cruel humor in his tone. "As soon as we loop back around to the ice-skating rink, we'll look for your husband. Won't that be nice? Have a lovely reunion? You do like your husband, don't you?"

Oh, dear heaven. That was his plan? To loop back around via Fifth Avenue so he could ambush Donner from his blind side? If only Washer hadn't searched her and immediately dumped her cell phone in the trash, someone could have done a GPS triangulation. Washer was too smart for that, obviously.

But not smart enough to search her for a gun.

"I like him in one piece, yeah," she spat out. "Whatever you have planned for him won't work."

Washer laughed, hustling her forward as he sensed she'd tried to slow down. So much for giving herself a few extra seconds to think.

"It'll work, Cassandra. Does he call you Cassy? I like Cassy. It suits you. You're so spirited," he said with inflection as if to mock what sounded like a compliment. Because he clearly didn't think it was a plus, or he'd never have taken her hostage.

"If you're mad about what happened at the rink, it was an accident," she told him, improvising as fast as her mind could come up with words. "I didn't actually think that karate-kick move would be that effective. My self-defense instructor was so impressed, he had me show the rest of my class."

Washer twisted her arm up higher against her back. Pain shot up her arm and caught fire in her shoulder as the unnatural angle strained her muscles and joints. "You and Oliver think you're so smart, don't you? It's not going to help. Self-defense classes won't save you in the end."

One thing in her favor—he didn't realize she and Donner were cops yet. Excellent. The less she gave him on that front, the better. Washer wasn't quite as smart as he thought he was.

Rory was smarter. She had to be. Her life depended on it.

"The classes and buying a gun, that was all Oliver's idea," she said casually, hoping Washer didn't have a good sense of Cassandra's personality. She was about to become an airhead. An overly impressed one at that. "I never thought it made a lot of sense. I mean, you're obviously a professional. What could a DJ and an event coordinator possibly do to stack up against a true, seasoned expert?"

She could feel the gun change angles again as Washer stood up a little straighter. "That's true, I am a professional."

Okay, good. He definitely wanted to preen a little bit. She could work with that. "I was reading about this famous serial killer online. He's hit victims at landmarks around town, and I told Oliver that Rockefeller Center is a landmark. Maybe we're his next victims."

"Figured that out, did you?" Washer snickered. "Maybe you should consider a different line of work. You're a lot smarter than the feds."

They passed the plexiglass-enclosed Fifth Avenue bus stop. They were almost halfway around the block. She was running out of time.

"Well, we did go to the cops after the first time you came into our tent, and they just took your gun, then told us they'd call us if there was a break in the case. Everyone knows that means it got buried in a lot of other crimes. This city is full of them. They should really do something about that."

Washer screeched to a halt in the shadow of the promenade, his fingers biting painfully into Rory's arm. "They took the gun into evidence? With my fingerprints on it? That was a very stupid move, Cassy."

Oh, no. Miscalculation. She scrambled. "Oliver insisted."

"You're very talkative for someone being held at gunpoint, Cassy." Washer's breath heated her neck as he leaned into the gun, the tip digging into her spine with a sharp bite.

He was getting antsy. Starting to question things. That was not good.

"I'm just nervous," she babbled. "I've never been held at gunpoint before. How did the others act?"

Put it back on him. That was her only shot.

"Terrified," he snapped. "I'm starting to think you're not aware of how dangerous I am. I'm going to kill you, Cassy. I just want Oliver to see it when I do so he can understand that it's his fault. He didn't have to drag you into this."

Rory blinked and bit back the defense of Donner that automatically sprang to her lips. She had to turn this around. "He didn't involve me. I involved myself. I love my husband. I don't want him to be hurt. Please leave him alone."

"Oh, I like it when you beg," Washer said somewhat thoughtfully. "You should definitely do some more of that."

She pleaded with him, letting all of her pent-up feelings about Donner tumble free. Just to keep him occupied. Meanwhile, she scouted for a plan.

The crush of people during the holidays meant that no one paid any attention to them, especially since most people were facedown in their phones.

They were about to hang a left on 50th Street. The metal pylons meant to keep drivers off the sideway curved in front of her, hugging the curb.

Bingo. She waited until Washer pushed her close to the pylon parallel with the edge of the building that marked the end of the row. Surreptitiously, she slid a hand up under her coat and closed her fingers around her weapon. Funny how Washer had immediately looked for her phone but not her gun.

The moment her foot hit the pylon, she planted her

other one on the top and flipped sideways, away from his gun.

Everything happened at once. Washer shouted. Rory rolled, hitting the ground, sweeping her leg against the back of her captor's knees. He went down, arms flailing, which flung his weapon into the street. She jammed her gun against his throat.

"You're under arrest."

Chapter 23

Not one face that passed through Isaac's field of vision matched the ones he was looking for. His eyes ached with the effort of sorting through so many visuals at once. Snow had melted against his coat collar where his scarf had torn loose, but he'd yet to take the time to adjust it.

Cold meant nothing. Fear meant nothing. Fatigue meant that he'd crash eventually, and that wouldn't work so he pushed through the physical cues his body had been broadcasting for an eternity.

If he collapsed like his body screamed at him to, Washer would win.

On the other side of the rink, Brennan Colton, the wiry one with the lighter colored hair, careened around the corner from the direction of 50th, hands in the air as he pointed with exaggerated motions toward Fifth Avenue.

Colton's voice reverberated in Isaac's earpiece. "Dispatch got a call. Active assailant with a firearm one block over."

Washer.

Isaac pounded the cement as fast as he could, meeting up with Colton near the gardens as they dashed in the direction of what would hopefully be Washer and his hostage.

There was no scenario Isaac would accept where they'd find Washer and his victim. The litany in his head turned into pleas sent out into the ether. His thoughts pinged around like targets in a video game, zagging from corner to corner, too hyped to settle.

People glanced at them curiously as they rushed past, one woman snatching her kid out of the way as if Isaac and Colton might've been dangerous.

If only they knew.

A glut of people in a frenzy erupted from near one of the shops, rushing toward him and Colton, their expressions panicked. Fleeing something. A man with a gun, if dispatch had gotten it right.

The other Colton, Cash, the one who looked like he never skipped a day in the gym, shouted into his earpiece that he'd gone around the long way up 50th. They'd cut off the head of this snake, no question. Washer wouldn't get away this time.

Isaac rounded the corner across from Saks and heard the other Colton shout, "I have a visual on Rory."

Rory. Air rushed into his lungs as he allowed himself a full breath for the first time in ages.

But when he turned again onto 50th, the scene took a decade off his life. Washer grappled with the detective on the cement, her firearm the subject of note as they both tried to get a grip on it. She'd lost her wig. Washer was on top of her.

Adrenaline replaced the ice in Isaac's veins as he roared his displeasure that filth like Washer had his body in a two-block radius of the detective, let alone covering her, holding her down. Good night, the man had to weigh at least thirty pounds more than her. Any man who would threaten a woman Isaac loved in the first place earned a very black mark in his book.

Enraged, he dove into the fray, mindful of the gun but determined to put an end to this.

Suddenly, Washer twisted, apparently aware that he had a new problem. He locked his gaze on Isaac and sneered. Hooking his arm around Washer's neck, Isaac dragged the killer off his partner as the smaller man kicked and struggled to break free.

One of Washer's flailing arms hit Isaac square in the face. He saw stars as his nose exploded in painful pin-pricks. Washer used that moment to wiggle out from Isaac's grip. He rolled and hit the pavement on flat feet, then fled down Fifth Avenue at a shockingly fast pace.

Brennan and Cash took off after him as Isaac gained his own purchase on the concrete, then he burst into a full run. *This is not happening again.* Washer would not escape this time.

Isaac overtook the Colton twins as his determination propelled him forward, closer to his target. Washer wove in and out of pedestrians, then veered sharply, straight into the street. A Lyft screeched to a halt inches from his kneecaps, but Washer scarcely registered it, throwing one glance behind him as he kept going.

Barely missing the Lyft himself, Isaac chased Washer past St. Patrick's Cathedral, yelling into his ear piece for the Coltons to call for backup. If they could get some squad cars up at 52nd Street in time, they could cut him off.

But Washer suddenly cut back across the street, barely clearing an MTA bus before it could splat him. He made it though, forcing Isaac to halt as the bus lumbered past. As soon as his field of vision cleared, Isaac spanned the west side of the street.

There. Washer was headed up toward 52nd again. The squad cars he'd called for started appearing on the scene, the officers splitting up to help give chase.

Isaac flung out a hand to stop a couple of old-school taxis from plowing him over and dashed after Washer. Brennan and Cash were still a half a block away, one of them shouting into his cell phone and the other motioning at pedestrians to clear the sidewalk.

The detective sprinted along between them, thank God, but when she saw Isaac, she broke away, waxing both of the twins in a gold-medal performance as she caught up with him. "You didn't think you were leaving me behind, did you?"

"Not a chance," he huffed as they chased Washer in tandem.

The killer was fast and had desperation on his side. But he and the detective had justice on theirs. Out of nowhere, a delivery man strolled from one of the shops on Fifth Avenue, right into Washer's path. The killer smacked into the sudden obstacle, knocking them both to the ground.

Washer scrambled to his feet, but the tumble had given Isaac and the detective exactly the opening they'd needed. In a burst of speed, Isaac caught up and tackled the filth.

He came up with Washer firm in his grip, both of the killer's wrists manacled by his hands. As he twisted them up behind Washer's back, he drew them together and held tight as the detective zip-tied him, pulling the ends extra tight.

"Got you," he told the killer grimly.

Washer registered that fact a moment later, lashing out with his foot, but Isaac moved out of his way easily.

"You're a dirty cop?" Washer's eyes bugged out as he absorbed what was happening.

Isaac waggled his eyebrows. "Call me as many names as you like. Detective Rory Colton and Detective Isaac Donner are the ones going in the press release as the officers responsible for dumping you in prison."

"This is not the end!" Washer screamed. "Maeve O'Leary is a genius, and her legacy will not be subdued. I will avenge us both, and then you'll see. You'll be worshipping at her feet like you should be."

"Sure," Isaac said with a smirk. "That's exactly what's going to happen. You have the right to remain silent—"

"I will never be silent," Washer spat back and went off on another tirade.

He might never be silent, but he wouldn't kill again. All of his victims could rest easy. The people he'd worked with in the FBI could begin the healing process of being betrayed by one of their own.

Isaac tuned him out in favor of seeking out the detective. One of the beat cops who had just arrived in an impressive show of tire screeching and sirens blaring could handle the Miranda portion of their program. He had more important things to take care of.

The detective stood just to the side, monitoring everything with her sharp gaze. Blood trickled from a nasty gash on her forehead, and he'd never seen a more beautiful sight in his life.

It meant she was alive.

Overcome and more emotional than he'd expected, he gathered her up in his embrace, not caring in the slightest that half of New York's camera crews had arrived on the scene and would probably capture the moment for all posterity on the six o'clock news.

"It's over," he murmured into her hair as he registered that her arms encircled him with half-hearted strength.

Pulling back, he eyed her. Was she hurt worse than he'd initially assessed? Had Washer done something to her that he couldn't immediately see?

She glanced up to meet his gaze, her expression unnervingly difficult to read. "I was handling it."

"Yeah, you were," he agreed readily, his fingers automatically smoothing over the place next to the gash, but she flinched, so he dropped his hand. "I wasn't worried."

"Other than the fact that you let him get away?" she asked with a sarcastic undertone. "If you hadn't pulled him off me back there, we wouldn't have had to go on this merry adventure down one of the most popular shopping destinations in the world."

Okay, this reunion wasn't going quite like it had in his head. This was the part where he swept the detective into a blinding kiss and they celebrated a job well done. Because that was what was most important—they'd captured the Landmark Killer. It was an accomplishment that would live on beyond them both.

The detective didn't seem to be on the same page, and the decidedly frosty vibe spilling from her had nothing to do with the snow. He released her and stepped back, scrubbing at the back of his neck.

"*I* let him get away?" he repeated, incredulous that this was the conversation they were having. "I'm the one who caught him just now."

"After you rushed in like the cavalry and tried to come out on top. Like always." She dusted her hands off and pulled out her phone as if they weren't in the middle of a conversation, texting as she talked. "Everything doesn't have to be a competition, you know."

Isaac recoiled. "What are you talking about? Everything is a competition. And I'm the one over here winning—by closing cases. That's what I do. Washer is in the back of a squad car. That's the very thing we've been working toward since day one. How are you not over here with me celebrating?"

"I'm celebrating on the inside, Donner," she said with a taut smile. "And I have a report to submit before Blackthorn throws a fit. He's already texted me twice for an update."

A report. That was what she wanted to focus on.

Sure, he'd have said the job was the most important thing to him too, but that was before he'd watched Washer take the detective captive before his terrified eyes, only to save her bacon at the last minute, then stand by her side as they arrested the most elusive serial killer the city had seen in a decade or two.

It had been one of the worst moments of his life. And the best.

The job could wait. "The case is over, Detective. You know what that means."

She glanced up, her expression cool. "We go back to our regular lives. No more Cassandra and Oliver. It was fun while it lasted. I'm sorry to give up the view, that's for sure."

"It also means we can talk about being together for real," he said tersely, wondering how on earth this conversation had turned tense so fast. "We can talk about being a couple because we make sense. We *work*, Detective."

Another squad car pulled up, blocking the traffic as a couple of grunts spilled out to start photographing the scene and collecting the scant bit of evidence there was left behind. A stark reminder they were still in the middle of a high-profile arrest.

Lots of people were doing their jobs, but not him. No, he was standing around arguing with the detective about whether she felt all of the same things he did or not.

"There's no more need to ensure we're selling the deal to Washer. It's over," she said.

"I'm not trying to sell it to anyone," he shot back and then jerked his head. "Well, except you, apparently. Yes, our marriage was fake, but nothing else was. You know that."

She stared at him, and the temperature dropped again. "You don't get it, do you? We *don't* work. Because you're never going to stop being that guy who has to be at the head of the line, even if it's to be first to get a bullet in your brain."

This time, his step back happened involuntarily. A flinch he couldn't control if he'd wanted to.

"Yeah. That's me. You know that too." But she'd made it sound like a negative. "I will always jump in front of any threat in order to protect you. If you're suggesting I should stop…"

"I'm not, Donner," she said tightly, something shiny glistening in her gaze. That was when he realized she was trying not to cry. "I would never tell you to be someone other than who you are. Be the best. Win at everything. You're a great detective. I couldn't live with myself if I stood in the way of that. But neither can I live with *you*. I would always be braced for that knock at the door, the one where I open it and find people I work with on the other side, heads bowed as they prepare to tell me what I already know—you've been killed in the line of duty."

The arrow found its mark and buried itself in his heart.

"That might not happen," he protested, already knowing it was useless. Because it *could* happen, even if it never did. He couldn't promise her forever. It wasn't a thing with cops. "But I could also say the same about you."

She nodded, and he swore as he internalized that potential reality. He would have to live each day wondering if it was their last together. That sucked.

"We're not meant to be, Donner. Let it go."

No. Not happening. Isaac sensed rather than saw Blackthorn appear in his peripheral vision, the lead detective's face jubilant as he clapped them both on the shoulders.

This conversation about their future wasn't over. But it had to be. For now. He refused to consider the matter closed, whether the detective liked it or not.

But as she turned to Blackthorn with a bright smile that he recognized as fake a mile away, he feared he'd actually lost her a long time ago, before they'd even met—back when his competitive streak had formed out of the dual trauma of Allison's death and his father's disappointment in him.

The worst part was that Allison would never know

if he'd avenged her memory, and his father would never suddenly become proud if he hadn't been thus far.

Nothing he'd done had gotten him what he truly wanted.

There might not be a happy ending to this story after all.

Chapter 24

Rory trudged up the stairs to her walk-up carrying a bag of groceries and wondering when a loaf of bread, chicken breast and some vegetables had gotten so heavy. Granted, she'd skipped a million days in a row of working out. She was out of shape.

That could've been it. Except the real reason was that Donner had carried the groceries home from the store when they'd lived together. She missed that. She missed *him*. Dang it.

She swiped at the stupid tear that had managed to sneak past her careful filters. Reality wasn't supposed to be this hard. She'd lived her entire life without Isaac Donner in it, and that mere blip in time where she'd spent a few days in another world with a fake husband shouldn't have left such an indelible mark on her heart.

Silly. She was being incredibly ridiculous.

But when she entered her apartment, the place she'd found not too long ago on the Lower East Side near the Williamsburg Bridge, it felt even drabber and more depressing than when she'd left it.

It was the lack of decorations, she decided. After putting her groceries away and ignoring how tiny her kitchen really was, she left without a backward glance and walked the long way through Seward Park to the Target on Grand.

This wasn't so bad. It wasn't the ritziest neighborhood and she certainly didn't have the most luxurious place to live, but it was hers and the park had a lot of trees that she enjoyed in the warmer months. But it was winter, so the wind had stripped them of their leaves and left a layer of snow along their bare limbs. Some enterprising neighbor had hung a few cheap plastic ornaments on an evergreen near the kids' spray showers, which had been shut off for the season.

Decorations. That was the ticket.

She hurried along the path and emerged into the mass of humanity that had braved a shopping destination the week before Christmas. The store only had a few boxes of ornaments left and a four-foot artificial tree that she could probably carry home without dying, so she purchased both and a couple strings of colored lights.

The tree did make her place a little more cheerful. And she did appreciate the solitude since tears ran down her face the entire time she stood there hanging ornaments and weaving lights around the tree's branches.

Goodness, she was a mess. She'd sent Donner on his way so she could get back to reality, and it turned out that she didn't like reality a whole lot. But what was the alternative? Let herself believe that everything would work out okay? That some love stories weren't destined to be a disaster?

That wasn't realistic, and yes, it sucked.

Her phone pinged, and she backhanded the tears from her cheeks before glancing at it.

Donner. She slammed the phone facedown on the couch before she could read the text. This was the third one he'd sent her this morning. She should read it. Washer had been behind bars for less than twenty-four hours, and she did have a job to do. The man was still her partner. They had to work together whether she liked it or not.

But she just couldn't read it. Not yet.

Funny how she'd been all about the job for so long and now that it was all she had…she wasn't so keen on it suddenly.

This was her punishment for getting way too involved with Isaac Donner, emotionally and physically. A classic case of making your bed and then having to lie in it.

Resolute, she ignored the text, same as she had with the others. She'd earned a day off. It was Sunday, for crying out loud.

But when she turned on the tiny TV set up on a stand in the corner, an ABBA song floated out from the speaker like a cruel joke. The universe clearly had it in for her. She switched it off before she could even register the product for sale in the commercial.

Her phone buzzed with a text again. Ridiculous. She stalked across the room and opened the freezer, but just as she slid the phone across the pizza box on top, intent on slamming the door on the infernal device, it rang. Sinead's name flashed across the screen.

Scrambling, she bobbled the phone out of the freezer and answered it. "Hey! Sinead. Um, hi. How are you?"

This was the first time her sister had called her. Ever. They'd worked together on the Landmark Killer case, of course, but their interaction had largely been via official channels. In-person meetings. Chats and Zoom calls.

This was personal.

"Hey, Rory," Sinead said, and she could hear the smile in her sister's voice. "I wanted to call and congratulate you on nabbing Xander Washer. That's some great work you and Isaac did."

"Oh, yeah, thanks."

All she'd done was allow herself to be taken captive and then almost arrest the Landmark Killer, only to have Captain Hero arrive to save the day.

She'd never get over the look on Donner's face as Washer had dragged her off. It had nearly killed him to be left behind in that tent. To not be the one in the dead center of the action. She knew beyond a shadow of a doubt that he'd wished he'd been the one captured instead of her.

That was who he was. Brash, bold and always, always, always the one wading into the fray, no fear, no regard for consequences. Especially when it came to breaking her heart. If not now, later, when he pushed the envelope too far, too intent on winning whatever contest he'd invented this time. Being first would always be a higher priority to him than she was.

"Would you and Isaac like to come to dinner again?" Sinead asked. "Wells has talked about nothing else but having you over again. But this time without the shadow of the case over all of us. We'll just relax and have fun."

"Uh, what?" *Brilliant response, Rory.* It was just

such an unexpected jolt. "Donner and I aren't doing the fake-marriage thing anymore."

"Oh, I know," her sister said, the slightest hint of confusion creeping into her tone. "That's why it'll be great. No work to get in the way. A totally laid-back double date."

"Donner and I aren't dating." And why in the world would anyone think that? "Did someone tell you we were? Did *Donner* say something?"

That rat. He'd gone to Wells behind her back to weasel his way back into her life. Fuming, she mentally composed a scathing text in response to the ones he'd sent thus far. By the time she was done, he'd know to never speak to her again.

"No, Rory," Sinead said quietly. "No one said anything to me. I just…assumed, I guess. You were so cute together the other night. Even Wells commented on it, and you know how obtuse he can be about this kind of thing. You told me you slept with Isaac, and I thought that meant you were… Never mind. I'm sorry if I overstepped."

Ugh, now her sister had regained that frosted tone from early on, the one that speared Rory right in the gut because it meant they weren't on good terms. They'd turned a corner recently, and her panic had started to unravel that.

Fix it.

"You didn't overstep. It's just—I don't know what happened," she wailed as everything overwhelmed her at the same time. "One minute I was the most professional of all professionals, and the next, he's spouting poetry at me and telling me I matter."

"Oooh," Sinead squealed. "I knew it. The sparks between you two almost caught my drapes on fire. You said you had it bad for him too. Why aren't you dating? It seems like a match made in heaven."

Just like Rory had thought about Sinead and Wells. Somehow they'd made it work, and they were both in law enforcement. Lots of cops married each other. Was she being too shortsighted?

"Let me ask you something. Don't you worry each time Wells walks out the door? What if he doesn't come back one day? What if today is the last day you'll ever see him and the next day, you're a grieving widow? How do you deal with that?"

The pause on the other end of the line unnerved her. Had Sinead never thought about this before? Surely she lay awake in bed at night, terrified that she'd end up a single mother.

"Rory, you lost your partner," Sinead murmured. "I get it. It's tough. I know it's tough, but I think you might be letting the loss of Zach Holleran color your relationship with Isaac. It's not the same."

"You're right. It's way worse!"

"But with bigger rewards," Sinead interjected gently. "Yeah, I do worry about Wells. Less so since he's taking more of a leadership role at the department, but it's still a huge risk. I could end up a widow at any time, but so could my next-door neighbor. Her husband is an accountant, but what if he has a heart attack? That happens more often than a cop is killed in the line of duty."

"Yeah, but I bet he's not bolting four cheeseburgers a day and chain-smoking in order to bring it on himself," she muttered, but Sinead's point wasn't lost on her. "This is not a case of me not understanding that I have issues—I know I do. That's why it's not going to work with Donner. It can't. I told him so."

Sinead sucked in a breath. "I hear you. We all have issues. The real question is whether you've found some-one who understands your issues and forgives them, who loves you anyway."

Well, that wasn't a question Rory had ever asked her-self. A bit dumbfounded, she scrambled for an answer and came up with a big fat zero.

"That's irrelevant," she insisted. "The real problem is that love is an illusion. Look what happened to your mother. She trusted our father and got a broken heart for her trouble."

Even Rory's own mother eventually regretted marry-ing the man who had swept her off her feet. Men were not to be trusted.

"Rory, seriously?" Sinead sounded annoyed and amused at the same time. "Not all men are like that. Do you honestly think Wells will do that to me?"

"Maybe." She frowned. "Probably not."

"And I'll flip that back on you. Do you think he's taking a risk on me? After all, my mother's marriage is my model for relationships. Wells should be terrified that I'm going to cheat on him."

"Yeah, yeah. I get it."

Intellectually, sure. Lots of people had normal rela-tionships, and no one got hurt. Everyone lived happily ever after. Just no one she knew. Yet. Wells and Sinead had been married for five minutes. Definitely not long enough to count either way.

"I'm gonna go out on a limb," Sinead said, "and say that Wells and Isaac are cut from the same cloth. Solid, good men. Give yourself a chance and Isaac a break. He cares about you."

Honestly, that had never been in question. That was what made it so hard. She knew what she was giving up. But she just couldn't see a way to leap over the pile of misery blocking her view from the path forward. Her heart couldn't take any more loss.

Sinead plugged her opinion of Donner a few more times and then said she had to go take care of Harry, her voice dropping tenderly. Boy, Rory's sister had really fallen into motherhood without a backward glance. She shuddered. There was only one thing worse than putting all your relationship eggs in someone else's basket—and that was a tiny baby putting all of his in yours.

What if she had a kid and then found out she was exactly like her father? Oh, she was sure she could be faithful. But what if she was killed in the line of duty? She'd be leaving a child behind just as surely as her father had done.

The thought upset her so much that she nearly missed Sinead's parting comment. "What was that?"

"I said come for dinner tonight anyway," her sister said. "Solo. No pressure. Just you and me hanging out. I'll send Wells away if you'd prefer. He can take Harry someplace and do the dad-bonding thing."

Yes. That was one thing that had come out of the Landmark Killer case she could grab on to with both hands and hug tight—her sister.

They'd become friends over the course of this investigation, and that was something she'd never thought she'd say. It was miraculous, and she'd be a fool not to do whatever she could to solidify that friendship. "I'll be there."

When she hung up, the text message alerts sat there flashing at her. Her heart fluttered as her eyes automatically slid over the first one: Have you eaten this morning?

Oh, man. Donner hadn't texted her about the case. He'd been checking on her. She tapped on it and read all the messages.

Have you eaten this morning?

Ten minutes later: If you haven't, here's a quick video on how to cook eggs. Try it. You're good at lots of stuff, so this will be a piece of cake. I mean a piece of egg. Or something.

A laugh spurted out before she could catch it, and that was the only thing that kept her eyes dry.

Thirty minutes later: If you couldn't follow that video, I found this other one that might be easier.

One minute later: Or I can just come by and cook for you.

Nothing after that. He'd been feeling her out, and when she hadn't responded, he'd let it lie. *Ball's in your court, Detective.* She could hear his voice in her head as clearly as if he stood right behind her, murmuring in her ear.

Okay, she had to get out of here before she weakened and texted him back. Because she wanted to. So badly. To just sink into Isaac Donner and never surface.

Instead of taking the day off like she'd planned, she took the subway to the precinct and buried herself in paperwork, of which she had plenty. Wells had told her she could deal with it bright and early Monday morning, and originally, she'd agreed, but only because she'd intended to avoid everything work related, mistakenly assuming the job would be the hardest thing to get back to after her fake marriage became a thing of the past.

Turned out it was breathing that had become impossible.

The other beat cops who worked on Sunday ribbed her mercilessly about the gash on her forehead, which she took good-naturedly, sending them all a particularly good video from a cable news channel that had featured the arrest of the Landmark Killer. It was both extremely normal and all so very surreal because the desk next to hers was empty.

It wouldn't be for long though. Tomorrow, it would be back to business as usual. She'd be given a new case, one she'd have to tackle with Donner because that was how being a cop worked.

She honestly didn't know if she could handle seeing him again. But she had to. The only other option was to quit. Or talk him into transferring back to his old precinct.

As soon as the idea sprang up, she liked it. That was the ticket. If she wanted to get her life back to the way it had been before Donner crashed into it, she had to get him out of it. Once and for all.

Chapter 25

Isaac stared at the text message from the detective for a full thirty seconds before his lungs actually started functioning again.

Text me your address.

The message had a thousand implications. He desperately hoped at least one of them led to fixing the hole that had been ripped in the fabric of his life.

His stupid thumbs wouldn't stop landing on the wrong letters though, so he painstakingly typed in the full address with an index finger and hit Send. Then quickly typed a couple of cross streets so it would be easier for her to find. And then realized that was dumb when he could just tell her it was near Seward Park.

As soon as he sent *that* message, the back of his neck heated. Lame. But not as lame as texting someone a volume of instructions when she not only had Google maps but a plethora of official police tools at her disposal. She didn't need his help navigating to an address.

The detective didn't disappoint him. She knocked on his door less than ten minutes later.

He disengaged all six locks that had come with the place and swung open the door to drink in the unexpected visitor on his doorstep.

"That was fast," he commented instead of yanking her into his arms like he ached to. "Did you have an Uber ready and waiting or something?"

"Are you kidding me right now?" she said, her hands on her hips. "You live two blocks from me. A fact I'm sure you already knew."

"I didn't." But it pleased him to no end to find that out. "You never mentioned where you lived."

"On the south side of the park," she told him somewhat grudgingly, as if she didn't want to admit it.

It was a far cry from 49th Street, but he didn't mind. As his gaze slid over her, he took in the small details, things he'd had no clue he would miss. The tiny flecks of gold in her green eyes. The gash Washer had torn across her fair skin, the sight of which put his temper on a slow burn. The way her hair curled under slightly at her neck and lay against her forehead in a tousled, artful mess—a look that lots of women paid big bucks to achieve.

The detective was naturally beautiful in a way that he'd never have said he'd prefer, but he did. By a very large measure. No other woman of his acquaintance could hold a candle to this one.

And he'd started to worry he'd lost her for good when she hadn't responded to his text messages this morning.

But neither did he believe for a second that this woman had come by for anything other than a reckoning. He tamped back his need to plow forward, to fix whatever was wrong between them, and crossed his arms so he didn't reach for her.

"You didn't give me a lot to go on in your text message, so I'll start with, are you hungry?" he asked with a lot more calm than he actually felt.

Because this was it. The continuation of the conversation they'd started across from St. Patrick's Cathedral after successfully bagging one of the most elusive killers this city had ever seen.

"We need to talk," she announced unnecessarily. "Not eat."

He sighed. "It is possible to do both, Detective."

"I really wish you wouldn't call me that." She brushed past him as she took off her hat, the cute one with the blue pom-poms. "Colton is fine. It's what all the other cops call me."

All the other cops. As if Isaac had been and always would be in the rank and file alongside the rest of humanity. Okay, totally new tactics needed stat, obviously. He shut the door.

Before she could move, he crowded into her space and did the one thing that would make or break this situation—and he had no illusions that he was already on thin ice. But he almost couldn't stand to be in his own skin a second longer if he didn't touch her.

Slowly, so she had enough time to acclimate and accept what she'd surely guessed would be his next move, he reached out and feathered a thumb across her cheek.

Her gaze went liquid and melty, searching out his and holding for an eternity, and that told him everything he needed to know. She wasn't here because she'd thought about it and didn't really have feelings for him after all. No. She was here because she had too many things inside that she didn't know what to do with.

That he could deal with.

"I'll call you whatever pleases you," he murmured. "As long as you're right here where you can hear me say it."

With that, she broke away, her gaze slicing away from his, the moment draining away as if she'd pulled some kind of plug.

"That's what we need to talk about," she said, her voice wavering.

Good. That small bit of contact had gotten to him too. It was nice to know they could affect each other. "I'm listening."

"I need you to transfer back to your old precinct."

His eyebrows rose. "So we don't work together any longer and can date freely? That's overkill, don't you think? The captain doesn't have a no-fraternization policy."

"No." She scrunched up her face in apparent frustration. "So we don't see each other any longer. Ever. We can't work together after being so…intimate."

An adorable blush stained her upper cheekbones, and he probably enjoyed seeing it far too much. "I beg to differ. That's what turned our partnership around. We're seamless because of what we've experienced together. I have a theory that we'll be even better once we get married."

The expression on the detective's face was priceless. He almost wished he'd gotten his phone ready so he could video it. Then he could take it out later and show her the exact moment when she'd finally realized what was going to happen between them.

"I'm not marrying you!" she sputtered, and that was when his nerves got a little frayed.

Before she could spew more nonsense, he steered her over to the couch his mother had given him from her own living room and sat her down, then knelt between her feet so he could speak to her from a position of reverence.

Because that was how he felt about her. As if he could spend the rest of his life putting her on a pedestal and never think twice about it.

"Detective," he murmured and then shushed her as she started to protest the nickname again. "Yes. *Detective*. Listen closely because this is important. I've been chasing ghosts for a long time. I'm ready to put my energy on something real. Something I can touch. You. For some reason, you seem to be operating on the idea that we're not going to be together. You couldn't be more wrong."

"Except I'm not," she broke in, her gaze full of fire and brimstone as she waved a curt hand at his supine position. "This is exactly the problem. You're down on your knees, probably a half second from proposing again—although as proposals go, that one didn't even count since it wasn't a question, more of a demand—and you don't even get my objections. You're always so focused on winning that you don't take a second to figure out that some of us aren't even in the game."

He hid a grin at her characterization of his perfectly valid statement that they would indeed be married at some point. Because as she'd pointed out, he did like to win. And the stakes here were the highest in his life.

"That's true. You're not in the game. You're the prize, and I intend to win you at any cost."

"That's—that's..." She struggled to come up with a response. "Ridiculous."

Not the comment he'd been going for. Clearly she needed more. He took her hand and held her fingers to his lips, admiring her stubborn streak as much as he wanted to stomp it flat. This was what he got for falling for a strong, independent woman who was every bit his match.

"Detective, you're—"

"Please," she pleaded, her eyelids slamming shut for a beat. "You can't call me that."

"Why, because you like it too much?" he shot back flippantly.

But when she opened her eyes, he saw that he'd hit the mark far more closely than he'd intended. The pain and longing in her gaze punched him in the gut, and he realized this was the time to lay it all on the line.

Or he would end up alone and miserable like he'd been for the last twenty-four hours. Only it would last forever, and he refused to accept that.

"Detective," he murmured. "You know why you like it when I call you that? Because you figured it out. All my feelings for you are locked up in that simple, vastly complex name. Every time I say it, it's my love letter to you. I love you, and you know that's what I mean every time you hear it."

Speechless, Rory stared at the man still on his knees in front of her. Silver-haired again. No longer blond. But still Isaac in every sense of the name.

This perfectly rational discussion about Donner transferring back to his old precinct had somehow morphed into a declaration of love, a marriage proposal, and she should probably just agree to having five kids right now because she had a feeling that was coming next.

What did it say about her state of mind that it seemed easier to confess that she loved him too than it did to bring up all the reasons her feelings didn't matter?

"You can't say that either," she whispered, shocked at how broken her voice sounded.

But why was that so shocking? He'd broken everything else inside. Even her resistance, which kept slipping through her fingers faster and faster.

"I can, and I will. A lot," he corrected. "I love you. You brought me back from a dark place, where I cared about nothing but avenging Allison so I could show my old man I'm better than him. I closed a difficult case, stopped a killer from murdering more victims, and the only thing I could think about was you. How you were doing. Whether you needed something. I'll do whatever you ask—transfer, quit the force, become a circus clown. Name it. As long as you don't walk out of here."

Oh, goodness. Rory's heart grew so big and full that her rib cage couldn't contain it a second longer, bursting open to let everything inside of her spill out at his feet. It happened so fast that her chest hurt.

"You can't quit being a cop, Donner," she cried, trying to stuff the huge thing that had just happened back into the box. "That's the most terrible idea I've heard in my life. You're a good cop. The best. If you quit, that will be on my conscience forever."

His gaze caught hers and held, a million emotions fighting for dominance. "Then tell me how to solve this dilemma. I'm laying it down. No more battle to be the victor. It's yours to win now. Because being the best isn't necessary anymore for me to be happy. You are."

The things he was saying…pure poetry. She wanted to believe. Oh, how she wished she could. But it couldn't be this easy. Her life didn't work like that. "How can you just stop being you?"

"Easy." His mouth tipped up in a tender smile. "I'm not the same me I was when I walked into the 130th Precinct for the first time. You remolded me into something different. A man who understands the value of staying alive."

She couldn't stop the laugh that spurted out. "A disco reference? Really?"

His grin widened. "That's how you know it's true love. You recognized it."

And for the first time ever, she started to think maybe her life *could* work out like this.

What was stopping her from believing in him? He'd done nothing but prove over and over that he cared about her. Basically everything that had happened since she'd arrived had cracked her heart open wider. She couldn't be more in love with Isaac Donner if she'd started out with that goal in mind.

But still. Nothing had really changed. She couldn't ask him to stop being a cop. She couldn't stop waiting for that other shoe to drop, where love died when she lost him.

"Smoke is pouring from your ears again, Detective," he murmured and brushed one of those amazing thumbs over her cheek, leaving a trail of sensation, like he always did when he touched her. "What can I say to convince you I'm serious? You don't want me charging into a bullet? Fine. I don't want that either. I'm a reformed adrenaline junky."

She shook her head. "That's the thing. I don't want to be responsible for changing you into a worse version of yourself."

"Me either." He laughed softly. "That's why it's a good thing I'm now the best version of myself. Who else but you could have held up a mirror and shown me that the reason I don't ever feel like I've won is because I've been competing against myself? Against my own high standard that was nearly impossible to achieve? No one else cares except for me. And I decided to reframe what winning looks like. Being Mr. Detective is it."

"Mr. Detective?" she repeated, dazed beyond all comprehension. "Is this some kind of announcement that you're planning to take my name when we get married?"

It wasn't until his smile nearly split his face open wide that she realized what she'd inadvertently said.

"It's handy that I'm already a detective. No one will even notice if I run around answering to Mr. Detective," he said and tipped up her chin to pierce her clear down to her soul with eyes the color of the sky. "Put down your stop sign and start connecting with me here. I'm dying."

She shut her eyes against the stark admission. Isaac was laying himself bare, offering himself up to her, and still she wavered, terrified to take a step forward, even knowing that step wouldn't be far. Or that difficult. What was she waiting for?

A sign. Something that she could trust that would tell her beyond a shadow of a doubt that she should take this leap. "How is this going to work? You're just going to keep being a cop and stop charging into the line of fire?"

Donner nodded, his gaze searching hers with intensity that took her breath. "I already started. That's why you spent so much time in Washer's company. I stopped myself from shooting off after him. It nearly killed me, but I figured that was better than being one hundred percent killed by Washer if I gauged his position wrong."

"You...did? That's—" *Everything.*

His revelation washed away the last of her willpower, and she launched herself into his embrace, flinging them both to the carpet.

It was okay. Isaac caught her easily, cushioning her fall as he rolled her deeper into his arms.

"Took you long enough," he growled, nuzzling her ear. "You're such a mule, Detective."

She shivered as he let the full force of his feelings for her unleash with that one simple, wholly complex name. Then she grinned. "Takes one to know one."

Epilogue

Rory put the final period on her report that detailed the arrest of Xander Washer, aka the Landmark Killer, and submitted it. When she glanced up, Isaac wasn't focused on his own laptop like he should've been.

No, he'd swiveled his chair toward her desk and sat with his hand on his chin, watching her. Unabashedly. As if the entire 130th Precinct wasn't right there, witnessing his attention on her.

She blushed. Curse of the Irish. "What?"

"You're cute when you're policing," he explained cheerfully. "I like to watch you. Sue me."

She rolled her eyes. "*Policing* isn't a word, and if anything, I'm detectiving. Which sounds even stupider."

"It is a word. And I one hundred percent agree, which is why I picked *policing*, Detective," he said with a laugh and pointed at his watch. "It's well past quitting time. Ready to go?"

She nodded, more than happy to stand up from her desk, a new thing she was still getting used to—being done for the day and actually leaving the job on her desk for a change.

Commuting in New York City kind of sucked, but Rory liked doing it with Isaac, especially when he did sweet things like sliding their fingers together as they walked or leaning in to murmur things to her, most of them racy and not fit for the average pedestrian's ears.

It was surreal to think that they'd be married in three short months.

They'd planned a trip to Hawaii, where they'd tie the knot on the beach. Sinead and Wells had graciously volunteered to come with them, finally getting their long-awaited honeymoon. It also allowed Rory to skip the big family wedding so she could make the day about celebrating love instead of being one long meet and greet.

But when you were a Colton, family still managed to eke its way into every aspect of life. Sometimes she wondered if Isaac truly understood what it meant to marry into one like hers.

"Are you sure you're up for the party tonight?" she asked him as they took the subway back to Rory's apartment, where they'd elected to live until they found a permanent place. Isaac's landlord had agreed to let him out of his lease if he found a subletter, and he had almost immediately in a stroke of luck—or fate.

Isaac raised an eyebrow. "Is there something happening at the party that you've neglected to tell me? A hazing ritual that requires me to give blood? Because that's not enough to scare me away, just in case you were concerned."

She grinned. "I kind of feel like you already gave up

the requisite amount the night Washer broke into the condo. You're paid in full. But the questions and the sizing up now that we're official? That gauntlet you haven't run yet. My cousins can be formidable."

"In case you forgot," he stage whispered, "I have a badge and I'm not afraid to use it."

Like that would help. But she let it go. She'd warned him, and now it was up to him to manage being engaged to a Colton.

When they got home—*home*, still a strange and wonderful concept—he unwound his scarf and hung it on the peg near the door, the one next to hers that had never been used until he'd moved in. Her heart filled instantly. That happened a lot lately, and she'd lost track of the number of small things that pushed it to the limit. She'd never been so happy or so incredulous that a scarf on a peg could cause it.

Somehow Isaac sweet-talked her into a dress again, and she let him because she liked the way his heated gaze on her legs made her feel. She equally enjoyed being able to drool over her fiancé in a suit, noting how the gray tones set off his naturally silver hair, which she much preferred over the fake blond.

Basically, everything between them was real, and it was amazing.

They arrived at Wells and Sinead's house at the same time as Ashlynn and her fiancé, Kyle Slater, who happened to be Xander Washer's half brother, a fact Rory had forgotten until this moment. Both Ashlynn and Kyle had been lying low for fear of Xander coming after them.

She hugged Ashlynn and smiled at Kyle. "I'm so happy to see you both here."

"We're pretty thrilled that we can move about freely now that Xander's behind bars," Ashlynn admitted as Kyle's arm tightened around her waist. They glanced at each other, a wealth of emotion passing between them. "We finally feel like we can start our lives together."

"What will you be doing next? Staying with the FBI?" Rory asked, genuinely curious if the wrap of this case might lead her cousin in a different direction.

"It's in my blood," Ashlynn said with a shrug.

"But she might take some time off," Kyle suggested quickly as he kissed his fiancée's cheek. "Maybe start a family."

Ashlynn chuckled. "That's definitely in the plans."

Sinead opened the door, shooing them all inside out of the cold, which Rory appreciated since the snow had stuck around, promising a whiter Christmas than normal.

"Congrats in advance," Isaac said with a genuine smile as he slipped off his coat and laid it on the pile draped over a chair in the corner of the foyer. "And I also want to thank you for the great digs you scored for us near Rockefeller Center. The condo was amazing."

"Oh, you liked it?" Ashlynn asked, her face lighting up. "I just heard that the US Marshals Service is selling it. They turn over their properties every so often as a policy so the addresses are not consistent. They don't list the properties with real-estate agents for a number of reasons, but if you're interested, I can put your name in. They typically go for a lot less than market price."

Isaac glanced at Rory, but she already knew what she'd see in his gaze. *Yes.* It was a huge yes for her too. "That would be fantastic."

A two-bedroom condo with an elevator sounded like

paradise to her. As long as Isaac Donner lived there with her, it could be a five-hundred square foot shack in Central Park.

Wells welcomed them all into the living room. Kyra and Patrick had beaten them to the party, and the couch, but no one minded if the new mother kept her seat. Sinead passed out drinks and then excused herself to answer the door.

The twins, Brennan and Cash, had arrived, both with their significant others. Stella, Brennan's fiancée, scarcely hit the threshold before she started hugging everyone with her trademark exuberant enthusiasm. Rory had liked her instantly the moment they'd met, and she couldn't have picked a better match for Brennan, who had eaten his words after swearing love would never be in the cards for him.

Since she'd similarly thought the same, she gave them both a pass. It had taken a special person to get past each of their barriers.

Cash's wife, Valentina, was the kind of woman you'd hate for being so beautiful, except she immediately won you over with her sweet personality and quiet intelligence. She and Cash had gone through a rough patch, even divorced for a bit, but had eventually realized that they couldn't be apart. They had adorable twin girls, and Rory was sorry they'd left them with a sitter. But they'd be bored silly at an adult Christmas party where likely everyone would talk about work.

Wells didn't waste any time getting to the shop talk either. He raised his glass to the room at large. "A toast to all of the people in this room who helped put Xander Washer behind bars. May he have plenty of time to reflect on the misery he's caused us all as he rots in jail.

Especially since it's not the same one Maeve O'Leary's in. I hope that sticks in his craw for the rest of his life."

Everyone clinked glasses together as the Christmas tree lights twinkled against all the crystal. As they toasted, the doorbell rang again and in walked another passel of Colton kin: siblings Sean, Liam, Cormac, Eva and their cousins Deidre and Aidan. They'd all played a part in capturing Maeve O'Leary and were delighted to be here to toast in Xander Washer's apprehension.

Isaac shook his head, wondering if he'd ever be able to keep all the Coltons and their respective significant others straight. But no time like the present to start getting acquainted…

Isaac cleared his throat and spoke to the room at large. "As the newest member of your esteemed group, I'd like to offer a slightly different perspective. I'm grateful that I took an interest in the Landmark Killer case because it brought me Rory, the love of my life. Who came with all of you fine people."

"You got the worse end of the deal, I'm afraid," Sinead commented with a good-natured laugh.

"She's worth it," Isaac said as he caught Rory's gaze and gathered her in tight against his side, clinking his glass to hers in a private toast that he whispered in her ear. As Rory's cheeks caught fire, he laughed softly. "Merry Christmas, Detective."

* * * * *

#2263 COLTON THREAT UNLEASHED
The Coltons of Owl Creek • by Tara Taylor Quinn

Sebastian Cross's elite search and rescue dog-training business is being sabotaged. And his veterinarian, Ruby Colton, is being targeted for saving his dogs when they're hurt. But when the resurgence of Sebastian's PTSD collides with danger, romance and Ruby's ensuing pregnancy, their lives are changed forever.

#2264 CAVANAUGH JUSTICE: COLD CASE SQUAD
Cavanaugh Justice • by Marie Ferrarella

Detectives Cheyenne Cavanaugh and Jefferson McDougall are from two different worlds. When they team up to solve a cold case—and unearth a trail of serial killer murders—they're desperate to catch the culprit. But can they avoid their undeniable attraction?

#2265 TEXAS LAW: LETHAL ENCOUNTER
Texas Law • by Jennifer D. Bokal

Ex-con Ryan Steele and Undersheriff Kathryn Glass both want a new start. When the widowed single mom's neighbor is killed and the crime is posted on the internet, Ryan and Kathryn will have to join forces to stop the killer before his next gruesome crime: live streaming a murder.

#2266 THE BODYGUARD'S DEADLY MISSION
by Lisa Dodson

After a tragic loss, Alexa King creates a security firm to keep other women safe. Taking Andrew Riker's combat and tactical class will elevate her skills. But falling for the ex-marine makes her latest case not only personal...but deadly.

YOU CAN FIND MORE INFORMATION ON UPCOMING HARLEQUIN TITLES,
FREE EXCERPTS AND MORE AT HARLEQUIN.COM.

HRSCNM1223

Get 3 FREE REWARDS!

We'll send you 2 FREE Books plus a FREE Mystery Gift.

FREE Value Over $20

Both the **Harlequin Intrigue®** and **Harlequin® Romantic Suspense** series feature compelling novels filled with heart-racing action-packed romance that will keep you on the edge of your seat.

YES! Please send me 2 FREE novels from the Harlequin Intrigue or Harlequin Romantic Suspense series and my FREE gift (gift is worth about $10 retail). After receiving them, if I don't wish to receive any more books, I can return the shipping statement marked "cancel." If I don't cancel, I will receive 6 brand-new Harlequin Intrigue Larger-Print books every month and be billed just $6.49 each in the U.S. or $6.99 each in Canada, a savings of at least 13% off the cover price, or 4 brand-new Harlequin Romantic Suspense books every month and be billed just $5.49 each in the U.S. or $6.24 each in Canada, a savings of at least 12% off the cover price. It's quite a bargain! Shipping and handling is just 50¢ per book in the U.S. and $1.25 per book in Canada.* I understand that accepting the 2 free books and gift places me under no obligation to buy anything. I can always return a shipment and cancel at any time by calling the number below. The free books and gift are mine to keep no matter what I decide.

Choose one: ☐ **Harlequin Intrigue Larger-Print** (199/399 BPA GRMX) ☐ **Harlequin Romantic Suspense** (240/340 BPA GRMX) ☐ **Or Try Both!** (199/399 & 240/340 BPA GRQD)

Name (please print)

Address   Apt. #

City   State/Province   Zip/Postal Code

Email: Please check this box ☐ if you would like to receive newsletters and promotional emails from Harlequin Enterprises ULC and its affiliates. You can unsubscribe anytime.

Mail to the **Harlequin Reader Service:**
IN U.S.A.: P.O. Box 1341, Buffalo, NY 14240-8531
IN CANADA: P.O. Box 603, Fort Erie, Ontario L2A 5X3

Want to try 2 free books from another series? Call 1-800-873-8635 or visit www.ReaderService.com.

*Terms and prices subject to change without notice. Prices do not include sales taxes, which will be charged (if applicable) based on your state or country of residence. Canadian residents will be charged applicable taxes. Offer not valid in Quebec. This offer is limited to one order per household. Books received may not be as shown. Not valid for current subscribers to the Harlequin Intrigue or Harlequin Romantic Suspense series. All orders subject to approval. Credit or debit balances in a customer's account(s) may be offset by any other outstanding balance owed by or to the customer. Please allow 4 to 6 weeks for delivery. Offer available while quantities last.

Your Privacy—Your information is being collected by Harlequin Enterprises ULC, operating as Harlequin Reader Service. For a complete summary of the information we collect, how we use this information and to whom it is disclosed, please visit our privacy notice located at corporate.harlequin.com/privacy-notice. From time to time we may also exchange your personal information with reputable third parties. If you wish to opt out of this sharing of your personal information, please visit readerservice.com/consumerschoice or call 1-800-873-8635. **Notice to California Residents**—Under California law, you have specific rights to control and access your data. For more information on these rights and how to exercise them, visit corporate.harlequin.com/california-privacy.

HIHRS23

HARLEQUIN
PLUS

Try the best multimedia subscription service for romance readers like you!

Read, Watch and Play.

Experience the easiest way to get the romance content you crave.

Start your **FREE TRIAL** at
www.harlequinplus.com/freetrial.